DEATH OF AN EARL

A Golden Age Mystery

Death of an Earl

A Golden Age Mystery

G.G. Vandagriff

Dedicated To

David Peter Vandagriff
My Companion, Editor, and Cohort.
This book should really have your name on the front, too.

Chapter One

1935

THE TIMES

EIGHTH EARL OF SEVERN DIES IN WOODSTOCK
—NIGEL FARRADAY, EIGHTH EARL OF SEVERN,
WAS FOUND DEAD BY HIS VALET IN HIS STUDY
YESTERDAY EVENING.

* * *

Catherine Tregowyn, poet and tutor at Somerville College, Oxford, read this headline with no idea how it would shortly affect her life. At the moment, she was eaten up with nerves over meeting her fiancé's family for the first time. Harry was calling for her in five minutes to motor her down to Hampshire for the weekend.

She told herself she was being ridiculous, but she did so want to make a good impression. Though not usually vain, Catherine checked her appearance once more in the glass. Her maid, Cherry, had insisted that her most becoming ensemble was her red belted suit with the pleated skirt and red and white polka dot silk blouse. Her matching hat with the peek-a-boo veil called attention to her best feature—her large velvety brown eyes set in her heart-shaped face. Lipstick of matching red completed her preparations.

Suddenly, she worried that she was too strident-looking. Too "Here I am—this is ME!"

There wasn't time to change. Catherine could only hope that the polka dots would convey the idea that she didn't take herself too seriously.

Cherry answered Harry's knock, and Catherine took up the bouquet of mixed chrysanthemums she was taking to his mother. Harry strode in, looking movie-star gorgeous as ever with his square jaw, auburn hair, and deep, dark eyes.

"Darling! You are the picture of a suitable daughter-in-law," he said. "So let us be on our way. You're going to wow everyone. No need to be nervy."

* * *

It wasn't until they were halfway from Oxford to Hampshire that Harry dropped his little bomb.

"You have a married brother who works at Oxford?" Catherine repeated. "Harry, what possible reason could you have for not telling me this before?"

Harry paused a minute before replying, "He only just came back from abroad. He's been with Bayer Labs. We haven't been close for years."

"Just geographically separated or estranged?"

Harry put his hand to his tie knot and adjusted it, stretching his neck. "He's been gone a long time, Catherine."

She noted the steel in his voice. And he never called her Catherine. She was going to have to tread carefully. Searching her memory, she said, "Bayer Labs. I think Wills used to talk about them. Aren't they in Germany? Haven't they just developed some new wonder drug?"

"Sulfa, yes. My brother, James, was in on it. Some fellow with a Polish name was the scientist who developed it. Word is that he'll probably get a Nobel Prize."

"He sounds like someone my brother would love to meet."

Harry's jaw relaxed. "What lab did Wills work for?"

"The Sir William Dunn School of Pathology."

"You will have a jolly time chatting with James, then. That's where he's working now. When is Wills returning from Kenya?"

They were approaching the chalk downs of Hampshire. Catherine quelled the nerves in her stomach. "It could be years. He's getting more funding all the time to take his clean water project throughout the country."

"Good for him."

She prodded, "Tell me about James's wife. Will we have anything in common?"

Harry hesitated a moment as though marshaling his thoughts. "You should. Anne's a Somervillian. Older than you by a few years."

"Excellent!" said Catherine. Her nerves abated somewhat.

She already knew that Harry's parents were large landowners and very accomplished. His father, a prosperous wool merchant, had recently received a degree from the London School of Economics, while his mother was a practicing physician. She had studied at the Edinburgh College of Medicine for Women. Catherine was prepared to like them and prayed they would like her, as well.

Her handkerchief lay mangled on her lap. After folding it up and putting it away in her purse, she removed her compact to check her lipstick. All was well there.

Harry took a hand off the wheel and put it over hers. "Don't worry, darling. They're going to adore you. I sent my mother your latest book, and she loved it."

She took a deep breath and squeezed his hand.

Moments later, they turned up the road to his Georgian home. She had already visited the mansion, so it wasn't new to her, but Harry's parents hadn't been in residence at the time. As his car pulled around the graveled drive, a tall, lean, gray-haired woman emerged from the house. She wore a long cardigan which she held across her body with one arm.

"My mum," Harry said, smiling. He stopped the motor in front of her and alighted. Stepping forward to embrace him, Dr. Bascombe looked ecstatic to see her son. Harry kissed her cheek and then came around to help Catherine out of the car.

She smiled and extended her hand. Dr. Bascombe took it in both of hers, saying, "Miss Tregowyn, how lovely to meet you at last! I have been so looking forward to this!"

Catherine said, "And I have been as well. Please call me Catherine."

"With pleasure. Since we are to be family, I insist you call me Sarah. Come into the house. Tea will be served on the instant! And don't worry about your luggage. It will be stowed away properly in your rooms."

The first time Catherine had seen the house, she was startled by its Art Deco interior, which provided a great contrast to the conservative exterior. She liked the white walls displaying colorful abstract art and the black and white leather and chrome furnishings. Catherine took off her gloves and hat in the hall.

Two men stood when she and the others entered a sitting room. Harry's father was easy to identify with his resemblance to his son—dark eyes, strong, square jaw, and muscular build.

"So this is my future daughter!" he said heartily. "Welcome to the family home. I hope you will be very comfortable. Meet Edward, our son-in-law. He's called Ned."

Both men shook her hand, and Mr. Bascombe clapped his son on the shoulder. Ned was broad and sturdy and had the look of an outdoorsman with tanned skin and squint lines around his blue eyes.

A woman who must be Harry's sister stood then and offered her hand. With fair hair and blue eyes, she was petite and very pregnant. "I'm Mary," she said, her eyes twinkling. "You can't imagine how we've longed to meet the woman who has tamed our Harry!"

Laughter bubbled out of Catherine as Harry said, "Don't you have a child somewhere who needs you?"

"It's lovely to meet you," said Catherine as she shook Mary's hand. "I look forward to meeting any children, as well."

"They are home with their nanny for the weekend," Mary said. "Now, you must sit and have some tea. Cook has made her divine cream cakes—Harry's favorite."

"James and Anne rang, and they won't be here until dinner," Dr. Bascombe said. "Some business of Anne's has held them up." The woman's voice was serene, but a furrowed brow betrayed worry or annoyance. "Tea?" she asked Catherine.

"Please. Just lemon," said Catherine.

Mary asked, "When is the wedding to be?"

"During the Christmas hols," said Catherine. "It will be small. Just family and a few friends."

"Are you being married at Oxford?" Mary asked.

"No. At Tregowyn Chapel in Cornwall. It won't hold many, but I don't want a lot of fuss. My father hasn't been well."

"I'm sorry to hear that," said Sarah Bascombe.

Catherine recognized the professional glint in the doctor's eye, so she elaborated. "His heart," she said.

Ned intervened. "I've been dying to ask you about the dig. Harry says you have a Roman excavation going at Tregowyn Manor."

Catherine smiled, and for the next quarter of an hour, they discussed the Roman ruin found on her family's property. Mary then inquired about her poetry. From there, the afternoon proceeded quite pleasantly. Catherine ascertained that Mary had two children—ages five and three. Ned managed the family woolen mill. When asked about her medical practice, Sarah spoke of having taken it over from her father.

Catherine realized the family had no issues about their place in society. They were like Harry in this—utterly secure in their social standing in the upper-middle class.

Mr. Bascombe insisted upon a turn about the garden after tea. Though it was October, frost had yet to bite, so there was an abundance of periwinkle asters, every shade of chrysanthemum, and even Japanese anemones.

"You will make my son a happy man, I think," the elder Bascombe said. "Do you garden?"

"I'm afraid not. That talent passed me by completely," Catherine said.

"My wife has little interest either, but gardening appeals to the farmer in me," he said. "Tell me, how does Baron Tregowyn feel about this marriage? Is it likely to be a problem for him?"

Surprised by his bluntness, she said, "He is quite fond of Harry."

"That doesn't answer my question," Harry's father said.

"He has grumbled a bit, but I think he's given up trying to control my choices."

"That's fine, then." Mr. Bascombe leaned down to deadhead a few asters with his clippers. "Have you siblings?"

"A brother. William. He and Harry are friends." For the rest of their ramble about the garden, Catherine told Mr. Bascombe about Wills' project to bring potable drinking water to the villages of his beloved Kenya.

Harry's father said, "What a commendable project! If he needs backing, I would seriously consider contributing to something like that."

"I'll let him know. He has a prospectus. I'll see that you get one," said Catherine.

* * *

When Harry and Catherine came down from their rooms to foregather in the drawing room for drinks before dinner, she sensed that the earlier ease had fled almost at once.

Harry's arm went stiff under her hand.

"James," he said. He bowed his head as though acknowledging a scarcely known acquaintance.

But Catherine only noticed his brother peripherally. Instead, a beauty sipping sherry and speaking to a frowning Mr. Bascombe caught her attention. With long black hair, an hourglass figure, and a perfect profile, Harry's sister-in-law would have caused a sensation in Hollywood.

"They have a nerve!" Mr. Bascombe was saying, his Hampshire accent more evident than usual. "Have you a solicitor, my dear?"

"Not yet," the woman said. "James is taking care of it."

Mr. Bascombe suddenly noticed Catherine and Harry's entrance. "We'll talk of this anon," he said. "Here is our affianced couple! It is their night tonight."

Dinner was more restrained than tea had been. Both James and Anne had greeted Catherine kindly, though their distraction was evident. Catherine kept an eye on Harry, who had a kind of false exuberance. She had never known him so ill at ease. He spoke of their adventures in California the preceding August, inquired of his mother after several of her long-term patients, traded jests with Ned, and tormented Mary until she blushed. He had no words for his brother or sister-in-law.

When there was a break in the conversation, Anne said to Catherine, "I have read your poetry with a great deal of interest. You have made quite a splash in the literary world. I have always longed to write. Tell me, have you ever met Mrs. Woolf?"

"Yes," Catherine replied. "She invited me to do a reading to her Bloomsbury Group. It was incredibly nerve-wracking. I don't think I could have been more intimidated by the king, himself."

Anne laughed. "I don't blame you. She seems quite formidable."

Catherine said, "Harry says you've just returned from Germany. What was it like to live there?"

"A bit scary, actually," said Anne. "I'm of the opinion that another war is likely and that instead of disarming, we should be rearming like mad. I'm afraid I'm not very popular in England right now."

The words sent a chill down Catherine's spine, and her throat closed up.

War! No. Impossible. Not again!

"Darling," said James. "Shall we give it a rest, just for tonight?"

"Sorry," Anne said, her voice terse. "I do tend to get a bit carried away."

Though Catherine had thought of herself as a pacifist and thought any person of sense would be, too, she was oddly anxious to hear what the woman had to say. If only so it could be disproven. She put her fork down and looked at her half-eaten dinner.

At Anne's words, there was a rush of conversation. Mary, who sat at Catherine's right, asked her how one went about constructing a poem. Harry's father rose and went to the sideboard for more food, and Sarah Bascombe asked her eldest son if he had any promising students this year.

Forcing herself to take a long, steady breath, Catherine said, "I'm sorry, Mary. What did you say?"

The woman glanced at Anne and then lowered her voice. "Don't let her get you down. It's her hobby horse. She's worse than Churchill. She thinks it's her mission to save England from Hitler."

"I'm a bit sensitive on the subject," Catherine murmured. "Let's talk of something else. First, tell me about your children."

CHAPTER TWO

The party got through the rest of the dinner and adjourned to the drawing room. The light-heartedness of the evening seemed forced to Catherine. Harry pounded the bowl of his pipe into his palm, which always betrayed his impatience. James silently watched him from across the room

What is wrong between them?

Anne kept drawing her eye. She spoke animatedly with her mother-in-law about something. Mary chatted with her brother.

"Did you know Ned is making me the sweetest cradle?"

Ned conversed with his father-in-law about the mill. Loathe to press herself on anyone at this point, Catherine had to force herself to interrupt Harry's pipe pounding.

"Darling, James's wife is smashing," she said in a low tone. "Can't you just see her holding court in Hollywood?"

Harry said only, "Huh!"

The words could not have carried, yet at that moment, Anne looked their way, and it seemed to Catherine that she exchanged a look with Harry. The woman walked over to them and apologized. "I'm sorry. I had a rather unpleasant experience this after-noon, but I intend to put it behind me and tell you how very pleased I am about your engagement." She shook Catherine's hand. "I've known Harry all my life, and I can tell you he'll make you an ideal husband."

Something about her words made Harry shift his weight as though preparing himself to enter a prizefight.

Afraid he was going to say something rude, Catherine said with a forced laugh, "I'm marrying him for his looks, of course. But I must tell you; I had to tear him away from any number of Hollywood types who wanted to offer him a film contract."

Anne and Harry both seemed to relax at the sally.

"Is the gossip true?" Anne asked. "Did you really help solve those awful murders? Harry's father said the news was all over *News of the World* because of your being from Oxford."

"Catherine did," Harry said, putting an arm around her waist and pulling her close. "She probably could have set up shop as a PI in Hollywood, but she chose to marry me instead."

"What on earth is a PI?" asked Anne.

"Private Investigator." Harry leaned forward as though confiding a secret. "The police in Los Angeles are so inept and corrupt that Hollywood people hire their own investigators. So having your own PI is quite the done thing."

"How very odd!" said Anne turning to Catherine. "Is he telling the truth?"

"He is exaggerating a bit," said Catherine with a laugh. "But we did rely quite a lot on PI reports in piecing the thing together. Unfortunately, two of those murdered were a PI and his secretary."

"Gruesome," said Anne. She shivered. "Let's change the subject. How did the two of you meet?"

Catherine threw a look at her fiancé, who was grinning.

"It was Catherine's poetry that brought us together, actually," he said. "I gave her first volume a scathing review. She hated me like poison."

"I did," Catherine agreed.

"But then I fell for her, of course," he said, smoothing the hair on the back of his head. "And have faced an uphill battle to win her regard ever since."

Anne laughed. "What a lovely story. You've needed someone to take the starch out of you for years."

"I think I'll wander off and find a whiskey and leave you two to tear my character to shreds," he said.

"How much of that is true?" Anne asked, her perfectly arched eyebrows raised.

"Every word," said Catherine. "It's been a lovely courtship interspersed with a few murders. Now, tell me about your family."

"Well, if you mean James and me, that's all there is. No children. But back a generation, I have a widowed father, no siblings." She shook her head and gave a rueful smile. "My father is rather a character in these parts—Rutherford Stapleton, Lord Rutherford. His title is only a life peerage, so I have no title myself. Not even an honorable! He's what one would call a Sherlock Holmes fanatic. Might you have heard of the Sir Arthur Conan Doyle literary prize for detective fiction? He's the sponsor, as well as the judge."

"I have heard of him," said Catherine, her interest piqued. "He received his peerage for outstanding leadership during the war, didn't he? And the Conan Doyle is quite a coveted prize."

"Well, he wants to meet you, as a matter of fact. Your exploits in Hollywood have made you famous. He wants you to write a book."

Catherine laughed.

"Now," Anne said, "I should like to recruit you for a league I'm forming. As yet, there are only four of us. It's an anti-fascist organization. I'm anxious to get it off the ground. It is so important. You might not believe it, but England has quite a number of people who admire Adolf Hitler."

Catherine's stomach turned queasy. "I . . . I don't know what to tell you. I'm anti-fascist, of course, but I'm also anti-war."

"Oh, my dear, that's only because you're uninformed. If you knew more about the man, you would realize that we must stand up to him. He's not afraid of war, I can tell you!"

Anne's eyes suddenly left Catherine's at the end of this speech, and she appeared to follow something across the room. Catherine turned to see Harry and James in a heated conversation.

"Oh, dear," Anne said, her features tightening. "I was afraid of this. I hope they can calm down eventually. They haven't seen one another since we got back from Germany."

Catherine thought the woman looked irritated rather than worried. "Have they always been at odds?" she asked.

Inhaling a long breath, the woman said, "It goes back a long way."

At that moment, Harry's mother appeared beside him and put a gentle hand on his arm. She drew him away, and soon she was pouring him the whiskey he had said he wanted.

"Darling Sarah," said Anne. "She's a gem. Now, if you'll excuse me, I must see to James."

Suddenly there was a small commotion as the ancient butler led two official-looking men in trench coats into the room. The men went straight to Anne. Conversation ceased as the elder one, who radiated authority, showed her the credentials in his wallet.

"Detective Chief Inspector Kerry," he said in a clipped voice. "Mrs. Anne Bascombe, I have a warrant to arrest you for the murder of Nigel Farraday, Eighth Earl of Severn. Sergeant, your handcuffs, please."

Producing a pair of handcuffs from his pocket, the younger policeman clipped them about Anne's wrists.

Sarah Bascombe gasped, and the color drained from Anne's face. James shoved the police aside and held onto his wife's upper arms. "I have you, darling. Don't faint. I'm sure there's some mistake."

Catherine watched the entire scene as though it were a charade, but Harry instantly appeared at his brother's side. "Where are you taking her?" he demanded of the police.

"To the lockup in Oxford. And we're leaving now if you'll excuse us."

With a policeman on either side of her, Anne was a few steps away when she slid to the floor in a dead faint.

Before anyone else moved, Harry pushed James aside and knelt beside her. "Anne, darling. It's going to be all right. I'll take care of it." He cupped her face in his hand and tenderly stroked her hair.

His mother said, "Get up, Harry, do. I must see to her." Harry got up with apparent reluctance.

Sarah turned to the police, "I'm a physician." Then, kneeling by her daughter-in-law, she took her pulse. "Faint and thready," she said. "I'm afraid you can't take her away like this. Carry her to the sofa; there's a good lad," she said to James.

"Fetch my bag, darling," she instructed her husband. "James? Anything I should know?"

"She's expecting. Three months along. She wasn't ready to tell anyone," said James.

The room was silent. Catherine noticed that Harry balled his hands into fists where he stood next to the sofa.

Harry's father returned with a black satchel which he handed to his wife. Opening it quickly, she withdrew a vial and unscrewed it under Anne's nose. Her eyes flew open, and she dashed the smelling salts away with her manacled hands.

"Silly of me," she said. "I don't know what's wrong with me. I've never fainted in my life!"

James smoothed her dark hair back from her face. "I had to tell them, darling. About the baby."

"Oh!" she said. "Not exactly how I'd planned it."

"I'm following you back to Oxford," her husband said.

"Much better find me a solicitor," she said.

"I think we can be of some help there," said Catherine. "I know a good man in London. Would you like me to call him?"

"Yes, please," said Anne as she tried to sit up. Her husband helped her.

"Still woozy?" he asked.

"A bit," Anne said.

Eventually, James's wife was able to stand and accompany the police. Catherine glanced at Harry. His lips were pressed tightly together, and his nostrils flared. She sensed not only frustration but anger as he watched James follow the police and Anne out of the room.

He wishes he were going, too.

Catherine pushed the idea out of her mind as she calmed herself with a deep breath.

"May I use your telephone to place a trunk call to London?" she asked Sarah.

"Please," Harry's mother said. "Poor, dear Anne. What a dreadful thing to happen. She knew Severn, of course. Their squabbles were a matter of record. But she would never kill anyone."

"What did she have to do with the earl?" asked Harry.

Harry's father said, "They're political adversaries. He's a great admirer of the Fuehrer. They've written dueling letters in the *Times*."

"I had no idea," said Catherine.

"Anne's scrappy," said Harry. "She always has been. Severn wanted to remake Britain in the style of Germany. Anne had a few choice things to say about life in the Third Reich."

"But surely that wouldn't lead to murder!" Catherine recalled herself to the task at hand. "Where is the telephone?" she asked.

Sarah led her to the butler's pantry. After asking the exchange to put her through to Mr. Spence on Half Moon Street in London, Catherine sat down to wait for the call. Her thoughts galloped through her head in an ungainly manner.

What is stuck in Harry's craw? He hasn't been himself ever since James and Anne arrived.

What kind of threat could an untitled housewife pose to an earl of the realm? Why would the Times even publish her letters?

At last, her call rang through. Catherine answered and spoke to Mr. Spence.

"I have yet another relation, or rather a relation-to-be, who has been arrested," she said after greeting the solicitor.

"Someone in Professor Bascombe's family this time?" His dry tone seemed almost amused.

"Unfortunately. It's Anne Bascombe. They're taking her to the jail in Oxford. It will be a while before they arrive. They just left Hampshire."

"Whom did she allegedly murder?"

"The Earl of Severn. But I know absolutely none of the details. I just met the woman."

"The chap in the morning paper. Well, well," said the solicitor." I shall make my way up to Oxford in the morning if that suits."

"Thank you, yes,"

"Shall you be involved in the investigation this time?"

"It's a bit sticky," said Catherine. "I just met the woman and don't know her at all."

"From what you said, she is soon to be family."

"That makes it doubly sticky," she answered.

"That seems to be your specialty, he said. "But of course, I'm happy to assist as needed."

As soon as she rang off, the little voice she had been trying to quell finally broke through the chaos of her thoughts. *What exactly is going on between Harry, James, and Anne?*

* * *

Harry's mother sat staring into the fireplace. Harold Bascombe, Sr., stood behind her, a glass of whiskey in one hand, the other on his wife's shoulder. Mary and Ned sat on the sofa, holding hands. Harry prowled the room, his forehead creased in a frown. Catherine didn't know what to do with herself. This seemed all at once a very private matter—one she had no business being part of.

"Catherine," Harry said. "There isn't any other option. Anne is innocent, so we must find the real culprit."

Her resistance to the idea was both instantaneous and strange. When had she not been keen to solve a mystery?

"Do you think you could do that?" inquired his mother.

"We've done it before," her son said. "Haven't we, Catherine?"

She made herself speak. "Harry, we don't exactly have an entrée into the earl's life. I wouldn't know where to begin."

"We'll find a way," he said. "We must find a way."

"This new Detective Chief Inspector in Oxford is supposed to be very competent. A great improvement over Marsh," Catherine told him.

"Not only was the victim an earl, but as such, he was a member of the House of Lords," Harry said as though she had not spoken. "There will be enormous political pressure on the DCI to wrap this up quickly. Look what's happened already! This morning they had no suspects. Now, in the space of a day, they've made an arrest. Anne of all people!"

"It's unfortunate, but they must have some strong evidence, son," said his father.

"Then that's where we start," Harry said. "We find the flaw in their reasoning."

Catherine felt as though her fiancé were on a stage, and she was watching him from the gallery. "You act as though you know just how to do that," she said.

"We've always managed before. We'll get the story from Anne's point of view and go from there. She and Severn were political enemies, you said, Mother. Was their relationship conducted only in the *Times*, or had they met?"

"I'm not sure," said Sarah. "His estate is near Woodstock, so he's next door to Oxford."

Harry's father said, "The fellow was a reactionary. He felt the aristocracy had a mandate from God to govern the country. Hated the whole idea of an elected body. He wanted to do away with the House of Commons."

"Good heavens!" exclaimed Catherine. "It sounds like the man was demented."

"Surprisingly, he had his supporters. The same people who think Hitler has the right idea about how to run a country."

"Did he think the British people would sit still while he implemented his ideas? He wanted a revolution from the Right!" said Harry. "No wonder Anne was so upset. This is just what she's been observing in Germany."

Mary spoke up, "But if that's so, can someone tell me how Hitler got away with it?"

"Good question," said Harry. "He did it by scaring everyone into believing they were on the eve of a Bolshevik revolution. Then, he came in on his white horse to 'save' the country."

"The devil of it is, the two factions *were* locked in a power struggle," Catherine said. "The Communists were a credible threat. Democracy had failed the German people."

"A powerful lesson in statecraft," said Sarah. "But bringing this all back to Anne, I can't believe the police think her politics would be enough of a motive for her to have killed Severn. She's not a radical. She's an Oxford housewife."

"We'll get to the bottom of it, Mother," promised Harry.

Ned broke into the conversation. "I need to get Mary home. Sorry to break up the evening so early, but she's been exhausted these past few days."

Sarah went to Mary's side and sat down next to her. "You haven't said anything, dear. Why don't you let me take your blood pressure before you leave? I need to watch you for pre-eclampsia."

Catherine noted that the pregnant woman did appear suddenly exhausted. The doctor already had her satchel out, so she removed her blood pressure cuff and took a reading.

"It's a little high, dear." She checked Mary's hands and feet. "A slight swelling. Ned's right. You need to go home and put your feet up and try to get some good sleep. I'll be by to see you tomorrow."

Mary smiled. "I'll be fine. But it certainly is nice to have a doctor in the family!"

* * *

As Catherine lay under her comfortable quilts that night, she went over her impressions of Harry's family. Dr. Bascombe was just like these quilts—warm and comforting. But she was intelligent, as well. Catherine believed she could become very fond of her mother-in-law to be. Her own mother was the hearty, cold-shower-before-breakfast type. She would have made a splendid games mistress in a girls' school. Catherine had never had anyone like Sarah Bascombe in her life.

Harry's father combined the qualities of a sharp mind and a hail-fellow-well-met personality. Catherine had been immediately drawn to him. Thinking over the evening's developments, she had no doubt that he knew precisely what was behind the tension between his sons.

She rolled over on her side and curled into a ball. As the evening had unfolded, particularly the arrest, Harry showed a side to himself that she had never seen—sharp-tempered, possessive, gripped by passion. Her Harry was an easy-going charmer with the trademark British reserve. What was his past with this woman?

Chapter Three

When she awoke the following morning, Catherine was surprised at how long she'd slept. Her wristwatch next to her bed told her that it was already after nine.

Even after a shower and applying makeup, she wasn't what one would call glamorous.

"Buck up!" she told herself irritably.

As she descended the staircase, she heard voices in the breakfast room and straightened her shoulders. When she entered the bright, sunny room with its view of the flower garden, she found Sarah dressed for church and conversing with someone she had never met.

"Catherine, dear, this is our neighbor, Anne's father, Lord Rutherford. Ford, this is Harry's fiancée, Catherine Tregowyn."

A tall, stork-like figure with a large head of white hair unfolded himself and stood, extending his hand. "I have looked forward to this meeting! I am a great fan of yours. I anticipate long conversations about these murders you've solved. But that must wait. First, there's this business of Anne's. Dare I hope you might lend us a hand?"

"Harry's determined that we will," said Catherine. "Did Sarah tell you that we've arranged for a solicitor who is meeting with her this morning?"

"Yes. And I appreciate it." He settled back into his chair. "The game's afoot, my dear. Where do you propose to begin?"

Catherine wondered if he wasn't relishing Anne's situation as a chance to play Sherlock Holmes. He seemed quite cheerful despite the fact of his daughter's arrest.

"I guess we will determine that after talking to Anne."

"Ah, yes. I imagine you will get along splendidly. She's a grand girl. I've missed her these years she's been gone in Germany. But she didn't waste her time there. I'm trying to set up an interview for her with Winston, but I suppose that shall have to wait until we get this other business settled."

"Perhaps you could tell me what you know about the man who was killed?" Catherine suggested.

"Before you start," said Sarah, "I really must leave for church. Harold is out in his garden, but Harry hasn't come down yet."

At that moment, Harry entered the breakfast room. He kissed his mother's cheek. "We'll be off by the time you return from church, Mother. Sorry, we can't stay the whole weekend, but we must see Anne and get started on this case. Lovely party last night."

Catherine's spirits took a dive. She wasn't ready to leave this lovely, nurturing home to embark on a new case. That was strange. She normally thrived on mystery-solving!

Harry greeted Anne's father, "Ford. I hope you're not too distressed over Anne. We'll soon have this sorted."

"That's what I'm counting on," the man replied. "And I'm going to help you. I'm not unfamiliar with the role of detective."

"Lord Rutherford was just going to tell me what he knows about the Earl of Severn."

"Very good," said Harry. "I'll just have a bit of breakfast then." He went to the sideboard and filled a plate with eggs, bacon, fried tomatoes, and toast.

As soon as Harry was seated, their neighbor began. "I can't say that I'm sorry he is dead. Man had dangerous views. Saw himself as the British version of Hitler. Unfortunately, there were quite a few people who listened to him. Aristocrats. People who were scared to death of Socialism and trade unions."

"I seem to remember he had some kind of manufacturing company, didn't he?" asked Harry.

"Yes. His firm does precision parts manufacturing. It's a big business right now. Parts for automobiles and airplanes, in particular. They've been trading with Germany since the end of the War."

"Harry's father said the earl wanted to abolish the House of Commons," said Catherine.

"Yes. Severn said the common man bent naturally towards Socialism which he felt would destroy the country. He was anti-democracy. Said we couldn't trust it. A thoroughly bad chap."

"He sounds like someone from the Dark Ages," said Catherine.

"Sounds like he traded on fear. Just like Hitler," said Harry.

"Right," said Lord Rutherford. From his pocket, he took a pipe. Meerschaum, just like Holmes. As he packed it with tobacco, he said, "Glad you're going up to see Anne. She shouldn't be in jail. Between us, I wish she'd married you instead of the gormless James. He'll be no help to her."

Catherine darted a quick look at Harry. He was suddenly hearty. "Then I couldn't have married Catherine. You do know she's my fiancée?"

Anne's father looked startled. "Well, yes. There is that." He lit his pipe, and for a few moments, there was silence.

Harry pushed his plate away. "Well. I guess we'll be going. We must get up to Oxford."

The peer stood. Catherine extended her hand. As the man shook it, he said, "I'll be in touch. I'll be up to see Anne this evening. Does Sarah have your number?"

"She has mine, of course," said Harry. "No need to bother Catherine."

* * *

They were almost out of Hampshire, and Harry had been silent all the way, his hands gripping the steering wheel so hard his knuckles shone white. Then, finally, Catherine said, "I think it would be wise if you told me a bit about your history with Anne."

Harry barked humorlessly. "She chose James. End of story."

Catherine persisted. "How long ago was that?"

He emitted a gusty sigh. "Eight years ago. Subject closed."

"I'm afraid not," said Catherine. "You're a completely different person today. I've never seen you like this."

"Things ended badly, Catherine. I'd rather not talk about it." He kept his eyes on the road, not even glancing at her. "It has nothing to do with you and me."

"It does. You're different than I've ever known you to be. The Harry I know has always been charming and devil-may-care. You're suddenly this intense stranger. I think you're keeping something from me."

"Don't be so dramatic! I've known Anne all my life. She's like a little sister. I'm worried about her, that's all."

He was silent the rest of the way to Oxford. Catherine looked out the window and then pretended to sleep. Harry had never been evasive. What was he hiding from her?

Should she just ask him to take her to her flat and go on to the jail himself? Perhaps that was unjust to Anne. For her part, she hadn't been at all encouraging towards Harry. And Catherine might not like it, but Anne needed their help.

And Catherine owed Harry for all the patience he'd shown over her past entanglement. Rafe had been a thoroughly bad lot. But like Harry and Anne, they had grown up together. His flaws were so familiar she couldn't even see them as such. Did Anne even have any flaws?

* * *

The police station was in the Oxford Town Hall. Harry parked on the street in front. Unfortunately, the sergeant at the desk said that Mrs. Bascombe already had a visitor, and only two visitors at a time were allowed.

"That'll be James," Harry said. "I'll go back first and tell him we are here."

Catherine sat on a bench while the sergeant escorted Harry back to the jail. How many times had she been in this place? She and Harry had worked on two cases here in Oxford, but they both seemed a long time ago. The first, concerning her brother, Wills, and the second involving an Oxford jazz band. But all that had been before their stint in California and the murders in Hollywood. That's where they had gotten engaged—on an unforgettable beach next to some wonderous tide pools.

James came out with the sergeant. He looked as though he hadn't slept at all with his rumpled evening clothes and hair falling over his forehead. His eyes looked as though they were set in craters.

"Splendid of you to come, Catherine. We're both so grateful. I'll dash off and have a wash and a brush-up while you and Harry are here."

"I'm happy to help," she said.

The sergeant led her back into the station's bowels, where she found Harry and Anne seated in one of the interrogation rooms with another policeman in the corner taking shorthand.

Anne's tired face lit at Catherine's appearance. "Thank you so much for sending Mr. Spence. He was quite helpful. I feel confident in his hands." The woman, though droopy-eyed, was still beautiful. She had pulled her hair back in an elastic, thus exhibiting a classic profile. Pallor suited her particular kind of looks.

Catherine said, "You've probably been interrogated 'til you're sick of it, but we need to know everything if we're going to help you. Tell us about your dealings with the earl. Did you only correspond, or had you met him?"

"Until the day he died, we only corresponded. First, privately. Then in open letters in the *Times*. James can show them to you. I saved all his letters and carbon copies of mine."

"Why did you see him on the day he was murdered?"

"He summoned me as though I were an errant schoolgirl. I shouldn't have gone, but I was curious. My besetting sin." She sighed. "Anyway, when I went to his house, he threatened my family and me if I didn't stop my 'persecution' of him. He said he was in a position to do us harm. He was a major donor to the University, so he could get James fired to start with. He also hinted that he could endanger my father's position in the Lords. Father is only a life peer, you see. That means that the king could strip him of his title, and he'd lose his seat."

"How did you respond?" asked Catherine.

Anne gave a short laugh. "I was pretty well speechless. When I could talk through my anger, I finally told the earl that I would publish his threat. He turned purple. I thought he might have a stroke. So I let myself out."

Catherine couldn't help her admiration of this ploy. "Jolly well done! What time did you leave?"

"My appointment was for four o'clock. Our conversation didn't take long. I couldn't have left too much later than four-twenty. The devil of it is that I went by the French doors in his office out into the garden, so I can't prove when I left.

Harry asked, "And the murder took place when?"

"It said in the newspaper that the valet who found him rang the police at seven. His secretary had left at five." Anne replied, giving a little shiver and running her hands down her arms.

"How was he murdered?" Catherine asked. "I'm afraid I didn't read the newspaper."

"He was stabbed to death with his letter opener." Anne shivered. "Gruesome. I don't think his murder was pre-meditated."

"Hmm," Catherine said. "I assume you were the last person known to visit him. But, that French door . . . It gives us a good window of time when the murderer could have entered and done the deed. Whom did you tell about your appointment?"

The woman closed her eyes as she thought. "I have that little group I was telling you about—sort of a nascent Anti-Fascist/

Pro-Armament League. We met that morning in James' and my flat when the earl's secretary called me and made the appointment. I couldn't imagine why he wanted to see me. So I told my group, and we tossed it around a bit, trying to guess."

Harry rubbed his hands together. "Ah hah! Can you give us their names?"

Anne bit her lip and looked at Harry under a lowered brow. "Is it really necessary? I don't want you questioning them. They're my friends."

Harry dismissed this, chopping his hand on the table. "You must see! They're suspects, Anne!"

"Well, it couldn't have been my co-founder, Oliver Anderson. He's a pacifist. I seriously doubt he could have stabbed anyone. He is ideologically opposed to violence."

"You don't know, Anne," said Harry. "It looks as though the murder was unplanned. I doubt they entered the earl's study planning to murder him. I have heard that Severn didn't like to be crossed. He had a vile temper. You certainly saw it. What if he threatened this Anderson the way he threatened you?" asked Harry, writing down the name. "Where can we find the fellow?"

"He's a tutor at Merton College."

"What else can you tell us about Mr. Anderson?" Catherine asked.

Looking down at her lap, Anne began pleating her skirt between her fingers. "It's Dr. Anderson. He's very sound. Oliver is fond of saying that the best offense is a good defense. So even though he's against war, he is for rearmament. He wants a show of strength."

"Hmm," said Harry. "That's a different line for a pacifist to take."

"He lost his brother and too many of his classmates and friends in the War. He doesn't want another one, but he thinks if Hitler rearms and no one else does, we're just asking for one."

"Very pragmatic for a pacifist. That sort usually has their heads in the clouds." Harry underlined the name he had written down in his pocket-sized notebook. "Who else?"

"Well, there's my good friend Red—Alexander de Fontaine."

"Oh!" said Catherine. "We know, Red. We're good friends. I sang in his band last year!"

Anne appeared startled. "You're a jazz singer? I thought you were a tutor at Somerville."

"I am," said Catherine, with a short laugh. "Harry and I were working a case where a member of Red's band was murdered. Harry, you remember Red?"

"A Communist, as I recall. He makes a splendid suspect!" He wrote in his notebook. "A pacifist and a Communist. We're moving right along. I can't imagine who else you've rounded up for this group of yours."

"Well, there are various Somerville students. I'm afraid I don't know all of their names off the top of my head. But I have them written down. They heard about the group from Dean Godfrey from Somerville. She's another of my allies who was there when I got the call from Severn's secretary. We've become fast friends. She's brilliant."

Catherine was surprised. She knew the new dean, of course, but she wouldn't say they were friends. The lady would not be surprised to find Catherine involved in another case. Nor would she be particularly pleased to be a suspect.

"That surprises me. I'm not certain of the political leanings of the Somerville Warden and the board, but I should think she might be risking her job."

"Elizabeth feels very strongly about this. Her mother is a close friend of Vera Brittain. She is certain, as am I, that Hitler is arming himself to the teeth and is going to drive his country straight into war."

"I had no idea about her friendship with Miss Brittain," Catherine said, mulling this over. Vera Brittain, a former VAD and the author of *Testament of Youth,* was one of the most passionate critics of the War, which had killed her idealistic, young fiancé. I wonder if she lost someone."

"Did you tell anyone else?" Harry asked.

"No," said Anne, smoothing her pigtail.

"Hmm," said Harry. "Well, this gives us a start."

"What did Mr. Spence say?" Catherine asked.

Anne sighed. "My arraignment is set for tomorrow. He's going to try to get me out on bail. My father rang, and he's willing to post it. He should be here in a few hours."

"Well, that's some good news anyway," Catherine said, standing. "We'll get started with this. Now, I'll leave the two of you to talk. I'm going out to get some air."

It was with some reluctance that Catherine realized she admired Anne greatly. It was easy to see why Harry had apparently carried a torch for her all these years. In Catherine's mind, there weren't very many men who could compare to Harry. But Anne had married his brother. How had that happened? Perhaps, Harry had been this other person then—jealous and possessive—when he and Anne were together. Catherine knew instinctively that Anne wouldn't have liked that. It would have been very wearing.

She decided to walk home. Catherine loved Oxford on Sunday afternoons. Without the everyday hurly-burly of traffic, it was easier to remember that this had been a learning center for six centuries. Fortunately, she was wearing her good walking shoes as she ventured upon her way. An autumn wind whistled through the buildings, feeling quite chilly, even though she was wearing her tweeds. The sky was a lovely intense blue with a few fast-moving clouds, serving as a perfect backdrop for the ancient honey-stoned buildings. She was happy this was her home, relieved to remember that Harry wasn't the whole of her life and that she had a challenging career as a poet and a tutor.

CHAPTER FOUR

Cherry, her maid, was pleased to see her.

"But where is your luggage?" she asked. "And where is Dr. Bascombe?"

The last thing Catherine needed was to be interrogated by her maid of long-standing. "He's at the jail. His sister-in-law has been arrested for murder. I desperately need a bath, Cherry. I'm chilled to the bone. If Dr. Bascombe comes by, please tell him I'm unavailable."

Cherry raised her eyebrows.

* * *

After her bath, Catherine pulled out the essays from her students on E.M. Forster and tried to immerse herself in the task of marking them. After an hour's attempt at this occupation, she acknowledged the futility of the job and put aside her student's work. She needed to get started on Anne's case.

She fixed herself a mug of Horlick's, wrapped herself in a down comforter, and sat before the fire, pen and paper in hand. Finding out that the murder weapon was a.) readily to hand, and b.) something anyone could use had changed her ideas somewhat. For some reason, she had gotten the idea that a pistol had been used.

A letter-opener seemed more like a women's weapon. There were two women under consideration already: Dean Elizabeth Godfrey and Anne Bascombe.

She didn't know anything about the dean's temperament, but Anne was certainly passionate about her cause. Severn had summoned her and commanded her to stop her assault upon him. He had threatened her with at least two things: a.) revenge to be carried out against her husband, costing him his job, and b.) revenge against her father by discrediting him in the Lord's and having his peerage taken away. Had there been something else she hadn't disclosed? Something against Anne personally? Something that gave *her* specifically a motive for murder? Anne struck her as being a bit of a *prima donna*, not the sort who would commit murder because her husband or her father were threatened. Besides, she had spiked his guns in that regard by threatening to publish his would-be weapons.

Catherine drew back from this line of thinking and examined herself. Why was she even thinking that Anne could be the murderer? Did she dislike her so much? Did she feel threatened by Harry's adolescent passion for her? If she pursued a case against Anne, she would lose Harry forever.

There was no one she could discuss this with but Dot, her closest friend. Dot knew her from the inside out. And she knew Harry. Catherine looked at the clock. It was 2:00 Sunday afternoon. She could be in London, where Dot had her flat by 3:30.

Was she losing her mind?

No. She needed someone who knew her well to untangle her motives and help her to move forward.

Catherine placed a trunk call to London. In ten minutes, she was speaking to her friend. Completely unflappable, Dot invited her for the night. Max, her American boyfriend, a Ph.D. student of Harry's, was leaving to get back to Oxford in an hour.

Cherry helped her to pack an overnight bag and, when it was packed, rang for a taxi to take her mistress to the train station.

* * *

London was a bit quiet on Sunday afternoon. Catherine took a taxi from the train station to St. John's Wood, where Dot had her flat.

Her friend greeted her with a worried frown. "Darling, when did you eat last? You're white as a sheet!"

Surprised, Catherine considered the question. "Breakfast this morning at Harry's parents' home. I hadn't even thought about food."

"You must have a puzzle on your mind. Don't tell me you're involved in another murder investigation!"

"Darling, I've so much to tell you," said Catherine. "But I could use some toast or something."

"And an egg?" asked Dot. "It's no trouble. And I just bought marmalade, so we have that."

Poking around in her small refrigerator, Dot found a tomato and a jar of pickles. Ten minutes later, the pair of women were seated at Dot's kitchen table, partaking of this unconventional repast, listening to music on the wireless.

"All right," Dot said as Catherine completed her supper. "We can leave the washing up for later. Let's go into the sitting room by the fire."

"That sounds wonderful," said Catherine. "You're probably going to think I've gone balmy showing up like this."

"No, really," said Dot. "I'm always a bit blue on Sunday afternoons after Max goes back to Oxford. It's lovely to have the company."

They settled themselves on Dot's navy blue sofa.

"Well, not to put too fine a point on it, I'm in danger of having Harry hate me forever," Catherine said, clutching a red throw pillow to her middle.

She recounted the events of Saturday night when Anne was arrested, Harry's reaction, and what they had found out that afternoon from Anne at the jail.

"I'm actually seeing how Anne could be as guilty as the police think she is. By her own admission, Severn threatened those she loves—her husband and her father. But I'm wondering if he didn't threaten her personally. She is a very assertive personality. An only child. I think she's used to getting her way."

"And Harry? He disagrees with you?" asked Dot.

Catherine shrugged. "I haven't even brought it up with him. He's not rational where she's concerned. I've never seen him like this. He takes his dialogue from Emily Brontë. If I try to investigate Anne, it will be over for Harry and me."

Dot caught her lower lip between her teeth. "I see your problem. Are you certain you're not prejudiced against Anne?"

"I'm not sure at all, which is why I'm here. This is not like me."

"Who are the other suspects besides Anne?"

Catherine held up her thumb and two fingers. "There are three, so far. Dean Godfrey from Somerville, Oliver Anderson, a pacifist, and our friend, Red. But the murderer could be anyone Severn has crossed swords with."

"Why are those three suspects, in particular?"

"They all knew where Anne was going at 4:00. But that argues premeditation and the knowledge that Anne would most certainly be accused of their crime. They are supposedly her friends." Catherine sighed and shook her head.

"One of them might be incredibly desperate," said Dot. "I think before you slander Anne, you need to find out about those three people first. Also, there is a motive staring you in the face that you've missed completely."

Catherine had been pleating the afghan in her lap. She looked up. "What?"

"Who stood to gain by Severn's death, Cat?" Dot leaned forward and looked Catherine in the eye.

Pounding her forehead with her fist, Catherine said, "His heir! The ninth earl!"

Dot nodded. "I don't think you need to worry about Anne just now. You have four other people to investigate. What's the new DCI like?"

"He settled on Anne awfully fast. He either knows something we don't know, or he's engaging in incredibly shoddy police work."

Dot seemed to hesitate for a moment. Then she said, "All right, now I have to ask you this question—how angry are you at Harry?"

Catherine was jolted out of her thoughts by the question. Her brow creased. "Do you think I've manufactured a case against Anne because I want to show him who she really is?"

"The thought has crossed my mind," said her friend.

"That's what I'm afraid of. That's why I came to see you. I knew you would give it to me straight, as they say in America. Am I really that awful a person?"

"I don't think you're awful. That's just the reaction I would have if the tables were turned," said Dot, putting a hand gently on Catherine's sleeve. "I grant you, the case looks bad against Anne, but why don't you just leave that to the police, Cat?"

"I don't know if I can do that."

"The least you can do is try to find alibis for the other four people, starting with the heir," said Dot.

"That's rather daunting. But maybe Red would know something. And I need to get my hands on a Debrett's and see who he the heir is."

They batted around ideas for a while and then left the subject and began to talk about Dot's new company and Max. It was so good to be with her friend. They had been confidantes ever since they were twelve years old. Now that Catherine had taken her thoughts and discussed them with her friend, they didn't look so damning.

When they finally got up to prepare for bed, Catherine's load felt lighter even though nothing had changed.

CHAPTER FIVE

On the train ride back to Oxford in the morning, Catherine tried to organize her thoughts dispassionately. If Anne hadn't killed the earl, it had been accomplished between 4:20 and 7 p.m. She wondered if the medical examiner had given a more precise time of death. What time did the secretary leave? Did he hear anything? Did the earl have any further appointments?

Perhaps she would need to go no further than the newspaper to find the answers to her questions. She hoped Cherry hadn't yet tossed out the newspapers for the past two days. When a murder happened, she liked to know what was going on. Maybe she had kept them.

It transpired that Cherry had taken the *News of the World* back to her bedroom, and the *Sunday Times* was sitting unread with the mail on Catherine's desk.

"Thank you, Cherry," she said.

"I'm glad you're back, miss. Dr. Bascombe has been ringing you. I didn't think you would want me to tell him where you were."

"Thank you. I will take his call if he rings again."

The *Times* gave a window for the time of death, calculated by the state of rigor mortis in the corpse, as between four-thirty and five o'clock. The police had interviewed the gardeners about comings and goings through the French windows in the earl's study. No one had seen anyone unusual.

The *News of the World* gave a sensational detail. What appeared to be a coded message was found on the victim's desk, spotted with his blood. What a pity that this particular newspaper couldn't always be relied upon. The *Times* had said nothing about this. It did sound rather bogus.

While she was considering this point, Harry rang.

"Darling, where have you been? I've rung all hours!"

"I went up to London and had an evening with Dot. You needn't have worried."

"Oh, that's a relief. How is she?"

"Spiffing," said Catherine brightly.

"I was back at college yesterday when it occurred to me that you would be needing your luggage."

"Thank you," she said. "Did you find out anything further from Anne?"

"No. I didn't stay long after you left. James returned."

Forcibly putting James's feud with Harry out of her mind, she said, "I don't know how it happened, but I completely forgot about the ninth earl! He would be the first suspect in the murder. I was just planning to go over to the library and check Debrett's."

"You're right! But surely the police have covered that angle."

"I wouldn't count on it. They were pretty quick to arrest Anne. Isn't she being arraigned this morning?"

"Yes. At ten. Shall I bring your luggage over?"

"If you don't mind. I shall probably be at the library."

"Can you wait a tick? I'll be over immediately. The motor's out in the street, so I can just nip over. We can walk over to the library."

"All right then. Cheerio," said Catherine.

When Harry arrived, and they were walking to Somerville together, he said, "I say, darling, you're not still angry with me about Anne, are you?"

He acts as though nothing is wrong. He seems to be back to the Harry I know.

"Should I be?" she asked.

"I was beastly to you while we were driving up from Hampshire."

"You were actually," she agreed.

"I'm deuced worried about Anne. You can understand that, can't you?"

"It needn't make you uncivil," she told him.

"I'm sorry." A glumness settled over him once again.

They walked to Somerville without speaking the rest of the way. Catherine was relieved when they reached the library.

Debrett's Peerage wasn't hard to locate. Catherine put the heavy volume on the table and looked up the eighth earl of Severn. Under heirs, she found Lord Bertram Netherton. Born 1855, St. Athan's, Wales. Residence: Cypress House, St. Athan's, Wales.

"Good heavens!" said Catherine. "The man's eighty years old! He's twenty years older than the eighth earl."

"A bit past killing with a paper-knife, one would think," said Harry. "He could have been overpowered quite easily."

"Let's find an atlas," said Catherine. "I don't know St. Athan's."

When they located the little town on the reference atlas, they saw it on the Bristol Channel, not far from Cardiff.

"Two and a half hours from Oxford by train, at least," said Harry. "I wonder how soon after the murder the police rang Lord Bertram."

"Yes. That's an interesting question," said Catherine.

"I do still have my obliging friend on the Force," Harry said. "Maybe he knows why the heir was disqualified as a suspect. I'll invite him out for a pint tonight."

"Good," said Catherine, feeling a little bit of their camaraderie return. "It's so helpful to have friends in interesting places."

They were situated back in the stacks of the library. Harry kissed her cheek and said, "Don't let Anne come between us. That was long, long ago and she's married to my brother now."

Catherine's only response was to pat the lapel to his jacket as he held her close. "The *News of the World's* story on the murder claimed that there was a coded bit of paper left behind on Severn's desk. Blood spattered."

"Sounds pretty bogus to me," Harry said.

"My thoughts exactly," said Catherine, glad they could agree on something. Are we finished here?"

"Yes. I think so," said Harry. "Seems to me that we need to talk to Severn's private secretary."

When they were out of the library, walking around the quadrangle, Catherine said, "He was full of ineffective quotes in that article—all about how Britain had lost a great man. His name was . . . Dawson, I think. Yes. Gerald Dawson."

Harry sounded out the name, "Gerald Dawson . . . Gerry Dawson . . .

Dawson . . . ! Yes, I do believe I know the fellow! He is a Christ Church alum. He was a first-year when I was third. Used to call him Hawk. Pesky sort. Always wanted to make certain he got his share of the spotlight."

Catherine said, "It sounds like he might not mind talking, then. But how will you get in with your last name being the same as his suspect's?"

"He knows me by my college nickname. Probably won't remember anything else. As for his talking, the problem will probably be the reverse. We won't be able to shut him up."

Catherine mused, "Don't you find in academia that everyone is always writing a book? Perhaps you should be terribly impressed by the Earl of Severn. You will need all of Mr. Dawkins's help to flesh him out for the book you're writing. Particularly his theories about the murder."

"I say, darling! That is brilliant! The only thing dimming my joy is that I shall have to act like a fascist."

"Fortunately, you're very good at dissembling," she said.

He looked at her keenly. "Why do I have the feeling that wasn't meant as a compliment?"

She managed a serene smile.

"You shall be *my* secretary, of course. I'm sorry to say that he is very misogynistic. Doesn't even think women should have the vote. Think you can manufacture some squiggles that might look like shorthand?"

Catherine sighed. "I suppose there's nothing for it. I shall make you pay in future, however."

Harry grinned. "That sounds jolly ominous."

How well he acts. Has our relationship been nothing but a charade from the beginning?

Catherine could feel herself being drawn in once again by Harry's charm. Had it never been anything other than superficial? "All right then. I'll leave it to you to breach the bulwark. I've got essays to mark before my tutorial tomorrow. If we could go afterward, that would be perfect. I'll expect to hear from you."

If he noticed her change of mood from warm to frosty, he never made a sign. "Thank you for doing this, Catherine. You have no idea how much I appreciate it."

"On the contrary," she said, looking him straight in the eye. "I think I do understand very well. Good afternoon, Harry."

They had reached the place in front of her flat where he had parked his motor. After infuriating her by kissing her cheek again, he took his leave.

She had plenty to think about that night as she tried to sleep. But a good nights' sleep was not to be had. Anne's father rang her at ten o'clock p.m., suggesting a meeting that evening.

* * *

Lord Rutherford arrived at her flat as naturally as though calling on a single woman alone at ten-thirty in the evening were perfectly acceptable. Cherry had been in her bed for a long time. The man looked even more stork-like and eager than he had that morning.

"I have an idea," he said. "I've been making inquiries about that secretary of Severn's—Gerald Dawkins. It seems he's not quite the thing. By all accounts, he's an over-ambitious lily-livered fop and a misogynist to boot. Not at all well-liked at his college. I think he is definitely suspect material. I intend to see if he had anything to gain by Severn's death."

"That's a good idea. We are going to try to get in to see him tomorrow afternoon, as a matter of fact," said Catherine. "We had the same idea."

"Capital!" said the peer. "Great minds and all that."

"Have you been to see Anne this evening?"

"I have. She's out on bail now. She's a game one, that daughter of mine.."

"Yes. She certainly struck me that way."

"I shall stay up here at the Randolph so that we can coordinate our investigations. Please let me know how it goes if you can get in to see Dawkins."

"We will," said Catherine.

Rutherford left shortly thereafter, as abruptly as he had come.

* * *

Harry's charm apparently worked on Gerald Dawkins, as he was willing to see them the following day at his office in Lord Severn's home on the Woodstock estate.

They were to join him for tea that afternoon. Apparently, he was to continue his role as secretary for the new Lord Severn.

Catherine found difficulty settling down to mark essays, but she knew she must. This was her second year teaching, and she had already decided she would vary her syllabus next year. She was very tired of Forster and Galsworthy. Thank goodness she taught 20th Century British Lit and not 19th like Harry. She much preferred the modern writers and they weren't so long-winded. Finally, after three cups of tea, she was able to buckle down.

* * *

Her tutoring session went well. The intellectual immersion in Forster was enjoyable. The consensus held that *Room With a View* was more successful than *Howard's End*. Catherine found herself championing the Free Thinker, George Emerson, and Lucy Honeychurch's fierce attraction to him. Was it possible that George reminded her of Red, the bandleader/Communist she had briefly flirted with when investigating another murder case? Quenching the thought, she quickly pressed on to a discussion of the enigmatic *Passage to India*. She wasn't about to submit to any life-altering embraces with Red among the bluebells.

When Harry came for her at four o'clock that afternoon, he was in a somewhat somber mood, leading her to think he had been with Anne.

"What's the latest with Anne?" she asked.

"She's home now. Her father posted bail. She lives in a flat near here."

Catherine told him of her visit from Lord Rutherford the night before and his desire that they keep him apprised of their progress.

Harry was not thrilled. "He's going to make himself a nuisance, I predict."

They said little the rest of the drive—the gloomy weather adding to Catherine's depressed spirits.

Severn Hall was a beautifully preserved Gothic work of art, the medium being golden Cotswold stone. Patches of fog clung to a garden of late-blooming annuals, and a drizzle persisted, making the whole scene like some dark lord's fantasy.

A butler took them down a long passageway to the back of the mansion, where they found their host waiting for them in a brightly lit yellow tearoom decorated with oil paintings of long-ago battles and several vases of rust-colored chrysanthemums. Gerald Dawkins was a small man with premature baldness, dressed in formal gray morning dress.

Harry's bad mood magically fled as he shook hands with his old acquaintance. "Wonderful of you to see us, Hawk. I imagine you are working full out during this transition. Good news about the new earl keeping you on." He turned to Catherine. "This efficient-looking party is my assistant, Miss Tregowyn. But, first, Miss Tregowyn, meet Gerald Dawkins, Lord Severn's secretary. I'm afraid he knows me by the sobriquet of McDuff."

Catherine was not offered a hand by their host but received a nod of the head instead.

"It's been a long time, McDuff. Sit down, please. Then let's get started, shall we?" Dawkins seated himself in a large leather armchair.

"Yes," said Harry. "I know my readers are going to be particularly struck by this gruesome murder. I've read the accounts in the paper, but what can you tell me?"

Dawkins sat back in his chair, and his fingertips met over his chest. "I can imagine with the research you have done that you understand why my employer had such bitter enemies. He was a brilliant man with a rare vision. He saw our country as being at a crossroads between the socialist's vision and his own view of Britain. He wished to capitalize on the strengths that made it the world's greatest empire. Needless to say, there is a great gap there." He leaned forward, elbows on his knees, and proceeded to expound. "His ideas were refreshing to many people like us. Severn's ideas would put those in power who want to see the nation be reinstated as a strong, well-armed world force again. Trade unions, which cripple the manufacturing process, would be abolished."

"Didn't he think Hitler might be the least bit alarmed if that vision was played out?"

"Severn had no quarrel with Hitler. He believes . . . believed our countries could rule side by side with mutual respect. He admired what Hitler has accomplished in Germany. It is a blueprint, as it were, for Britain. But we don't need a new party like the National Socialists in Germany because we have the House of Lords . . . " Severn's minion continued in this vein for some time, causing Catherine to squirm. The late earl's view had been distinctly feudal.

The man really must have been delusional. Who could take him seriously?

Harry finally asked, "And I'm sure you believe that his murder was meant to stop the progression of this great dream of Lord Severn's?"

"There is no doubt in my mind. He received threats every day. By mail, mostly. Sometimes by telephone."

"What about on the day that he was killed?"

"There was one mysterious caller who rang. He didn't identify himself. He said he needed to deliver a message in person to my employer from the German embassy. His voice was heavily accented. Of course, Severn was not surprised. He has been corresponding with the ambassador. He was to have gone to a reception there next Friday. So, I don't think the five o'clock visitor was an enemy who killed him."

"Did you see him?"

"No. I had an errand for my employer which took me out of the office as soon as that infernal woman arrived . . . " his face fell and, for a moment, he stared at Harry as though seeing him for the first time. "The devil! How could I be so gullible! Bascombe! You are her husband! You aren't writing a book! You are seeking information!" He stood.

Harry said, "I am not her husband."

"Nevertheless, I'm afraid I must ask you must leave. At once. But I have one more thing to say to you! Have you never wondered why he wanted to speak to the saintly Mrs. Bascombe? Why the police were in such a hurry to arrest her? He knew things about her that would blister an elephant's hide. And not just Mrs. Bascombe. The earl knew *everything* about her little group of anti-fascists. Things that could ruin all of them. And he knew other things about people in power. He wasn't someone you wanted to tangle with. Now, I have nothing further to say to you. The right person is in custody. My duty is done."

Harry's whole body was rigid, and she could feel hate emanating from him in waves. He rose. "Thank you, Hawk. I'm afraid we can't stay for tea."

Catherine stood. "Farewell, Mr. Dawkins," she said. "It would do you good to remember that blackmail is a crime."

CHAPTER SIX

"Well," said Harry with an air of pseudo-cheer as they drove down the gravel drive. "Don't think we'll get much more out of Dawkins. However, we do have another line of inquiry. The stranger who rang. Sounds like the name of a thriller. I wonder if the police know about him."

"Harry, we must talk about the threat to Anne. I know you'd rather not, but are you going to ask her about it?"

He was white-knuckling the steering wheel again. "Do you suppose he was telling the truth then?"

"Definitely. We wondered how they got on to Anne so fast. Completely ignoring the heir. Has she spoken about what he threatened *her* with? It would have been easy for her to make up the threats to her husband and father."

"No. No, she hasn't. I can't even imagine what it must have been."

"Don't you think we need to know?" she asked, voicing her words just above a whisper.

"I know she's innocent," he said stubbornly. "That's all I need to know."

But Catherine could see the anguish in his face. Poor Harry was torn nearly in two.

She changed the subject. "Just suppose *The News of the World* got it right about that coded message. It could have been from someone at the German embassy."

"Too *Boys Own Magazine*," said Harry distractedly. "Even the Nazis wouldn't play such ridiculous games."

"It appears to me that if he thought it was possible to reinstate the aristocracy as our ruling class that he was deluded enough to relish something like that," said Catherine.

"You know, Hawk was the type to manufacture gossip so he would get noticed. He may have made up that bit about Anne," Harry said.

Catherine prudently avoided comment.

"There are plenty of Oxford grads who are balmy with some theory of their own devising. But, fortunately, most of them don't get taken seriously. Dawkins could have said what he did about Anne simply to make her suffer. She could have slighted him in some way."

Catherine sighed, "I suppose that could be right. Where are we going?"

"I think we need to report to Anne and see if she has any ideas about deep dark secrets in her anti-fascist group."

Catherine's heart dropped. Instinct bade her keep her distance from the combination of Anne and Harry. But how could she go forward with the investigation in that manner?

"Perhaps she could meet us at the Cheshire Cat. I was expecting tea, and I'm famished," she said. Perhaps if she suggested the venue, she would feel more in control of the situation.

* * *

Catherine had eaten an entire steak and kidney pie before Anne made an appearance at the pub. Her first look at the woman breezing through the entrance in a suit of Delft blue turned Catherine's meal to lead in her stomach. She was followed by the tall figure of her father, whom Harry said she had insisted on bringing.

Her fiancé stood and welcomed his sister-in-law and her father to their cozy booth in the corner of the pub. Anne didn't even resemble the person Catherine had seen languishing in the Oxford jail. Her red lipstick left a print on Harry's cheek as she kissed him. Catherine clenched her teeth.

Harry asked the newcomers what they wanted to drink.

"A shandy will be fine. Thank you," Anne said.

Lord Rutherford said, "Whatever's on tap."

Harry went to get their orders.

"We have visited Severn's private secretary," Catherine said, taking the bull by the horns. "We learned there was a visitor due after you, Anne, but I don't think Dawkins told the police about him. He thought he might have been someone from the German Embassy."

Anne replied, "I'm not surprised he was in correspondence with them. As I've told you, he thought highly of the lot of them."

"Hah!" said Lord Rutherford. "Von Ribbentrop has been visiting. It could have even been him! Hitler's foreign secretary, don't you know."

Harry returned at this comment with the drinks and overheard the peer's remark. "Severn was due to go to some sort of reception on Friday. It was probably for von Ribbentrop. I imagine they had a lot in common. He would have relished a meeting with a German aristocrat."

"Hmm," said Anne. "I wouldn't be at all surprised if von Ribbentrop made the journey from Germany just to meet with Severn. My contacts there say the Nazis thought very highly of him and probably had an exaggerated idea of his popularity in this country."

"Dawkins also said just as we were leaving that someone in your little group apparently has a guilty secret," said Harry. "I don't know if Dawkins knows it, but he claims Severn did."

"*My little group?*" Anne asked, raising her elegant brows.

"I assume he was talking about your anti-fascist bunch," said Harry and sipped his lager with elaborate casualness.

"I really do need to come up with a name for us," said Anne.

"I don't know everything about my members, though I known enough to call them friends. They wrote me after my letters to Severn appeared in the *Times*. We've only met on a few occasions."

Catherine said, "You said they all knew you were going to Severn's. According to the experts, his murder supposedly happened between 4:30 and 5:00. That means any of them could have come in after you. The secretary was gone. He wouldn't have known."

"Oh, dear," said Anne. "How awkward."

Catherine said, "Yes. Murder does tend to be awkward." Harry threw her a reproving look, but she didn't regret her cattiness.

Lord Rutherford said, "You probably know more than you think you do. You need to apply a little reason and deduction to the situation is all."

"Oh, Father, I'm not sure this is the time for Holmes."

"Anne, love, you are under arrest," said Lord Rutherford. "There has never been a better time for him. So. Tell us about the members of your group, and we'll see what we can deduce."

"Don't be ridiculous," she chided.

"You really do need to tell us about them, you know," said Catherine, getting out her notebook.

"Well, you already know Red. He's a Communist, Father, and has a jazz band. He's very open and above board about it. He's fomenting union discontent. He wants unions to have the right to strike again," said Anne. "He wanted to be part of our group precisely because of Severn."

Harry intervened, "Catherine, can't you see your Red knifing the good earl? Wouldn't Severn's agenda threaten everything he holds most dear?"

Catherine considered this. "He is very fond of saying thus-and-so type will be 'up against the wall come the Revolution.' I suppose it's possible that Severn was so egregious to him that he jumped the gun, so to speak. But, despite his theorizing, I have never been able to picture Red as a violent man. Would a violent man sponsor a jazz band?"

Rutherford said, "I would have to talk to him before I gave my opinion."

"Nothing easier," said Harry. "We can go to the Town Hall on Friday or Saturday night and listen to his band. Of course, we'll have to dance."

Catherine knew she was not ready to see Anne dancing with Harry. "Would James like to join us?" she asked.

"He's not much of a dancer. Neither am I to tell the truth," Anne replied.

"I think it much better if we call on him at his house. He lives here in Oxford," said Catherine.

"Well, it would be slightly ridiculous for all four of us to descend on him," said Harry. "Much better to invite him to join us for a drink. Is everyone available this evening?"

They all agreed to this plan. Then Anne said, "We might invite Oliver and Elizabeth as well," said Anne. "I'll ring them all from the flat when I get back. Eight-thirty, don't you think?"

Everyone agreed.

* * *

Catherine had to admit that she was more than a little curious to see Red. When she had been "undercover" singing for his band, they had hit it off. However, his politics had always stood between them. Not to mention Harry.

When she arrived back at her apartment, Cherry informed her that Dot had rung. Immediately, Catherine put a trunk call through to London.

When the exchange rang through, she settled herself on her Art Deco sofa--a white leather cushioned creation that swallowed her slender build.

"Cat, I had to ring to find out how everything is going and to ask you if I can stay with you this weekend. I'm coming up to see you and Max."

"Well, Harry and I are doing some investigating together. But now that she's out on bail, she's joined us."

"Is he still doing his Heathcliff impersonation?"

"He's better," she said. "But I don't know what he's like when he's alone with her."

"How does Anne respond to him?"

Catherine thought about that. "You know, I can't figure her out. I don't know if she takes his attentions as any more than her due. She's an exceptionally beautiful woman."

"Well, what are you going to do?" Dot wanted to know.

"There's not much I can do."

"How is Harry acting toward you?"

"Aside from our spat in the motor I told you about, he's treating me the same as usual. However, when I contrast it to the way he acts toward Anne, it makes me wonder if he's ever felt much of anything for me at all."

"Crikey. I thought you and Harry were solid. I'm glad I'll be there over the weekend."

* * *

When Catherine spied Red, she smiled. He was a handsome man. Not as good-looking as Harry with his movie star jaw and deep, dark eyes, but certainly attractive. Under his plentiful red hair, his face had bright blue eyes, a wide, inviting smile, and a closely trimmed beard. He kissed her on the cheek.

"Greetings, Comrade," she said, stepping aside so he could say hello to the others. "I don't believe you've met Anne's father, Lord Rutherford." She introduced the two, and they all got settled with drinks.

Next to arrive was the dean. With her was an attractive, distinguished looking man who was far too finely turned out to be an academic. Catherine recognized him from the Michaelmas Term sherry party a few weeks before. The dean introduced her companion as Mr. Stanley Oveson. He bowed over Catherine's hand in a courtly manner. She recognized the Christ Church tie.

"So lovely to meet you," he said. He had the sharp eyes of an observer who took in everything at a glance.

"Dr. Anderson was unable to make it tonight," Anne said. "He had another engagement."

They pushed two tables together. Anne sat between her father and Harry. Catherine sat with Red and the dean across from the threesome. Mr. Oveson sat on the other side of the dean.

"Do the two of you know anything about this business other than what was in the newspaper?" asked Red of Catherine and Harry.

Catherine caught everyone up by taking them through their interview with Mr. Dawkins the day before. She didn't mention the specific threat to Anne.

"So there was someone else due to see Severn after Anne, but no clue as to who he was?"

"Dawkins thought he was a messenger from the German Embassy. Severn was fairly thick with them, apparently," said Harry.

"Of course he was," said Red. "The fellow fancied himself to be the British Hitler. I don't for a moment think you're guilty, Anne, but I have to confess I'm jolly glad he's dead."

"I say," said Lord Rutherford, "Do we have any reason to believe this secretary fellow might be guilty? He was conveniently to hand."

"Not unless we can think of a hidden motive. It was in his interests that Lord Severn stay alive," said Catherine. "Dawkins was very involved in the earl's movement, not to mention what I am now guessing was a thriving blackmail concern."

Catherine felt the dean stiffen beside her. "He was blackmailing people? How do you know that?" asked Dean Godfrey.

"Dawkins as much as told us so. And he hinted that he would be continuing the blackmail, as well."

"Heavens," murmured the dean.

"Nasty sort of blighter," said Mr. Oveson.

It occurred to Catherine to wonder if the elegant, cultured dean had anything she could be blackmailed over. It was impossible to imagine her with any sort of murderous inclination.

"Dean Godfrey tells me you are new to teaching," said Mr. Oveson. "20th Century Literature, isn't it?"

"Yes," said Catherine. "What there is of it."

"Who is your favorite author?"

"Well," said Catherine. I'm a poet, so I am inclined in that direction. I have a weakness for the War Poets in general and Wilfred Owen in particular. What is your business?"

"I'm a drudge, I'm afraid. I work nine to five as an engineer."

"Here in Oxford?"

"Close by. I design precision machine parts for the former Earl of Severn's company."

Catherine sipped her cider, hoping her surprise didn't show. "Oh! And who will be taking over the plant now?"

The man lit a cigarette. His movements were careful and precise, his hands long-fingered and beautiful. "It's for sale. I'm trying to organize a consortium to buy it, as a matter of fact."

They spoke for a moment about the products the plant produced. "Our biggest customer is Krupp in Germany. I wish it were our own government, but they aren't interested in weapons manufacturing at the moment. I hate to say it, but now that Severn has passed on, maybe there is a chance that will happen."

Was this man going to marry the dean? Did he know if she had a secret dire enough that she would have wanted the earl dead? She couldn't see the dean killing anyone, but this man's long-fingered hands looked as though they would easily wield a deadly letter-opener.

Lord Rutherford left the table and came to stand by Catherine. "Would you mind trading seats with me? I'm interested in furthering my acquaintance with Mr. Oveson.

"Stanley, please." He held out his hand, and Rutherford shook it.

Catherine stood up and went to sit by Anne in her father's place. She was disappointed not to be able to talk with the dean.

Harry's sister-in-law was chatting with Red. "Darling, are you going to wreak havoc in the Severn Works now that the owner is gone?"

"That would be telling," said Red. "I'm terribly cut up about your arrest. The police are idiots."

Anne gave a brittle laugh. "Well, we all know your opinion of them. Do you have any ideas about the murder?"

"The Trade Union Congress absolutely hated Severn. He was very outspoken in his support of the Act of '27, which attempted to abolish strikes," said Red. "Unions have indeed been trying to organize without success at his manufacturing plant, but I hardly think a disgruntled unionist would think killing the man would further their cause. I've been consulting with them, as a matter of fact. We had a strike scheduled for this week."

The table went silent, contemplating this.

Had Severn gotten wind of it and called Red on the carpet? Was Red the earl's mysterious appointment after Anne's? Had he threatened Red with something from his past?

"Then there is the whole House of Commons who he wanted to abolish," Harry said.

"I'm having a hard time believing anyone actually took this man's views seriously enough to see him as a credible threat," Catherine said, watching Red's face. He grinned, not one whit abashed.

"Oh, he was a threat, all right," Anne said. "Maybe he wouldn't have ever achieved all his goals but look at Hitler! He started out as a small-time bully in Munich. No one took him seriously."

"This isn't Germany," Catherine said. "I don't think the House of Commons is exactly quaking in its boots."

"There are those in the aristocracy who *are* quaking in their boots. The Labor Party aims to get rid of them," Anne said.

Catherine felt Red's eyes on her again and knew he dared her to stand up for the aristocracy. Harry was looking down at the wooden table, tracing its grain with a thumbnail. Who knew what he was thinking? It seemed his mind was elsewhere.

Lord Rutherford wasn't looking the least bit perturbed, but then his views on the aristocracy were very cavalier. Being only a lifetime peer, he had no stake in its continuance. Catherine thought him to be very liberal in his views.

She wondered what Anne's political views were. Conservative? Liberal? Labor?

"And would that be such a loss?" asked Red, his tone lazy.

Anne said, "If we are to maintain a democracy and not slide into an autocracy, all the parties need to stay healthy. We can't be motivated by fear to abolish the Right or the Left."

Catherine said, "Now there, I agree with you. But it seems a bit of a reach to think someone would kill Severn to protect democracy."

"We shall see," said Anne's father. "Let us not forget Holmes' maxim: 'When you have eliminated the impossible, whatever remains, however improbable, must be the truth.'"

"I hardly think we're at that point yet," said Catherine, irritation sharpening her voice.

"Temper," Harry advised her.

I shall clobber him in a moment.

"I think we have you teaching in the wrong field," the dean said to Catherine. "You ought to be teaching politics."

"Another round of drinks, anyone?" asked Red in the best of spirits.

In the end, the conversation with Anne's peers was unproductive. If Anne weren't under arrest, Catherine would give up on the investigation altogether.

After they all stood, the dean moved over next to Catherine and said in a low voice. "If you would like to drop by my office sometime, I'll tell you something about Severn that might be helpful. I don't want it generally known, however."

"I'd be happy to," she said.

DEATH OF AN EARL

Mr. Oveson helped Dean Godfrey with her coat and ushered her out with a hand at her back.

Red invited her to share a taxi with him as the night was too cold for walking. Harry didn't even seem to notice how she was getting home, which thoroughly nettled Catherine. Jealousy didn't become her, and she knew it.

CHAPTER SEVEN

Wednesday's lecture "Feminist Writers Before the Vote" passed uneventfully.

Afterward, Catherine decided to go to the offices of the Oxford *Daily Mail* to read local accounts of Lord Severn's activities in the weeks before the murder. She also wanted to read their story about the murder to find any clues she didn't have.

To her satisfaction, she found something new. Two days before the murder, Lord Severn had held a small press conference in Oxford after an address that he had given at Merton College. The reporter from the *Mail* had asked him about his *Times'* correspondence with Mrs. Bascombe.

According to the report, Severn had said, "Why should I care what an ignorant housewife thinks of my scheme to save our country from the tyranny of small minds? Mrs. Bascombe surely illustrates the terrible misstep our government took in giving the vote to women!"

Phew! If Anne were thought to be at all unstable, this statement would indeed offer a motive for some sharp retaliation. Catherine was surprised neither Anne nor her father had mentioned this incident.

She read on and was startled by the next question. "We understand there is a strike planned for next week by your workers.

Their leader, Mr. de Fontaine, is quoted as saying that the working conditions in your plant are appalling. He likened them to the worst of Victorian vintage."

Severn had replied, "Mr. de Fontaine is much given to exaggeration. I am engaged in private negotiations with the man and am confident that there will be no strike."

Why didn't Red mention this? What sort of "private negotiations?" The kind that could have led to his murder?

The *Mail* dated the day after the murder included an account of a strange blood-spattered note appearing to be written in code atop the victim's desk.

So, it wasn't merely a bit of sensationalism on the part of *The News of the World*! Catherine wondered if it was an authentic item or whether someone had left it with the intent to mislead. Probably the mysterious caller who came after Anne had left. The murderer.

To her surprise, she arrived home just as Red was calling on her. Pleased to see him, she invited him in, asking Cherry if there was anything suitable for tea.

"I'm not exactly a tea drinker," said Red.

"But I bought ginger biscuits at the bakery today," interposed Cherry.

"Ah! Ginger biscuits," said Red. "Now that's another story. I am partial to them, as it happens."

Catherine removed her hat and gloves and took Red's from him, putting the lot in Cherry's waiting arms. Then she bade Red be seated.

"I had an idea in the night," he said. "Perhaps you will think it ridiculous, but it would be fun, and I think it might help."

"Tell me," said Catherine.

"I thought I might go behind the scenes anonymously at Severn's machine plant. I know several of the rabble-rousers there from when we were organizing the strike that never happened."

"I was just reading in the mail about the last press conference that Severn gave. He said he was having 'private negotiations' with you. You never mentioned them." Catherine said.

Red looked uncomfortable for the first time in her experience with the man.

"There was a good reason. Those negotiations never took place. I didn't show up. All part of my tactics."

"Ah!" said Catherine, but she wondered if he was telling the truth. Must she be wary of the man now? She didn't like the question. "I hope for your sake that you have an alibi for the time of the murder," she said.

Red said nothing, but he looked at her with a face gone suddenly serious. Unfortunately, at that moment, Cherry entered with the tea tray. "Thank you, Cherry," said Catherine.

Red ended by having a cup of milky tea with his biscuits and said, "This is all very cozy. It reminds me of the nursery."

"Does it?" She was feeling a bit uneasy.

"My nanny used to find me quite handsome," he said with a naughty grin. "Of course, that was before the beard."

Catherine thought him a dangerous flirt. There was a knock at the door at that moment, immediately followed by Harry's entrance.

"Darling, could you spare a cup of . . .?" Her fiancé stopped at the sight of Red sipping tea. "Sorry . . . am I intruding?"

"Of course not," said Catherine, her words sounding overly hearty. "Red's just been telling me that he's going to go behind the scenes at Severn's company."

Harry took off his hat and gloves, giving them to Cherry. "I thought you said that was a dead end," he said to Catherine's guest.

"Thought I might as well do it as not," said Red. "One never knows. There might be a hothead in the bunch."

Catherine's fiancé sat in his usual black leather club chair. She poured him a cup of tea with milk and sugar.

"Incidentally, I found out a couple of things of interest today," she said. "In the *Oxford Mail*." She told them of her discoveries about the press conference and the coded message.

"I'd love to have a crack at that code," said Red. "I used to tinker with those things when I was a kid. I liked the mathematical ones."

"I'd be surprised if this were anything that sophisticated," said Harry.

"Why is that?" asked Catherine.

Harry said, "I have the feeling it's just an amateurish attempt to throw us off the true scent."

"That's a rather large assumption," said Catherine.

"What do you think it's about?"

"I have no idea. A manifesto of some kind? A warning?" she said.

As was her wont, Cherry entered the room with a contribution to the discussion. "Something like this?" she asked, handing the afternoon edition of the *Mail* to Catherine, folded into a rectangle.

Startled, Catherine looked at the paper. There was a photo of a page of type which appeared to be cut out of magazines. The caption read, "Note sent to this newspaper by the morning post."

You are looking in the wrong direction. Who stood to lose the most if Severn wasn't stopped?

She passed the paper around. "Thank you, Cherry. That is most appreciated."

The maid gave a mock curtsey and went back to the kitchen.

"She fancies herself as Bunter to my Lord Peter Wimsey," Catherine said.

"Do you suppose the murderer sent this?" asked Red. "Foolhardy, certainly. One would think he would be happy to have Mrs. Bascombe in custody."

"This is frightfully vague," said Harry. "But I would venture a guess that it was sent by someone who doesn't like to see Anne in custody. So it probably isn't the murderer. What interest would the killer have in the investigation being solved?"

"Not only does it point the investigation away from Anne. It tries to steer it toward the upper classes. Someone with a grudge, possibly," said Catherine. "The aristocrats were the only ones who stood to gain from Severn's agenda."

"I think its purpose must be misdirection. I.e., anywhere but at Anne," said Harry.

Red stood and went to the mantel where he lit a cigarette with the lighter Catherine kept there for Harry's pipe.

"The devil!" blurted Harry. "We've lost a thread here! Remember what Dawkins said as we were leaving, Catherine?"

She set down her teacup. She knew at once what Harry meant. "Yes. He said there were those closer to home that might have done it." In Red's presence, she didn't mention the specific threat to Anne.

"The same ones who knew she was off to see Severn that afternoon," said Harry. He looked Red straight in the eyes. "And that includes you, de Fontaine."

"This Dawkins had something against me?"

Catherine bit her lip. Had she allowed Red to misdirect her? Was Red cultivating her company because he was worried about what she might uncover? After taking a deep breath, she said, "We don't know for certain. It could have been you. Or the dean. Or Oliver Anderson. You all knew when Anne was going to visit Severn. According to Dawkins, Severn knew something about one or all of you. Things that might have led to his murder."

"You have got to be joking!" Red exclaimed. Turning to Catherine, he said, "You can't believe that!"

Drawing herself up, she said, "I'm afraid I must keep an open mind. Do you, in fact, know anything to the others' discredit?"

"Of course not! Neither of them would have committed murder! There is nothing the least bit reprehensible to know. And you already know the worst of me—I wish to uproot the status quo. But I didn't take Severn and his ridiculous agenda as a serious threat!"

"Even though his role model, Hitler, came to power because of widespread fear of the Bolsheviks?" Catherine asked.

"The reverse is true as well. In Russia, the Bolsheviks came to power because of hatred of the monarchy and the aristocrats! But the whole thing is irrelevant because you know I'm not a Bolshevik! I'm a homegrown Communist," Red insisted.

Catherine did know that about Red. But she didn't suppose it made a bit of difference to Severn. Red was all the more dangerous because he didn't seem scary. That could well have occurred to Lord Severn. And Red could have all manner of secret plots for all Catherine knew.

Could she have really grown close to someone like that?

Yes. Because there was an air of honor about Red. It came from his being raised a gentleman. A peer. She conveniently managed to forget that he had renounced all of that upon embracing Communism.

Would one take tea and ginger biscuits with Stalin? Not likely.

Rising, she tossed her wavy hair back out of her eyes, uncertain what to do. It wasn't your average social problem: How to get a Communist out of your sitting room?

As though sensing her dilemma, he rose, too. "I'll take my leave."

Instead of calling for Cherry, Catherine went to the cupboard and retrieved his hat and gloves herself. Because she couldn't think of what to say, she said nothing as she handed them to him.

Red said, "Do you still want to know if I find anything unsavory going on among the workers at Severn's plant?"

"Yes, please," she said, bowing her head rather than looking him in the eye.

"All right, then." Putting on his hat, he left.

Once she had returned to the sitting room, Harry asked, "What was de Fontaine doing here?"

"He just came by to flirt with me, I expect."

Harry scoffed. Then he asked, "Got any more ginger biscuits?"

Catherine called for Cherry, and he put his request to her directly. Catherine's maid was very fond of Harry.

"How is Anne today?" Catherine asked.

Harry poured himself another cup of tea. "Holding her own. James is taking it a lot harder. He's ready for Bedlam."

"Poor fellow," said Catherine.

"Anne sent him off to the lab. He's better when he's working. Now, if we could just get her father to go home. He's intent on solving this. It's a sort of game to him. These are delicious biscuits, by the way."

"I shall convey your praise to Cherry. How do you propose we visit with this Oliver Anderson?"

"I imagine Anne can make arrangements for us to meet Anderson."

"Dot's coming up from London this weekend," Catherine said, deciding to steer the subject away from Anne.

"It's not exactly the time for frivolity," he said.

Catherine curbed a sharp retort and managed to say civilly, "Have you any other ideas about the direction we should take?"

"Something will come to me in the night," Harry said, standing.

"You don't look very rested, Harry. Would you like to take home a bit of Chamomile tea? I swear by it for sleep."

"Don't fuss," he said, as though mentally swiping at a pest. "I shall be all right when Anne is free."

Annoyance and hurt wrestled for prominence in Catherine's breast. "You know your way out," she said, heading for her kitchen.

Chapter Eight

Though Harry had upset her, she was more disturbed by her blindness concerning Red. Just how dangerous was he? Was it possible Red was the murderer? She needed to find out if he had an alibi.

She knew that most of what he did would be considered rabble-rousing. She had read accounts of his speeches from time to time in the newspaper. Red might have tried to write off Severn as a credible threat, but was that really so? The earl seemed like he would have proved an irresistible target for the Communist. Had he been causing trouble with the earl's labor force? Had the victim, in fact, attacked Red in the House of Lords? Did he know something material that would result in Red's imprisonment?

There was one way she knew to begin queries on this. The Somerville College library indexed *The Times* and *The Oxford Mail* by featured names. And it was open until ten o'clock. So she would go there now.

* * *

Catherine's search was painstaking but fruitful. She found that Red had been a busy man. He had written letters to *The Times* protesting speeches the Earl of Severn had made in The Lords during the Scottish coal strike, setting forth all the reasons why the workers deserved a pay increase. But, of course, the strike had ultimately failed. Red had written scathing letters lamenting this "on behalf of the workers of the nation."

The reporter had also given coverage to a speech he had made at Magdalen College—Severn's alma mater—about the suffering that would inevitably occur if changes in socio-political society were not made voluntarily. He spoke of the political strife in other countries in Europe.

"The day of the worker has come. The workers, not the politicians, warm our homes, produce our electricity, put food on our tables. They do so for a pittance, while others, from no other reason than an accident of birth, live off the backs of the poor. While the government supports this practice, our country is ripe for a revolution, possibly like Russia. Or we will fall into the other extreme of fascism as we see in Germany and Italy. This latter is what our own Lord Severn is already advocating.

"The masses are not happy. And the masses outnumber the upper class. So it is only a matter of time before they act. Let us act first. Let us support our working class, so they have comfortable homes and enough to eat. Let us not make them have to choose between food and fuel to heat their homes. Let us give them educations so they can pull themselves out of poverty. Unlike Germany or Russia, Britain has a functioning democracy. We have the opportunity to make these changes peacefully. Or we face a Revolution."

Red gave other such threatening warnings in the universities in the North as well as Scotland and Wales. He always mentioned Lord Severn by name, sometimes giving particulars of the earl's proposals, such as abolishing the House of Commons.

At union meetings, Red advocated strikes, even though the Act of 1926 prohibited them. And strikes inevitably followed, even if they were not successful most of the time.

This was the true Red. Not the man Catherine knew socially. Not the Red who had tea in her sitting room. This was an angry man, committed to a course that, if followed, would inevitably result in violence. This was a man who could commit murder. Even if the murder was largely symbolic.

Unfortunately, when she had come this far, Catherine saw the warning flash of the lights. The library was closing. She would have to come back the next day to check the *Oxford Mail*. Cherry had been saving those since the day of the murder. Catherine would comb through some of them at home that evening.

As she walked home in the brisk night air, she pulled her fur coat around her and thought about what she had learned. She should have checked on Red first thing instead of letting him woo her. Now she was angry with herself.

Cherry was awaiting her at home with a fire going in her bedroom. "It is that cold out there, miss. It's not summer anymore. Would you like some Horlick's?"

"Yes, please, Cherry. But first, draw me a bath, if you don't mind."

Later as she sipped her Horlick's under her quilts in bed, Catherine read through everything she could in the *News of the World* and the *Oxford Mail*. She didn't know exactly what she was looking for, but she had the feeling that events concurrent with the murder might tell her something. There were scandals in Hollywood concerning people she had met; there were scandals in London among people she hadn't. Royal Societies had convened and had lectures about their abstruse specialties.

The Oxford paper was more localized. There were college alumni weekends, a review of a Chopin performance in the music hall, a meeting of the Oxford Birders. Catherine's father was a birder. More from curiosity than anything else, she read the article.

A moment later, she sat up straight in bed. The Oxford Birder's Society report concerned an outing they had made the day of the murder. It had been conducted in a wooded area belonging to the Earl of Severn with his consent. She skipped through the account of rare species they had spied. There was a telephone number at the end of the article for people interested in joining their society.

Since it was eleven o'clock at night, Catherine knew she must wait until the next day to ring. She tried not to get too excited, but birders carried binoculars, and some of them even telescopes.

* * *

Cherry brought her tea at seven o'clock. It took her a moment to remember what she had been so excited about before she fell asleep. When she did, Catherine decided to ring the number in the newspaper after she rang Harry.

After eating a roll, drinking her tea, and dressing in the conservative clothes she taught in, she sat for Cherry to do her hair.

"You seem awful restless this morning, miss," her maid commented.

"I'm sorry. I'll try to sit still." She told Cherry about the birders while Cherry deftly waved her hair with the iron.

"Are you going to ring all of them? That's a big job."

"Maybe Harry will take half the list. I don't know. I haven't spoken to him yet."

After Cherry was satisfied that her mistress's hair looked its best, Catherine rang Harry.

"I think we may have happened onto a bit of luck. The Oxfordshire Birder's Society was spending the day of the murder combing through Lord Severn's woods. As you know, they carry telescopes and binoculars. So perhaps one of them saw someone around the grounds who wasn't a gardener."

"Spiffing!" said Harry. "What in the world made you think of that?"

"Just an article in the *Mail*. There's a number to call. I'm hoping someone has a list of members."

"Does the number belong to a man or a woman?" Harry asked.

"A man. I'm hoping I can charm him," said Catherine. "If it were a woman, I would leave it up to you."

He laughed. "Jolly good. There's sure to be a long list, always supposing we can get our hands on it. It would go faster if we split it up."

"I agree. I'll be in touch. I just didn't want you to disappear. You have a tutorial today, right?"

"Yes. Same time as yours—eleven o'clock."

"I'll wait and ring this Mr. Swanson after mine."

They decided on this course. It occurred to Catherine that this was the most normal exchange she had had with her fiancé since he had seen Anne last Saturday night in his parents' drawing room.

* * *

Mr. Swanson came across as a precise and fussy-sounding man on the telephone. As membership chairman, he didn't know if he was justified in sharing the names and telephone numbers of the Society.

"Have you heard that the Earl of Severn was murdered on the very day of your search through his forest? Don't you suppose he would want you to help find his murderer?"

"Well . . ." he said.

"My future sister-in-law has been arrested, but she didn't do it. There was another person—an unknown man—who had an appoint-ment with the earl after hers. No one knows who he is, but one thing is that he came and went by the French doors which lead to the back garden and the forest. If you were in my place, wouldn't you want to find out who that person is? You are a vital link, Mr. Swanson. An essential link."

The man finally said, "Well, I won't give the list to you over the telephone. You will have to come and copy it down from my record book."

"I shall. My . . . uh . . . fiancé and I will be over to do that this afternoon. You are such a wonderful help. Now, what is your address?"

* * *

Harry and Catherine drove over the gentle hillside of Oxfordshire to the address in the village of Brimscombe and found a charming Cotswold cottage. A few pink roses clung to the climber that embraced the old wooden front door.

A small, stooped man opened to their knock. Catherine thrust out her hand. "Hello, Mr. Swanson. I'm Miss Tregowyn, a tutor from Oxford, and this is my fiancé, Dr. Bascombe."

Their host seemed instantly reassured by Harry's presence.

"You had better come in," he said. "I have the membership list in the sitting room. There is a table there where you can write."

"Thank you so much for letting us come," said Harry. "This is frightfully important."

The sitting room was small and quaint, with a fire burning in the grate. Meticulously arranged, the room was furnished with period pieces, mainly from Queen Anne vintage. Lithographs of birds hung above the mantel, and a somewhat worn Persian rug covered the gleaming wood floor. On the table, a ledger lay open, and two chairs had been drawn up.

Harry pulled two legal tablets out of his briefcase. "This looks very legible. Our work should go quickly," he said. "Do you mind if I just move this chair? Miss Tregowyn can copy the left-hand page while I do the right."

"Certainly," said Mr. Swanson. "I will be right here if you have any questions." He sat in a leather-covered wing-back chair next to the fire.

Harry and Catherine worked quickly. Fortunately, Mr. Swanson's handwriting was legible. When they had finished, they had close to thirty names. So they had quite a task before them.

Catherine delivered the man a small paper-wrapped parcel. "Thank you so much. Here are some ginger biscuits for your tea."

Mr. Swanson actually smiled, showing an impressive array of dentures.

During the ride back to Oxford, Catherine longed after her

own tea. Fortunately, Harry suggested they stop at one of the charming village tearooms found in the Cotswolds.

With a thatched roof, it was painted slate blue with white trim. They had a small table vacant in a cozy corner with a ceramic cat seated on its scrubbed oak table.

Catherine ordered Earl Grey tea and scones while Harry wanted gooey cakes and China tea.

"When do you think we should ring these people?" he asked.

"Well," she said, "Since the only people we want to speak with were at the Severn estate on Friday, I would say most of them aren't employed. So I would think tomorrow morning before our tutorials and then in the afternoon before tea."

"Well-reasoned. If any of these birders saw anything helpful, we should arrange to call on them. Telephones are so unsatisfactory," said Harry.

His manner toward her today had been strangely formal. It brought an ache to her heart.

"How is Anne doing today?" she asked.

"She was bucked up to hear about the birders. I hope something comes of it."

After a brief struggle with herself, she decided she wouldn't give him the information she had found about Red just yet. She couldn't have said why, exactly.

"Is Anne's father still staying at the Randolph?" she asked.

"I think he's there for the duration; more's the pity. Anne could do without his antics. How are your parents? Do they know about this investigation?"

"Good heavens, no. You know my father would never approve, and just worrying about it would be bad for his heart."

"My mother is being very meddlesome," Harry said with a frown. "Since Anne's expecting and has no mother, she thinks Anne should be down with them in Hampshire. But Anne, of course, has to be near the action. Being so far away would be the worst thing for her."

Catherine took a deep, steadying breath and said, "Are you ever going to tell me what happened between the two of you?"

Harry's eyes narrowed, and his brow gathered in anger. "I told you. She preferred James. End of story. They were married and gone off to Germany when I returned from my Grand Tour of the Continent. No one had written me. But I was moving from place to place on a whim, and I had no fixed address. So, I can't blame them."

She couldn't help asking, "But how could she marry someone else without telling you? And how could your brother let her?"

"I gather the job with Bayer Labs had to be taken up immediately, and it was too good to pass up. That's the explanation James gives. I've never discussed it with Anne."

Catherine thought the whole thing exceedingly strange. But it explained why Harry had acted so differently with her than he did with Anne. Clearly, he didn't want to be wholly emotionally invested in another relationship after how that one had ended. Worse still, Catherine worried that Harry wasn't entirely over Anne. The last time he had seen her before Saturday had been years ago. And then he had been passionately in love with her.

It followed that the man she was engaged to was not the complete Harry. The realization nearly sank her. She couldn't touch her scone. How could she have known him for a year and a half and not sensed this?

A teashop was not a place to break an engagement, so she said nothing.

"You don't want your pastry?" he asked.

"I'll take it to Cherry," she said, wrapping it in her paper napkin. Harry was finished with his tea. She said, "Tell me one more thing. Have you asked Anne about what Dawkins meant by his accusation?"

"I did. She acted indignant, and I felt like a heel. It came down to who I believed. I chose to believe he was trying to get us riled. Unless we find out otherwise, I believe Anne."

I don't. Dawkins was too gleeful. He knows something.
But what can I do? I can't go to the police! Harry would kill me.

"I think we should go now."

"Right," said Harry, his voice clipped.

They didn't speak the rest of the way to her flat. Harry turned her legal pad over to her when he walked her to the door. When he had left, she took the scone into the kitchen and crumbled it viciously in her hand over the sink. Then she dusted off her hands and walked back to her bedroom, where she undressed and put everything in its place instead of waiting for Cherry, who was at the market.

When she was done, she hauled out her students' essays and tried to lose herself marking them.

Chapter Nine

She wanted Dot. But her friend had to be up early for her job at the advertising agency and would be in bed by now. Dot would be here at the weekend. That would have to do. She would have to deal with her inner conflict until then.

She drew a hot bath and put in a liberal sprinkling of citrus bath salts made for Dot's fledgling business of creating and selling bath products. After soaking until the water was cold, she dried and dressed languidly, made herself some Horlick's, and went to bed without dinner. Catherine escaped into a deep sleep.

* * *

She rang the first of the birders on her list after eating a piece of toast the following morning.

"Miss Liddell, this is Catherine Tregowyn calling regarding the Bird Watcher club."

"Oh, yes?"

"Did you happen to go out with the Birders last Friday? To the Severn Manor grounds?"

"Of course! I wouldn't have missed it for the world! And I'm so glad I went because I saw a Dodo! Such a splendid display of plumage. There are not many of them left, you know, outside the zoo."

"You must have a fine pair of binoculars! What a find! I need to ask you something important. Of course, you know the Earl of Severn was killed that afternoon?"

"Yes, poor man. He was so kind to allow us on his land. I felt truly dreadful when I read the news in the paper. I shed tears over it." She sniffed a little, and Catherine thought she might be silently weeping again.

"You could be an important witness, Miss Liddell. Did you go anywhere with a view of the rear of the house?"

"Oh! You wonder if I saw anything! Sadly, I didn't. I stayed in the forest. I was nowhere close to the house."

Catherine was disappointed but not surprised. She said a kind goodbye and rang the next person on her list.

Birders loved to talk about their hobby. Consequently, before leaving to teach her 11:00 tutorial, she could only speak with four people. None of them had been within sight of the manor house.

* * *

The tutorial—building on the material her Tuesday group was studying—was quite demanding. This group was over the moon about *Howard's End* and had several different interpretations to offer. They had identified the feminist theme and the obvious fact that it was the story of class struggle.

Following the class, she ate in the Somerville dining hall, hoping to catch sight of Dean Godfrey, but the woman was not seated at her usual place at High Table. Still heavy-hearted, Catherine was not in the mood for chatter and wished she had simply gone back to the flat.

When she finally arrived home, Cherry told her that Dr. Harry had rung and wished she would return the call. Though very reluctant, Catherine did so.

"Cath?" he answered. Her heart squeezed a little at the endearment.

"Yes?"

"Did you have any luck this morning?"

"No. How about you?"

"I have a probable. He's pretty sure he saw someone just before he packed up to leave. He's local, so he's going to meet us at the pub. If he can describe the man at all, I think we need to take him to the police. We'll need their sketch artist."

She had been hoping to avoid Harry for a couple of days, but it looked as though she would have to see him today. At least they would be in company and not alone.

"What time are we to meet him?" she asked.

"At about three o'clock."

"The Bird and the Baby?"

"Right."

"Good. That will give me some time to get down further on my list. It would be good if we could get at least a couple of witnesses. Thanks for ringing. I'll see you at 3:00."

"I say, Catherine. You're not brooding, are you?"

"About what?" she asked, her heart starting to race and her hands instantly clammy.

"Anne."

"If I were, I certainly wouldn't talk about it on the telephone," she said. "Cheerio."

Hoping that this case would reach a swift resolution, Catherine went back to ringing the people on her list. Before two-thirty, when she had to leave, she had spoken with five more people. Unfortunately, they were all "sorry, no's," so she left the last seven to ring in the morning.

She dressed quickly in her mauve tweeds. Cherry did her hair, and she carefully placed her fur hat over her waves. Assuming her matching sable coat, she set out for her walk to the pub.

* * *

Harry and a man she took for the bird-watcher were just entering the pub when she arrived. Harry introduced her to a bald Dr. Clement, a professor of biology from St. John's College.

Bluff and hearty, Dr. Clement offered his hand to Catherine. "Dr. Bascombe tells me you are a tutor at Somerville. I'm happy to make your acquaintance."

"And I, yours," said Catherine. "Shall we sit?"

Harry took drink orders, and they made their way to a high-backed booth.

"Just what is your interest in this murder?" Dr. Clement asked Catherine.

"Dr. Bascombe's sister-in-law has been arrested by the Oxford police, partially because she was the last person known to see the victim. A mysterious phone call and appointment were made for five o'clock, but no one saw anyone come. The secretary was off on an errand. We are trying to find the person who kept that appointment. No one from inside the house saw anyone."

By this time, Harry had returned with drinks. Lager for Dr. Clement and himself, and a shandy for Catherine.

"Well," said Dr. Clement. "I hope I can help. The person I saw was definitely a man. He caught my eye because he was dressed as a gardener, but he was entering the house by the French doors. My immediate thought was that he was up to no good."

"How far away were you?" asked Harry.

"I was at the edge of the forest, but I caught sight of him through my binoculars."

"So you got a fairly good look at him?" Catherine asked. *Could things be this easy?*

"Of what there was to see. He was a very hairy individual. Heavy brows, mustache, beard. Longish hair. All gray. It has occurred to me since that he might have been in disguise."

Catherine sighed. *Of course, he was.* "I don't suppose you noticed his ears? It is impossible to disguise ears."

"His ears? Well now. Let me think." The professor took a sip of lager. "I believe his hair was too shaggy for me to get a good look at his ears. But at least you know that it was a man."

"Why did you assume he was a gardener?" Catherine asked. "What was he wearing?"

"Dungarees. Old dungarees. Oh! And here's something!" The man's eyes lit with excitement. "The reason I thought he might have been trespassing was that his boots were off. They were sitting on the terrace, next to the door. He was wearing only socks."

"That's jolly important," said Harry. He downed a good bit of his lager, put his glass down emphatically, and grinned. "I'd wager a great deal on him as our murderer."

"Could you tell if he was heavy or slight?" asked Catherine.

"He was tall. Big shoulders. Large belly."

"Excellent!" said Harry. "I say, would you mind going to the police with us and cooperating with a sketch artist?"

"Certainly. Miss Tregowyn said your sister-in-law was arrested for the murder. I hope this will sow some doubt in the minds of our constabulary."

"As do I," said Harry. His countenance was brighter than Catherine had seen it since before this whole business began. Though she still had her doubts about Anne, she was grateful for the break in their case.

* * *

The police could not be rushed. It transpired that the Detective Chief Inspector was unavailable. The Detective Sergeant working on the case took some convincing before calling in their sketch artist. The artist was not available until the following morning. Harry became surly, and the professor was a bit insulted that his evidence was being taken lightly. Once the appointment was made for eleven o'clock the following day, they all left the station. Harry, who lived close to the police station, offered to drive the professor and Catherine back to their residences. They agreed.

Harry drove to Catherine's flat first, which relieved her,

preventing her from having a private visit with him. She thanked the professor for his help and said good night to both men. She was feeling snappish, and Harry had no idea how grateful he should be for having escaped a display of her temper.

Once she was inside her flat, Cherry greeted her with the news that Dot had rung and wished her to ring back whatever the hour. Once Catherine had changed into her red silk lounging pajamas, she settled in for a visit with Dot.

"How are things going?" her friend asked.

"The case is going well. I think we've had a real breakthrough. But things with Harry are tenuous. I'll have to tell you about it when you come. I don't want to talk about it on the telephone."

"How are you holding up?"

"Oh, I'm doing well. It will be tremendous to see you."

"Max is picking me up on the seven o'clock train. I refuse to drive in the surge of traffic out of the City on Friday night. Join us for dinner?"

"No, thanks. I'll see you afterward here at the flat. Take your time."

"All right, darling. Kisses. See you tomorrow!"

Catherine decided to finish her calls to the birders that night so she wouldn't dwell on Harry and Anne. Unfortunately, no one else had seen the man in the dungarees or anything else.

* * *

Friday morning, Catherine got a good start on marking this week's essays, as Catherine hoped to be involved with Dot and Max over the weekend. It was going to feel jolly strange without Harry to make up their usual foursome. She remembered he had labeled that idea as much too much "frivolity."

Catherine showed up at the police station at 11:30 to see if she could view the sketch artist's work. She was hoping she wouldn't recognize Red beneath the disguise.

Because he was involved in finding the witness, Dr. Clement, the Detective Sergeant evidently thought it would be all right for her to see the sketch.

To her frustration, there wasn't enough facial structure visible beneath all the hair for her to tell if it was Red or not. A well-placed pillow could have suggested the portly belly. Red had broad shoulders, but that was hardly an identifying detail on its own. She couldn't even see the size of his hands as the subject wore gardening gloves.

"I'm sorry," she told the policeman. "I think he must be wearing a disguise. It's impossible for me to know whether I've ever seen this man before. Did he have any idea about his height?"

"The witness said the man was probably at least six feet. Maybe more."

Impossible to know if it was Red.

Harry arrived just as she was leaving.

"Any joy?" he asked.

"I'll be interested to hear what you think," she said. "The man was entirely too hairy for me to identify him. He could have been the rag and bone collector or the local chemist for all I could see."

She was curious to see what Harry thought, so she waited for him in the station's lobby. She didn't feel like facing the flat and her student's essays on this gloomy day.

Harry wasn't long. "I see what you mean," he said. "But at least we know he is a man. That should help get Anne off."

"If we can prove he came in before and not after the murder," she felt she had to add.

His jaw tightened. "You're right. We need to find this fellow. Let's go out to the Severn estate and have a look 'round the garden."

"What do you hope to find?" Catherine asked.

"I don't know." Harry pursed his lips and scratched the back of his neck. "Something. Anything."

"Don't you think the police will have found whatever there is to find?" she objected.

"Think, Catherine! They arrested Anne almost immediately.

They weren't looking for anyone else. If they had been at all thorough, they would have discovered the bird-watchers! They simply weren't looking for anyone else. We owe it to Anne to be as exhaustive as possible."

He was right, but that didn't prevent her from feeling another jab to her heart.

"Well, let's go, then," she said. "But I have to be back by evening. Dot's arriving."

Walking swiftly toward where he'd parked his car, Harry might not have heard her.

During their short drive to the Woodstock estate of Lord Severn, Harry was silent, but Catherine could almost see the wheels turning in his head. He was so utterly unaware of her; she wondered why he had bothered to invite her to come with him.

Finally, she asked him, "Harry, where are you?"

He glanced over at her. "Oh, sorry. I'm just wondering how the gardener who wasn't a gardener got to the estate. My guess would be a bicycle."

"That sounds reasonable. If he's from away, he could have arrived by train. In third class, they let you bring a bicycle along with you."

When they got to the estate, he said, "Let's just drive around a bit and see how he could have approached the back of the house without being seen."

A gravel road branched off the main avenue which had taken them up to the manor. Turning there, Harry drove slowly around to the back, through the forest. There was a graveled spot that appeared to be recently churned up.

"Birders," Catherine said. "It was only a week ago."

"If the murderer had come this way, he would have seen that the place was crawling with bird-watchers. I think he must have gone by a different route," said Harry.

Driving back the way they came, Harry then found a footpath on the other side of the mansion, curling around to the backside of the residence.

"I think this must be it. He could have parked the bicycle behind this hedge. He would have been focused on the house and would not have seen the birders in the forest."

Harry parked the car and helped her to alight. As she stood, Catherine saw a bit of torn paper under the hedge.

"Hullo! There's something here." Stooping, she pulled the paper out. "It's a bit of train ticket. What luck! This had to have belonged to the murderer. Look! It's dated the day before the murder."

She handed it to Harry, who squinted at it. "Third class. So he could have brought his bicycle. Hmm. St. Athan to Oxford. Why does that place ring a bell?"

"Idiot child!" she said. It's where the heir lives! The ninth earl."

Harry placed the ticket stub in his wallet, and they walked carefully toward the back of the house. The gray fingerprint powder still covered the doorknob, and there were signs that many feet had trodden the grass through the area around the French windows. However, there were no more clues to be had.

Harry said, "What we need is a good photo of the police sketch. Then we must make a journey to wherever this St. Athan is. I brought my camera with me. Let's go see the dear Detective Sergeant. I think we'll keep this train ticket to ourselves for a while, hmm?"

"I agree," said Catherine.

CHAPTER TEN

While Harry went off to deal with the police and get his photo, Catherine went to the college library to look at the ABC railway guide. She found that there was a rail line between Cardiff and St. Athan. The train journey from Oxford to Cardiff was only 2 hours. Not deepest Wales then, thank heavens.

She went back to her flat to get things ready for Dot's visit. Catherine didn't expect Harry for some time, as he was taking his film to a photographer friend who could develop the film in a darkroom set up in his flat.

Cherry was doing a heavy cleaning of the premises. The maid adored Dot and was always thrilled when she came.

"I see we need another jar of Horlick's," Catherine said. "You know how Dot loves it. I imagine she'll be dining with Max tonight, so we needn't worry about dinner."

Though Catherine saved Dot's bath products for special occasions, she got them out of the cupboard now and displayed them prominently in her bathroom. She had chosen the lilac line, which was Dot's favorite.

"I'll just run out and get some flowers, Cherry. And the Horlick's. If Harry rings, tell him I'll be back shortly."

* * *

Harry and Dot arrived at Catherine's flat at the same time. Her friend had taken a taxi from the station as Max had been tied up.

"Oh, Cat! It's lovely to see you," said Dot. "You, too, Harry! Will you join Max and me for dinner tonight? We're going to Carmichael's."

Catherine could read Harry very well, and at the moment, he was trying to hide his annoyance.

"Catherine and I are in the middle of a case. I need to go over to my brother's tonight to see his wife and report. She has been arrested for murder, but fortunately, she's out on bail."

"Yes, Cat told me," Dot said briskly. "I never even knew you had a brother!"

"He's been abroad for years. Working in a German lab. They just returned to England a few months ago."

"Lovely for you. But what an unfortunate business this is. I look forward to hearing about it," said Dot.

Harry poured himself a stiff whiskey. "Catherine, what did you find out?"

"St. Athan has rail service from Cardiff. One can get there in two hours by train."

Harry's features lightened. "Wonderful! I have a good photo of the police sketch. Anne and I will go down there tomorrow and question the villagers. We'd best not waste any time."

His words smote her so hard Catherine was breathless. *Anne?*

Her face must have mirrored her feelings. Harry scowled and tapped his foot. "Come now. You have Dot to stay! You don't want to go chasing down to Wales."

Catherine pulled herself together. "Of course. Will you take James with you?"

"James works seven days a week at the lab. He's under a lot of pressure right now to develop a drug he was working on in Germany. It cures external infections. Could have saved a lot of lives in the war."

"Marvelous," Catherine said in a flat tone. Then she smiled. "It really is. How brilliant he must be."

"It's a bit hard on Anne, but she bears up well. She claims she does better when he's not hovering over her at home. I do what I can to cheer her up," Harry said.

"I'm sure it means the world to her," said Catherine. Then, lest he read her words as sarcasm, she added, "I hope you have success tomorrow."

Harry tossed off the rest of his drink. "Thanks. I'll be off then. Have fun. Give my regards to the cowboy."

As soon as the door closed behind him, Catherine collapsed onto the sofa. "I can't believe it!"

"Crikey! That is definitely beyond the pale!" said Dot, sitting down beside her. She put an arm around Catherine's shoulders. "I can see why you are disturbed. What a colossal idiot he is!"

"You should see her, Dot. She's the complete glamour girl. She'd fit right in back in Hollywood. Their families are friends down in Hampshire. He's probably known her all his life. I'm quite sure she is his first love."

"Tell me about this case. Is she really in danger of being hanged?"

Catherine breathed a heavy sigh and caught her friend up on the case down to the latest discovery.

"Cat, that business with the secretary could be nasty. It sounds like he gave whatever it was to the policeand that's why they arested her. Are you sure she hasn't told Harry what it is?"

"Well, almost sure. The thing is, at this point, if it's something awful, I think he would protect her rather than tell me. He'll go on working to get her free no matter what, I think. But he has his doubts about whether I will."

"You have the right to know," insisted Dot.

"Not really."

"That ring on your finger, Cat. That gives you some rights. And it's probably wrong of me to say so, but by taking Anne with him tomorrow, it sounds like he is adding insult to injury."

Catherine firmed her lips as anger started to seep through the hurt. "You're exactly right."

"Well, let's ring Max and go out for cocktails at that new little club on the High Street. Then we can go to Carmichael's. We have a reservation for half-past eight."

"But wouldn't you and Max rather be alone? You haven't seen each other all week."

"Cat, I'm sure we'll have a great time. You need to let your hair down a bit. And Max is so easy to be with."

Catherine embraced her friend. "Thank you. Now. I'm sure you want a bath after the train. It always smells of cigarettes."

* * *

The evening with Max and Dot went as well as could be expected sans Harry. The four of them had enjoyed delightful times in Hollywood, and Catherine had grown very fond of Max—an American cowboy with a hankering for British literature, not to mention Dot. When they were seated at Carmichael's, Oxford's elite restaurant, Catherine was surprised to see Red dining alone. He immediately came over to join them. She and Red had dined together at the restaurant on another occasion.

"The band's not playing tonight?" Catherine asked.

"The Hall is in use for some municipal meeting that always takes precedence over the jazz band," said Red. "Hello, Max, Dot. Good to see you again. Where's Harry?"

"I haven't the first notion," said Catherine. "He's been misbehaving."

"Why don't you join us?" asked Dot.

"Thank you. I'd enjoy that," said Red.

Catherine was of two minds about the situation. She didn't want to encourage Red, but his company was welcome. It always amused her that for all his communist leanings, Red enjoyed his creature comforts.

They all ordered raw oysters on the half shell to start with, and Max soon had them laughing about his adventures on the Tube in London when he fell asleep and ended up in Epping, where someone took grave exception to his cowboy boots and hat. He was writing an article for the *Los Angeles Times* Sunday Supplement called "A Cowboy's Misadventures in London."

While they were eating their entrée, Catherine asked Red, "How can I get in touch with Oliver Anderson?"

"I assume you're talking about the pacifist chap?" Red asked. "The one in Anne's anti-fascist group?"

"Yes." Catherine briefly told Max and Dot about Anne's project.

"He tutors at Merton College," Red said. "I think it will be worth your time to talk to him. He and Severn had a couple of run-ins."

"Why don't you tell Max and Dot about the earl?" Catherine asked.

They spent the next half hour listening to Red's anecdotes about the late peer. As usual, his dry humor was entertaining. It was difficult for Catherine to remember that Red was actually a dangerous individual and Severn, a murder victim. In fact, Red was a suspect himself. It still bothered her that he hadn't given her an alibi. Her spirits took a dive.

When the men were sitting over their brandy and the women their coffee, Red said, "This evening needs a little jazz. Why don't we go back to your flat, Catherine, roll up the carpets, and dance to the wireless?"

Catherine said, "Dot has had a long week of working, unlike us academic types. I promised her an early night."

Red seemed to notice her change of mood. He stood. "All right, then. Good luck with that chap, Anderson. Good to see you, Dot, Max. 'Night."

* * *

When they got back to her flat, she left the sitting room to Max and Dot and went back to her bedroom. Dot came in a short time later.

"You certainly cut Red off at the knees tonight, Cat."

"I suddenly remembered he doesn't have an alibi for Severn's murder."

"Is there a chance he murdered the man? What is his motive?"

"He doesn't need a motive like an ordinary person. It could have been political. He's quite a dangerous person."

"Somehow, I have a hard time remembering that," said Dot.

Saturday, Max took Catherine and Dot punting on the Cherwell, where they enjoyed the splendid colors of the autumn foliage.

"Darling, do try to enjoy yourself," urged Dot. "Harry is behaving like a perfect beast, but I know he loves you. This is just a temporary fit of madness on his part. As you said, he has known Anne all his life. He is probably accustomed to running to her aid."

"That's what I'm afraid of," said Catherine. "He has no idea that he's out of line. Where Anne is concerned, he's like Pavlov's dog. Her distress is his dinner bell. Part of him belongs to her, and I don't think it will ever be any different. Can you imagine this happening if we were married, for heaven's sake?"

"Maybe it will take some time, but don't you think Harry is bound to remember that he is no longer an adolescent but a grown-up professor?"

"You must remember, he has known this woman all his life," Max responded.

"You know, I don't even like him when he's like this," Catherine said.

"Of course not. How do you think Anne feels about him?" asked Dot.

Catherine considered the question. "Well, I hardly know her, but I think he's a habit. She's used to him coming when she rings the bell."

They fell into a silence, listening to the laughter from the other punts and the occasional splash. Dot dozed while Catherine brooded.

* * *

After their interlude on the Cherwell, Catherine returned to her flat, insisting that Dot and Max have the rest of the day and the evening alone. Cherry was giving Catherine a manicure when the telephone rang.

"Hello?" she answered.

"Cath, it's Harry. We've run into a spot of trouble. I need you to ring Spence and get him to come down here post haste."

Catherine ignored his presumptive manner and asked, "Mr. Spence? Whatever for?"

"The local bobby was alerted by a resident when we questioned her about our suspect. She was suspicious of us for no good reason and rang the Oxford police. Apparently, as a condition of her release on bail, Anne wasn't to leave the county. We're in Cardiff now, and Anne and I are in jail here! It's ghastly! Anne has seen a rat."

Catherine wanted to laugh, but she knew that Harry would be incensed. "Luckily, I have Mr. Spence's home number. I will ring him for you. Did you get anywhere with your inquiries?"

"No. They were a washout. It's my opinion that our bit of evidence was a blind. We've been manipulated. I think, to lead us to the heir."

"Have you met him?" she asked.

"We should have done that the first thing, I know. I came off without even an address. I would have eventually asked someone, but then we ended up here."

Finally, Catherine laughed, unable to restrain herself. Oh, she was wicked. Harry and Anne in jail! With rats!

"Well you may laugh," Harry said. "But we're freezing cold. I don't think anyone's been in this jail since before I was born."

The warning pips sounded, signaling their three minutes were up. "I'll see you," she said cheerfully.

Mr. Spence was not at all pleased to have his afternoon

interrupted. "I thought the woman had brains! What does she think she's doing haring off to deepest Wales? And it's Saturday afternoon of all times! And what about Bascombe? He's in jail, too? What has he done?"

Catherine chuckled to herself at his fury, which Harry richly deserved. "He was just trying to get some information on the case. I agree; he certainly didn't go about it in the best way."

She listened to further invective until Mr. Spence realized he'd have to move quickly if he was going to get a train to Cardiff that afternoon.

Dressing warmly, she decided to go for a walk and pay a visit to Blackwell's for medicinal purposes. The largest bookshop in Europe could easily swallow up the rest of her time that afternoon.

The air was crisp, but Catherine walked so briskly that by the time she reached Blackwell's, she needed to shed her jacket. She loved the iconic shop. There were books on every surface and in every cubbyhole. She descended to the underground level, where she often found the best gems. As Catherine was writing her doctoral dissertation on recently-published poets and the literary movement they signified, she sometimes had to dig deep to find the new writers' offerings.

Kneeling on the floor deep in the stacks, she found a treasure trove. While she investigated this, she had no awareness of what went on around her. It was thus that Lord Rutherford found her.

CHAPTER ELEVEN

"Your maid told me I'd find you here," he said. "I was just about to give up."

Surprised, Catherine stood up. She was going to have to have a word with Cherry.

What have you got there?" Rutherford asked.

"Poetry," she said. "I'm researching my dissertation. Was there any particular reason you wanted to see me?"

"Anything that's any good?" he asked.

"I don't know yet. Why are you here?" she asked again.

"I'm being left in the dark. I need to know what's going on. Let me buy you a cup of tea, and you can bring me up to date."

Catherine sighed. Did she have any choice? "I've been here for hours. What time is it?"

"Teatime. Let me carry the books."

After she had paid for her selections and seen them wrapped in brown paper, Lord Rutherford took her to a nearby tea shop and treated her to a high tea. There were scones, eclairs, raspberry tarts, cucumber sandwiches, and savory biscuits.

"Did you know that your daughter broke the terms of her release and went down to Wales with Harry Bascombe to follow up a lead?"

Lord Rutherford rolled his eyes. "I should have suspected she would do something like that. She is nothing if not impetuous. What was the lead?"

There was nothing for it but to tell him the story of the birders, the stranger in dungarees, and the train ticket.

"I don't quite believe in that train ticket," he said. "A bit too obvious."

"Not worthy of Sherlock Holmes?" Catherine said caustically. "This is a real murder we're talking about. Not something written by Sir Arthur Conan Doyle." Unable to withstand the temptation, Catherine took a raspberry tart from the tea tray.

"Is my daughter still in jail?" the peer asked.

"Yes," said Catherine.

"She never was very good at keeping rules. Has anything come out about the coded message that was found on Severn's desk?" he asked.

"No." She didn't tell him that she didn't believe in the message. "That sounds like your specialty. Why don't you follow up on that?"

"I will, then. It could be important," said Rutherford. "What's your next step?"

"I'm going to look in on Oliver Anderson, I think. He's one of the people who knew your daughter had an appointment with Severn."

"That sounds like a good idea. Do you need some help?"

"No, thanks. I think I can manage. I'll ring him when I get home." Catherine realized she had been putting off this action until Harry was available, which was idiotic. She was perfectly capable of pursuing the matter herself.

"Now, tell me about your daughter. What was she like growing up?"

The man looked away. His brow furrowed in annoyance. "Oh, just your average girl. Maybe a bit more curious than most. I thought she might make a better marriage than she did. She didn't show much sense there."

Catherine felt her first bit of sympathy with Anne. Rutherford's statement might have come out of Catherine's father's mouth. Not a very emotionally present father—one that it wasn't easy to please.

She gathered her package of books and her purse. "Thank you so much for tea. I must go now. Let us know how you are coming along with the mysterious message."

He rubbed his hands together. "I'll do that," he said.

* * *

Back at the flat, Catherine rang Dr. Anderson at Merton College. It was six o'clock, and she hadn't much hope of reaching him, but she had to do something. Lord Rutherford had made her feel guilty about taking time off the chase.

To her surprise, the tutor answered. "Anderson here."

"Dr. Anderson, this is Miss Catherine Tregowyn. I'm a friend of Anne Bascombe. You've heard about her arrest?"

"Anne's been arrested? For what?"

Catherine realized she'd stumbled upon one of those Oxford tutors who lived in an Ivory Tower away from what was going on in the real world. "Murder. The police think she killed Earl Severn."

"Ridiculous!" the man pronounced in lofty tones.

"She was the last known person to see him before he was killed," Catherine told him. "I'd like to talk to you about the anti-fascist group if you could spare me a little time."

"I suppose I could. When did you want to meet?"

"How about tomorrow afternoon?" she asked.

"About two o'clock?" he suggested.

"That would be lovely," said Catherine. "I do so appreciate your help. Anne's brother-in-law, Dr. Harry Bascombe, and I are trying to get the charges dropped."

"I know Bascombe. Sound chap. Will he be with you?"

"I really can't say at this point. We're pursuing different angles."

"I see. Pity. Well, where shall I meet you?"

"I'm a tutor at Somerville College. Would you mind meeting me in the Junior Commons Room?"

"That would serve adequately. You'll leave word with the porter?"

"Of course," she said. "I look forward to meeting you."

Catherine spent her evening reading and annotating all the books of poetry she had bought that day. At eleven o'clock, she called it a night and went to bed.

In the morning, she and Dot followed their custom and went to the services at Christ Church Cathedral to hear the world-famous choir. Catherine allowed herself to be carried away on the strains of ethereal music weaving in and out of the cathedral's beloved columns. For a time, she let herself forget that a man had been murdered, that Harry was being beastly, and that there might be another war.

Max and Harry met them to her surprise as they followed the stream of worshippers out into a rainstorm after the service. Harry looked like a thundercloud, and there were dark rings under his brown eyes. He kissed Catherine's cheek perfunctorily.

"I say, thanks for calling Spence to come to rescue us yesterday. Unfortunately, he was only able to spring me. Anne has to wait in jail for a detective sergeant to come down from Oxford to take custody of her. She's headed back to the Oxford jail."

"Bad luck," said Catherine.

"No, it's not bad luck. I deserve to be in that jail instead of Anne. It was asinine of me to think she wouldn't suffer for breaking the rules of her bail agreement. I haven't the least idea why I thought she needed to go down there with me. Mind if I share your umbrella?"

When Catherine shook her head, he moved closer to her and even put his arm about her waist. "Spence gave me a tongue-lashing, and it was not *pleasant*," he continued. "James was with him. I'm afraid I have lost what remained of his goodwill toward me. I had to listen to his chastisement of Anne, as well. Poor woman."

Max interrupted Harry's *mea culpa*. "We actually came to

extend a Sunday dinner invitation to you. They're serving roast beef and Yorkshire pud in the dining hall. Say you'll come."

Dot looked at Catherine, raising her brows in a question.

Catherine replied, "Max, you're coming on with the accent. I'd almost swear you were Oxford-born and bred. Dot and I would love to come."

Harry looked a bit less out of sorts but was still miles away from being cheerful. Dot put her arm through Max's. Catherine was tempted to take his other arm and leave Harry to bring up the rear, but she restrained herself. Harry trudged beside her in the rain.

Once they arrived indoors at the college, Harry excused himself to get out of his wet things. Max chuckled once his friend was a safe distance away. "I know the gender is wrong, but he is as angry as a wet hen."

"Poor Harry," said Catherine. "He is rarely so out of sorts. In fact, I have never seen him this way."

"He's usually the life of the party," said Dot.

During dinner, Catherine exerted herself to bring Harry out of his mood by telling him about the new poets she had discovered the day before. He allowed himself to be coaxed. As they sat over their baked apple and custard at meal's end, he apologized, "I'm sorry I've been such a cross bear. But I'll wager no one likes being dressed down by a first-rate London solicitor."

Catherine thought his brother's words had probably hurt him more, but there was no further mention of James.

She said, "If you like, you can join me in my interview with Dr. Oliver Anderson this afternoon. He is a fan of yours. That should prop up your morale a bit."

"Oliver Anderson?" Harry echoed.

"The pacifist who works with Anne in her anti-fascist league. He was one of the ones who knew she would see the Earl of Severn the afternoon of the murder. I want to see if he qualifies as a suspect," Catherine said. "But you have to promise to leave off this mood."

The waiter cleared their plates, and Harry took out his pipe and began to fill it.

"Forgive me, Cath. I promise to behave and not be such an idiot."

"Good. He's meeting me in half hours' time, so we had best be off. Do you want to motor, or should we take the bus?"

"We'll motor."

Catherine pulled on her gloves and crossed her fingers that Harry's repentant mood would last. She was relieved when he produced an umbrella.

CHAPTER TWELVE

Oliver Anderson proved to be a long, thin scholarly type, balding with a beard and thick, heavily framed glasses. He arrived at the rendezvous carrying a brief case and an umbrella. As soon as introductions were handled, the three sat down in the leather chairs that furnished the college's Junior Commons Room.

"I could hardly believe it when you told me our Anne had been arrested! Something must be done! She is not the type to go around murdering people, no matter how much she might disagree with them. The very idea!"

"We are trying to find the real murderer," said Harry. "Since the police do not appear to be interested in doing so."

Catherine told him about the man the bird-watcher had glimpsed. Harry produced the photo of the police sketch.

"I don't recognize him, but it's clear he's up to no good," Dr. Anderson said, folding his long hands over his middle. "Severn was a dangerous man. He has made a lot of enemies, I would think."

"Did you know him personally?" asked Anne.

"We had never been introduced, but the man was notorious. He was beastly to his men in the war, and he's never changed. To my mind, he was evil incarnate with all his ideas of making us a carbon copy of Germany! Whoever killed him has done this country a favor, but it wasn't Anne. She is anti-violence—anyone will tell you that. Not at all the sort of person who goes around murdering people."

"You don't have to convince us of that fact," said Harry. "I know Anne very well. She is my sister-in-law."

"Then you know she could never have killed Severn. She reminds me a lot of my late wife."

"I'm sorry," said Catherine automatically. "Did she die recently?"

"No. No." The old professor waved a hand. "But she belongs to another life. She was French. I married her after the war and lived in France until she died a few years ago."

Catherine stood and poured tea into the cups the scout had left brewing for them. "How did you and Anne become connected?"

"Uh, milk, no sugar, please," said Dr. Anderson. "It was rather a quirky thing. We met through Winston Churchill, you might say. We were both down at Chartwell to meet with him." He took his tea from Catherine's hand. "About rearmament."

"Oh?" said Harry. "I didn't know Anne had met with Churchill. She never said."

"They are thick as thieves. She knew that bloke in Germany, von Ossietzky, who exposed Germany's rearmament back in '31. You have heard of him. He was awarded the Nobel prize this year for publishing his work. He's been sent to prison and tortured for it. Before he was arrested, Anne had been meeting with him secretly. I imagine that is the real reason she and James left Germany. She was about to be arrested, as well. Not to put too fine a point on it, Anne was Churchill's spy."

Stunned, Catherine stopped pouring tea and sat down hard. Turning to Harry, she said, "And you didn't know this?"

"No," her fiancé insisted, his face flushed. "She kept completely mum. I wonder what other secrets she has been keeping from me."

"Oh, dear," said Dr. Anderson. "I see I have been terribly indiscreet. I am just such a champion of Anne. She takes action.

She does important things while the rest of us just sit about and complain. She even had sources inside of Krupp—the weapons manufacturers."

Catherine had never seen Anne in a heroic light. Now she wondered if she had misjudged her. Or was Anderson just exaggerating?

"And what business brought you to Chartwell?" she asked Anderson.

"I keep my finger on the pacifist pulse. Please keep that to yourself. I shouldn't like to be exposed. They will do anything to keep Churchill from being believed. They want peace at any price."

The sudden flood of unexpected information winded Catherine. She almost forgot that this man was a suspect in their investigation.

Something he had said tugged at a corner of her mind, but she couldn't retrieve it. Maybe Harry had noticed it. But when she looked his way, she realized he was looking shell-shocked. The news about Anne and Churchill had probably blown away any idea that he was in her confidence. The fact that Anne and James had essentially escaped from Germany in the face of an arrest was another stunner.

"You have certainly given us a lot to think about," said Catherine. "Have you any idea who killed the earl?"

"He had offended so many people. I honestly don't know. His death was by way of being a sort of assassination, you know?"

"Does anyone actually believe Severn's movement could possibly have gained universal acceptance in modern Britain?" Catherine asked.

"Politics are uncertain all over Europe right now," commented the professor, sipping his tea serenely as though he were at a garden party. "Fascism and communism are fighting it out. Democracies don't seem to be able to offer any hope to people who are still suffering from the upheaval of the Depression. There is an unfortunate appetite for drastic action. Then there is the worsening class struggle. The bad old ways are still hanging on in some respects. Nothing shows that more than the following that Severn managed to gather."

"So," said Catherine. "Who do you think killed the man?"

"I'd look into the secretary. He strikes me as a wrong 'un."

"When did you meet Dawkins?" asked Harry. He got up and absently poured himself a cup of tea.

"We belong to the same club," said Professor Anderson. "He's an insinuating little creature."

"I can't say that I took to him," said Catherine.

"There's gossip that he's a blackmailer, and I must say, I believe it. He's just that sort. And he was privy to a lot of things the titled rich would rather have kept secret."

"Do you believe Severn was a blackmailer, too?" asked Catherine.

"Let's just say he would have had the knowledge needed," the professor said, putting down his teacup. "Now, I really must fly."

"Thank you for coming, Professor Anderson," said Catherine.

"Where is Anne at the moment?" he asked. "I'd like to let her know I'm thinking of her."

Harry answered, "She's in the Oxford jail. "She'd be glad of a visit, I'm sure."

Dr. Anderson was startled. "I thought she had been released on bail!"

"It's my fault. I talked her into an excursion to Wales. She violated the terms of her bail."

"Oh. Bad luck."

When the professor had taken his leave, Catherine relaxed back into the leather chair and exhaled a long breath. "Phew!" she said. "Anne, a spy for Churchill who had to leave Germany to avoid arrest? Dawkins and Severn blackmailers? I'd say we got a lot more than we bargained for out of Professor Oliver Anderson."

"Including the information that he is not a pacifist, but a spy for Churchill as well," said Harry. "He either trusted us completely, or he is incredibly indiscreet. It's hard to imagine him as a spy! I think we need to verify all this with Anne."

"Agreed," said Catherine, rising to her feet. "Can you give me an hour? I'd like to say goodbye to Dot before she goes. She's at my flat packing up."

"Jolly good. Shall I meet you at your flat at 4:30? I'll drive you down to the police station."

"Excellent."

* * *

Dot was packing when Catherine arrived at her flat.

"Sometimes I hate your job!" she said to Dot. "It would be so much better if you stayed here. I don't feel like we've had a chance to talk at all."

"I know," said Dot. "If my business succeeds, I do think I'll move back to Oxford. If you're still here, of course."

"I'm sorry. I haven't even asked," said Catherine. "How's the business going?"

"Well. Those contacts I made in New York and Chicago have paid off. They've agreed to distribute my products as of the first of the year."

"Dot! That's wonderful news!"

"Yes, I'm pleased."

"And how are things going with Max?"

"We suit each other down to the ground. If only it weren't for that pesky Atlantic, we'd be happy as clams." She slammed her suitcase closed and locked it. "Now, tell me about Harry. I'm not used to seeing him so moody."

"You know, it's rather frightening, because I'm beginning to think I don't really know him," said Catherine.

"If it were me, I'd have a straightforward talk with him. About more than just the investigation."

"I know. I'm beginning to think I must postpone the wedding. My decision to marry him was based on false premises."

"That's a big decision, darling. But I can certainly see why you would feel that way. Perhaps you need to give the relationship some more time."

Catherine was aware of the anxiety pooling in her middle. Coming on top of her big Sunday dinner, it was making her nauseous.

"How is the investigation going?" Dot asked.

"It's getting more complicated—spies, blackmail, you name it."

"Oh, Cat, do tell."

Catherine outlined what they had learned from Oliver Anderson.

"It seems the messier your cases get, the closer you always are to a solution," Dot said.

"I think we're a long way from that. I haven't told you about Anne's father, Lord Rutherford. He's a Sherlock Holmes devotee. He is determined to solve this. At the moment, he is trying to get a look at a complex coded message that was left at the scene of the murder."

"It needed only that," said Dot. "If it weren't so serious, it would be comic."

There was a knock at the bedroom door. "Time to go, Dot," Max called out from the hall.

Catherine's friend kissed her cheek. "Call me when you've talked to Harry," she said.

"I will," she promised.

CHAPTER THIRTEEN

For the first time since Catherine had met Anne, the woman looked bedraggled and down in the mouth. Her hair wanted washing, and she was so pale there was a greenish tinge to her skin. Her father was sitting with her when they called. He rose and greeted them.

"It's the sleuths! Good afternoon. I hope you have brought new leads!"

"Darling!" said Harry as he looked at Anne. He was oblivious to the viscount's greeting. "You look as though you haven't had a wink of sleep!"

"I haven't," she said. "We didn't reach here until early this morning, and then the questioning began again."

"What were they questioning you about this time?"

"I was just telling Dad. The Germans. Did I know how close Lord Severn was to them? What did I do with my time when we were in Germany?"

Harry said, "I must tell you, your friend, Professor Anderson, came clean about where and how he met you." He nodded toward the constable taking notes of the conversation in the corner of the room. "You could have told me, you know."

"Oh, bother! I'm sure that has nothing to do with all this." She looked at the constable. "That's confidential."

Catherine referenced her feelings on this subject. Anne was right.

"To change the subject, then. Have you ever had any reason to believe that Severn or Dawkins, his secretary, were guilty of blackmail? Professor Anderson thought they might be. He's heard rumors, but nothing concrete," said Catherine.

"I don't know Dawkins and have never met him, so I can't say." Anne looked away from her visitors, biting her lip. Her hands were clutched together in her lap. "Surely Severn wouldn't have needed to blackmail anyone. He had no need for money. He was practically made of it."

Catherine watched the woman as she parsed her words. She hadn't actually said that Severn wasn't a blackmailer. Just that he didn't need to be. Catherine decided to keep her own council for the moment, but she wondered whether Severn had been black-mailing Anne.

"But the thing he wanted more than anything was to have influence," mused Catherine. "Could he have blackmailed some-one—say a noted aristocrat—into coming out in support of his program? That could be quite a coup."

"Oh, my," said Anne. "I see what you mean." Her tone was artificial. Catherine could tell she had hit the nail on the head.

Catherine went on to press her point, "It makes far more sense to me that the murderer was someone who was being blackmailed to use his influence rather than because Severn was any kind of realistic threat to the country."

"Amen to that," said Rutherford. "As far as I'm concerned, it's the best motive for his death that anyone has come up with. What do you think, Anne?"

"That makes more sense to me," said Anne. "But we have to remember that murderers aren't always sensible. Emotions are running high in this country right now."

Catherine marveled at how easily the woman dissembled, drawing attention away from Catherine's theory. But she knew she would never convince Harry of it.

Her fiancé said, "I think you're right. But all the same, we should keep it in mind."

Catherine pressed her lips together. Was Harry trying to throw her some kind of sop because the all-wise Anne disagreed with her?

"I think I would still try to get to the bottom of that business with the train ticket," Anne said. "But the murderer needn't have left St. Athan, dressed as a gardener with the wig and so on. He would have had to change trains in Cardiff, which is a big city. It is far more likely that he assumed his costume there where no one would notice his comings and goings."

Catherine forced herself to think of this. It made sense. If Anne were right, the murderer could have left St. Athan undisguised. But then why didn't he stay in Cardiff in the first place?

"What was St. Athan like? Was it fashionable or just an old, sleepy place?" she asked.

"Most of the residents are old," said Harry. "Of course, we didn't get to talk to many. The lady in the second house was the one who called the constable."

"It was trying to be fashionable," said Anne. "There was an adorable tea shop and a quaint bed and breakfast. It is right on the channel."

"So, it's a place where visitors would probably be noted," Catherine said.

"Yes," said Anne.

"I must tell you; I'm convinced that whole train ticket business is a false lead," said Rutherford.

Anne gave a short laugh. "You just don't like an obvious clue," she accused her father. It's the Holmes in you. You always want things to be obscure. But I'm convinced it's a genuine lead. It makes sense to me that it could have been the heir's ticket."

"Anne and I were going to try to meet him when we were down there, but, as you know, the police had other plans," said Harry.

"I'm going to follow up the German angle," said Rutherford.

"They have got to be involved somehow. And now, I must be gone. The peer gave Catherine a nod. "Keep up the good work."

Did Catherine imagine it, or had Anne gone rigid at her father's words about the Germans?

"I'm going to leave, as well," said Catherine. "I'm behind on everything."

Neither Anne nor Harry seemed to notice as she slipped away from the room.

* * *

Monday morning came too early for Catherine after a bad night. She had been unable to sleep. She felt that the direction she wanted to go—after Anne and her connection to the Germans—would be totally unacceptable to Harry. And she was angry at herself for minding about that. She had taken two baths, given herself a facial, and done deep breathing exercises. Finally, she had written him an angry letter which she tore up and fed to her bedroom fire.

The day was gray, of course. She dressed in her red trousers and a black jumper and decided to give herself a break from Anne's case. So, deep in her study of her new poets, she didn't even hear the door. Cherry came in to tell her that Lord Rutherford was in the sitting room. Catherine reluctantly left an intriguing poem about a beehive.

Lord Rutherford's long face was beaming. "I got a copy of the cipher from the police yesterday when I told them I worked out ciphers as a hobby. The code itself was child's play, but since it's in German, that made it a bit of a challenge."

"German?" said Catherine. "You deciphered it? Is it from the embassy?"

"I did. And it is. At least it tells of von Ribbentrop's arrival, so I think it must be."

"Good. Could you tell me what else it said?"

"It looks like Severn was in cahoots with the Germans. The cipher thanked him for agreeing to get information for them.

Then it went on to mention the delivery schedule for the weapons Severn had purchased once they received the requested information."

"Crikey!" said Catherine. "Treason." She walked in circles about the room as she thought. "But if the German's were the killers, they would never leave evidence like that proving his connection. I'm bound to think it was a plant. But I suppose the police will follow up on it."

"You're right, of course. The simplicity of the code makes it seem as though it was a phony meant to set us off in the wrong direction. But who put it on Severn's desk?"

"Probably the murderer. There was that call from the German embassy setting up the 5:00 appointment," said Catherine. "That could have been from the murderer."

"Who told you about it?"

"Dawkins, the secretary." Catherine mused on the unlovely man. "But if he's the murderer, I'm guessing there was no call. And that cipher sounds like something he would think of. He fancies himself clever."

But what about the phony gardener? Had the call been made to ensure that Severn was at his desk waiting for his appointment? Or was the unsophisticated cipher genuine but a German attempt to deceive Severn with false promises in order to get information?

She put clenched fists to her temples. "There are way too many possibilities here!"

"Yes," said Lord Rutherford. "I can see that. And, of course, there is no way we can tell if the cipher was genuine. One can't exactly ask the Germans if they sent it."

Catherine stopped her pacing. "Forgive me for asking, but how good is your German?"

"Not that wonderful, actually. I had to rely pretty heavily on the dictionary," said Anne's father.

"Do you mind if we get Harry to look at your translation of the cipher? He is fluent in German. I gave up on the language after only one term. There are so many things you have to get just right—case, gender, and all that. It would be easy for a non-German speaker to make a mistake."

"Certainly. I'll ring him if you'll allow me to use your telephone," the peer said.

Harry wasn't in, but Lord Rutherford left a message with the porter to ring him at the Randolph.

"I'll be off, then. I'll just stop by the police station to drop off this transcription, and then I'll go back to the Randolph. I'll let you know if Harry takes issue with the translation."

"That will be wonderful. May I also make a copy of the transcription? I'd like to have it to refer to."

The peer agreed, and taking out a piece of her stationery, Catherine hastily wrote out another copy.

"Thank you so much, Lord Rutherford."

"You don't need to thank me. I haven't been the best father to Anne. The least I can do is to give her a hand now."

Catherine said her farewells and went back to her poets.

＊ ＊ ＊

Her telephone was silent until late in the afternoon. By that time, Catherine was utterly absorbed in her studies.

It was not Lord Rutherford on the telephone, however. It was Harry.

"Cath, they've just brought Red into the jail. Apparently, he was fomenting unrest among the workers in Severn's company. I almost didn't recognize him without his beard."

"Oh no!" she cried. "Are they charging him?"

"Yes. Under the Unions Act of 1926. Apparently, he crossed the line. Why would he do something so stupid?"

"He was trying to help us, I think. I'll be right down."

It was only as Cherry was frantically buttoning her into her most conservative black frock that she realized Harry must have been at the jail visiting Anne when Red was brought in. The idea stoked her growing insecurity.

In the interest of time, she took the bus instead of walking, but even so, she chafed at its slow pace. Did Red have a solicitor? She knew he had formulated this plan to infiltrate the workers at the manufacturing plant for Severn's products, but she should have insisted that he tell her what he hoped to accomplish.

Finally, she arrived at the police station in the City Hall. She couldn't see Red right away because he was with his solicitor. This was a relief rather than an annoyance. She had to remember that Red probably didn't need her help. He certainly knew the ropes. He'd been arrested many times before.

Instead of merely waiting to see Red, she decided to take the opportunity to show the translation of the decrypted cipher to Harry if he was still there visiting Anne. She asked the desk sergeant.

"Yes. He is still visiting Mrs. Bascombe."

"I would like to see her, as well," she requested.

The sergeant took her back. When she entered the interview room, it was to see Anne pull her hand hastily out of Harry's grasp as it lay on the table. Catherine's heart took a sharp dive. It appeared that matters between her fiancé and his sister-in-law had progressed to the point where neither of them was trying to hide their feelings. Tears stung Catherine's eyes, and for a moment, she couldn't say anything.

Finally, she thrust her copy of the cipher's translation at Harry.

"Anne's father brought this to me today. It's his translation of the cipher, which he decrypted. He said it was rather an obvious code."

"I don't know why you're wasting your time with that silly thing," said Anne fretfully. "What I need you to do, Catherine is to go to Wales and look further into that ticket stub. That's where you're going to find answers."

Catherine's face burned at the woman's audacity. Before she could say something rude, she turned and left the room.

She scarcely heard Harry's "Catherine, wait!" as she walked

down the hall. She wouldn't wait to see Red now. She felt as though she were choking.

Air! I've got to have air!

No sooner was she out in the street than she felt a hand grasp her arm. "Catherine,

Stop! Listen to me!" Harry cried.

"Let go of me, or I shall have you up for assault!" she said through her teeth.

"Anne didn't mean to order you about like that! She's terribly tense, just now," Harry said, his voice pleading.

"I am no one's errand boy," Catherine said. In a swift movement, she pulled off her engagement ring and put it in Harry's handkerchief pocket. "Go back to your woman. I'm finished with two of you."

Before Harry could protest, she stepped out into the street and hailed a cruising cab. "Train station," she said to the cabbie. She had to get to Dot and away from any place where Harry could find her and hurt her further.

*　*　*

The express train took only forty minutes to get to London. Catherine's jaw was rigid during the entire journey, and her hands clenched as she glared out the window. *What right did that woman have to treat me like her employee? How far had things gone between her and Harry? He was not generally a demonstrative man, but he had been holding her hand, leaning toward her. She was his brother's wife! And he was engaged.*

By the time Catherine arrived in London, she was ready to explode.

It was five o'clock. Dot would head for The Spotted Pig after work. Catherine splurged on another cab. When she got to the noisy pub, crammed with people celebrating the end of the workday, she grew anxious when she couldn't see Dot. Her friend must have seen her; however, as only a moment or two into her search,

Dot gripped her arm from behind. Catherine whirled to face her, and she went limp at the sight of her friend.

"Cat? What is it? Your face is white as a ghost!"

"Can we go?" Catherine asked. "I've just given Harry the push."

"Good for you, I say!" her friend guided her out of the pub as though Catherine was blind. She hailed a cab and sat holding hands until they arrived at Dot's cozy flat.

While Catherine sat on Dot's kitchen chair staring straight before her, Dot made tea. She added three lumps of sugar and put it in Catherine's hands.

"That'll do you good, Cat. Drink up."

Catherine said, "I don't know why I'm behaving like a schoolgirl. This is ridiculous. I'm sorry to appear out of the blue like this."

"You've had a shock. What happened?" Dot asked, sitting across from Catherine with her cup of tea.

"This was bound to happen the way he has been behaving. I walked in on them in the visitor's room at the jail. They were holding hands, and when I came in, they fairly jumped apart. Then Anne proceeded to give me orders. As though I were her underling, and I was hers to command. I walked out. Harry came after me. I stuck my ring in his pocket and jumped into a cab before he could say a word. He's been moonstruck ever since this started. Well, it's over, Dot."

"He has been behaving like an idiot. You're right—this *was* bound to happen," said Dot. "But I think all this business is just a temporary regression on his part. He's not acting like the Harry of 1935, but more like a silly undergrad."

"I'm afraid it's more than that. His whole attitude toward me has changed. How could he let her talk to me that way?"

"I'm glad you're angry," Dot said. "That's better than tears."

For the next hour, she filled Dot in on all Harry's acts of perfidy since the night of their engagement party and Anne's arrest. She had hoarded each one carefully.

"I didn't know he was capable of this type of devotion. He's certainly never displayed it with me.

"You did the right thing," Dot said finally. "Now he is stuck with her in reality; she is no longer a fantasy, but a pushy woman who is married to his brother. Let him see how he likes them apples, as Max would say."

"What a marvelous turn of phrase," Catherine commented. "You always know what to say."

"Ready for some dinner? I have lamb chops."

"Perfect," Catherine said. She was aware of pain starting to peek through the anger and knew it would be keeping her company for a long time.

"I need to call my mother and tell her to stop her preparations for the wedding and the luncheon that was supposed to follow," she said. An unwelcome thought struck her. "You know, looking forward, I've been seeing life with Harry as my future. We had such plans. Now I must change the whole concept of what lies ahead." Catherine pressed her lips together to keep from crying.

"I would wait on that," Dot said. "You are perfectly entitled and capable of having a wonderful future without Harry, but I expect he will come around within the week."

"Hah!" said Catherine. "I don't. I'd rather pay the price in pain for a couple of months or even a year instead of a lifetime. He didn't love me, Dot. We were partners. We enjoyed being together. We were comfortable. But I never stirred him the way Anne does. I don't think he wanted to go there again. His feelings for me were safe."

"Or his feelings for Anne are nothing more than a boyhood fantasy," said Dot. "I think this Anne is a person who inspires worship. What is her relationship with her husband like?"

Dot began preparing lamb chops as she talked. Catherine got up and scouted out the refrigerator for traces of vegetables. She found a carrot, some leftover peas, half a tomato, and half a lettuce head. She began making a salad.

"He certainly doesn't worship her. He works seven days a

week in his lab on the development of a vital medicine. He seems to tolerate Harry making a fool of himself."

"Hmm. Interesting," said Dot. "His brother's aloof manner may have been a challenge for our Anne. Maybe it was even refreshing."

"You could be right. She's very independent. Turns out she was a spy for Churchill while she was in Germany. She knows quite a bit about German rearmament. She may concentrate on that business and her anti-Nazi league while her husband works. They had to leave Germany because of her activities. They're lucky not to be in prison there, according to one of her friends."

"Sounds like our Anne lives for thrills."

"I think she does. I rather think she likes teasing her husband with Harry's adoration. I'll wager you anything you like that her marriage to James was the result of a careful campaign on her part. She was probably angry at Harry for preferring a Grand Tour to her charms."

They ate their dinner, did the washing up, and then listened to the wireless. Red was in the news as a prominent Communist who had been arrested at the Severn plant. He was now out on bail, which was a relief to Catherine.

"Are you planning to go back to Oxford on the eleven o'clock or stay 'til morning?" asked Dot.

"I need to ring Cherry. She must be worried. I'll go back tonight. I have to tutor in the morning."

"Will you continue with this case?"

"No. Harry is on his own now."

Her resolve lasted until the nine o'clock news bulletin. Dawkins, Severn's private secretary, had been found murdered. Red's notecase was found at the scene. He was back in jail—this time for murder.

Chapter Fourteen

Catherine returned home after midnight. The day had been fraught with emotion, and yet she couldn't sleep. Her anger with Harry hadn't abated, her future was up for grabs, and she was also worried about Red. There was no doubt in her mind that he had been framed. Did the same person commit the two murders? She would wager money on it. And that was enough to get her back on the case.

At dawn, she decided to get out of bed and get ready for a visit to the jail before her 11:00 tutorial. She was at the police station by 8:00, a pastry in hand for Red.

When he was shown to the visiting room where she waited, Catherine almost didn't recognize him without his beard. He was devastatingly handsome with a square-angled jaw and a dimple when he smiled.

"Catherine!" he said.

She put out her hands and grasped both of his, though they were manacled. "Red! This is a terrible thing. Tell me what you know about what happened."

As they seated themselves behind a table, Catherine noticed his blue eyes were bloodshot. She figured he'd had about the same amount of sleep she had. None.

"I don't know what's happening," Red said. "I was released

from jail late yesterday afternoon. Apparently, the secretary chap was murdered a few hours afterward, and I find myself back in here. When they gave my personal effects back to me when I left yesterday, my card case was not among them. I didn't notice at the time. I rarely carry it, you see, so I have no idea when it was taken. It was probably lifted from my home, come to think of it. The police found it at the murder scene."

"You were on the BBC news last night," she told him. "Even the bit about the card case."

"Huh," Red responded.

"What is your motive supposed to be?"

"I am a dangerous Communist who murdered Earl Severn to rid the world of his fascist agenda. Dawkins supposedly knew that and was blackmailing me."

"How appalling! Do they have any evidence at all beyond your card case?"

"They're not telling me, but then they wouldn't, would they?"

Catherine shook her head. "And you don't have an alibi?" she asks.

"I do. I was eating an early meal with one of my comrades at her flat. But since she's a Communist, as well, they discount that. Also, they think she had another motive for protecting me because she's a woman."

Catherine said, "I guess the only way I'm going to be able to disprove this is by finding out who the real villain is."

Red looked at her with a speculative gleam in his eye. "Don't think I don't appreciate it, but are you going to take this on by yourself? What happened to your partner?"

She glanced away from him and down at the floor. "I broke my engagement," she said flatly.

"Well, that's good news anyway!" he said, grinning. "Am I allowed to ask why?"

"No. It's none of your business. But tell me, have you any idea who killed Severn? Or Dawkins?"

"I thought you had someone in your sights."

She pulled the photo of the police sketch out of her purse, unfolded it, and presented it to him. "This is a visitor Severn had right around the time of the murder. A birder spotted him who got quite a good look through his binoculars."

"Dash it. Except for the paunch, the guy looks way too much like me before I shaved."

"Don't go around saying that. He could be anyone. But the fact is, someone was there at that time besides Anne. Also, there was a coded message on his desk, supposedly from the German Embassy. Dawkins claimed they called the office and scheduled a 5:00 appointment."

"Has anyone been able to decode it?" There was finally a light of interest in Red's eyes.

"Lord Rutherford, Anne's father, did. But it may not be genuine. According to Rutherford, it was rather a crude code. Harry has it now. If he can find the time, it's his job to tell us whether the German translation is grammatically correct."

"What did Rutherford give as the translation?"

"Evidently, it said that if Severn gave the embassy information about what certain peers had to say about Germany's plans for the U.K., they were prepared to give him weapons. It was all quite nebulous, though. And there was no reason why this should be conveyed by code in a written record. He met with people from the embassy all the time. Why couldn't they just have told him in person? Certainly, it would be better than documenting something like that, even in code."

Red rubbed his chin. "Yes. It doesn't sound like the careful Germans to me. More like the *Boys' Own Magazine*. Do you have any other evidence?"

She told him about the train ticket. "Anne Bascombe thinks that's the key."

"Too bad I'm locked up. I'd love to run down to Wales with you and do some sleuthing. You have that sketch."

"A friend of Anne's thinks there may be blackmail involved. By either Dawkins or Severn or both."

"And who is this friend?"

"You know him, actually, now that I think of it. You told me how to get in touch with him—Oliver Anderson."

"I wonder what made him think of blackmail?" Red stroked his naked chin again.

"We both disliked Dawkins a great deal and thought he would be just the sort to resort to blackmail. He even made a veiled reference to the fact that things with certain people weren't all they appeared. Then it occurred to both of us that Severn may have been blackmailing other peers into showing support for his fascist movement."

"Ingenious. He just came up with that idea, or he had some evidence?"

"No evidence that I know of. Did you ever meet Dawkins?"

"No. That is what makes this charge against me particularly ridiculous."

Catherine tried to think of the proper adjective. "He was smarmy," she said finally. The kind who would have been preyed upon in school and who would think up schemes to get back on his tormentors. He seemed to especially love the power that being Severn's secretary gave him. Oliver Anderson had him pegged for the murder of his boss."

"And what do you think?" Red asked.

"My opinion is that he liked his position too much," Catherine answered. "Now, tell me, is there anything you think I should look into since you're locked up and can't do it yourself?"

"Besides the probably bogus cipher, the only real evidence you have is the sketch and the train ticket, right?"

"Yes."

"Then, I guess you're going to have to follow that up," he said. "I'll let you know if I think of anything else. Unfortunately, being a communist, I'm the likeliest type of person as well as being the handiest to have murdered a blood-curdling fascist."

"It's unfortunate, indeed." She looked at her watch. "Oh my, I must be off. I have a tutorial! If you want to help, put that mighty brain to work!"

* * *

Fortunately, Catherine's tutorial concerned her favorite era of twentieth-century literature—the War Poets. She always liked to begin with Rupert Brook. His romantic poetry typified the approach to war taken by all the idealistic young men coming out of university to fight the Great War. He died of sepsis before he could fall into the despair and disillusionment his colleagues later felt and expressed.

There was no better testament to the futility of the high human price of that war than the work of the War Poets. She felt a sense of mission when she taught about them and their work. They made her problems shrink into proportion.

When her tutorials concluded, she always liked to lunch in the dining hall with her students. Harry was far from her mind when she found him waiting at her flat afterward.

"What are you doing here?" she demanded.

He looked up from the engagement photo he was holding. His heavy-lidded eyes appeared sunken.

"Catherine, can you ever forgive me? I've been the devil of a fool."

For a moment, she was speechless. Her anger was in danger of melting, revealing the pain beneath. She said, "I am glad I saw you with Anne. It has made me realize I don't know you at all, Harry."

"I can see why you would feel that way. But you must let me explain."

"You don't need to explain, Harry. I understand you now, for perhaps the very first time. You are a completely different person than the one I fell in love with."

He stiffened and drew his brows together. "What do you mean by that?"

"You've been hiding the fact that you are one of those

melancholy heroes you study. Straight out of Brontë—a star-crossed lover."

His face grew red. Then he turned away from her, his eyes on the floor.

"You have never felt that kind of passion for me, Harry," she said quietly, sudden pain surging on a wave inside her. "What you offered me was only superficial, but obviously, there was a whole lot more to you underneath. I will not try to compete with Anne. You are welcome to pine after her all you wish. Now. Please go."

"I have been insufferable," he said, turning to look at her again. Reaching out to touch her, he drew his hand back as though realizing his unworthiness. "I've been a schoolboy."

"I'm glad you realize that," she said. "I don't know this person, Harry."

"That's because I'm an adult in real life. And you are my real life."

"I don't believe it," she said, her voice low. She walked to the other side of the room, using the sofa as a barrier between them.

"The moment she spoke to you like you were her servant, the schoolboy grew up in a hurry," he said. "I tried to reach you until midnight. Finally, Cherry told me you were in London. Did you go to Dot?"

As she thought of the night before, her anger rose again. "It's not really your concern. I'd like you to leave now, Harry. I promised Red I'd try to get him out of jail, and I've got to get to work."

"But don't you see?" he pleaded. "The Dawkins murder is an extension of the Severn case. They both died by the same means. Only this time, the murderer brought the knife with him. It was in the paper this morning."

He continued, "We can work together. Like we always do."

She rushed on, as though he hadn't spoken. "It took me until now to see that your charming manner is just an act. I don't think it covers any deeper feelings. You've never given me any evidence that it does, but I assumed it did. I can't believe I didn't learn my lesson with Rafe! But when I saw you with Anne, I realized you had feelings and attitudes I had never seen before."

"You are wrong about *me*, Catherine. But for what it's worth, it took seeing Anne next to you for me to realize I had always been wrong about *her*. She's a classic narcissist. I responded to ancient cues and played right into her hands."

Catherine felt a small victory. "Well, I'm glad you realized that, at least."

Rushing to her position behind the sofa, he tried to take her in his arms. She pushed him away. "Harry, don't you see? We're not right for each other!"

She walked away from him, calling over her shoulder, "Please go now!" Catherine went to her room, shut the door, and locked it. Leaning on it, she felt the tears fall. *Why am I crying? He's not worth it!*

"Catherine," he called through the door.

Long after she heard the front door close behind him, she paced the floor, trying to resurrect her anger, but all she felt now was searing pain.

Chapter Fifteen

Catherine couldn't seem to pull herself back together. She was only able to sleep in fits and starts and woke up more exhausted than ever.

The wall she had built against Harry was showing some damage. She pressed her fingertips to her temples as she tried to think. *Concentrate.* She must put away all her sticky feelings and concentrate.

At least he had given her one new fact concerning the case: both murders had been committed the same way. Either the murderer was the same person or wanted it to look like it was. Anne would probably be released now that the police thought the murders were linked and had physical evidence that Red had done them.

Catherine opened one of her poetry notebooks, and rather than writing a list, she gave her creative brain an assignment to write her stream of consciousness about these crimes. Maybe she could get to a breakthrough that way.

Whoever the murderer is tried to make it look like a German/Severn alliance was a threat. Communist conspiracy? That is undoubtedly what we are meant to think. Even the guy in dis-guise—working man's kit, bushy beard— was made to look like a Bolshie. Who would want to kill Severn and Dawkins both?

Considering that Dawkins lacked stature and power, he must have been killed for the only thing he did have— information. Was he blackmailing someone? He said quite boldly that he and Severn knew secrets about the anti-fascist group Anne was forming.

We know it wasn't Anne who killed Dawkins (worse luck!) because she was in custody.

I don't believe it was Red. So that leaves Anderson and the Dean as people who knew Anne was meeting with Severn that afternoon if that should prove important. Why haven't I spoken with Dean Godfrey? Obviously, that's the first thing I must do!

As usual, writing had cleared her head. She took up the telephone and rang the dean's office for an appointment after her lecture.

To her immense surprise, before she left for the college, a bouquet of roses arrived from Harry.

He had never been given to extravagant gestures such as these. The delivery softened her heart a bit, but she remained wary. She wasn't going to let him win her back with hearts and flowers. The hurt and doubt went too deep for that.

* * *

Detractors of the academic life would say that Dean Godfrey was far too beautiful for that profession. She was short and slim with wavy blonde hair. She was also only one level below Catherine's employer, the Bursar. Catherine must step carefully here.

"Miss Tregowyn!" the dean exclaimed. "How delightful to see you again. I hope one of your students isn't in trouble this time."

"No." Catherine smiled. "Though, this is rather a delicate matter, Dean. It concerns the murder we talked about the other night. There's been another one. Severn's secretary. The police are certain they are linked."

Dean Godfrey invited her to sit down. "Why is the police of the opinion that they are linked?" she asked.

"The method was the same—stabbing. And there is a possibility that the motive was the same—to end blackmail by the victims."

Catherine laced her gloved fingers in her lap and crossed her ankles.

"I have good news, too," she said. "I believe Anne Bascombe will be released from jail this morning. You know they have Red in custody?"

"Mr. de Fontaine? No, I thought he had been released on bail. He's supposed to have sowed discontent among the workers at Severn's plant; am I right? I know he's rumored to be a dangerous man, but I think he's a lamb."

"I think you're right," Catherine said. "You know him from your anti-fascist league, don't you?"

"Yes. However, I don't know him terribly well. We're a new group."

"Well, he's been arrested for Dawkin's murder now. I don't think he is guilty, and he's rather a friend of mine. I'm trying to get him released. Do you know anything about Severn or Dawkins that might help? There's been talk of blackmail."

"Really? Oh my goodness," said the dean. "But, on second thought, I wouldn't put it past that awful creature."

"You knew him?"

The dean broke eye contact with Catherine and tucked a strand of hair behind her ear. "I was curious about Earl Severn. I wanted to see what he was like. I pretended that I was thinking of having him come to speak at Somerville. I made an appointment with him. He was very discourteous and made me wait." She gave a short, mirthless laugh. "I had to wait in Dawkin's office. He was insufferable."

"He was. I met him, as well. So, what did you think of Severn?"

"He is . . . was delusional, of course. But then, so is Hitler, and he's succeeding like mad."

"I found the whole idea of the man frightening," confessed Catherine. "But I never met him."

"He was surprisingly charismatic." Dean Godfrey tapped a place above her eyebrow with a fingertip. "He was trying to draw me in, of course." She wet her lips and moved forward in her chair. "I'm afraid I underestimated him."

"In what way?" asked Catherine.

"The slightest investigation of his calendar will show that he was meant to speak to the students this coming Sunday afternoon. I arranged that, as you can probably guess, but it was at his insistence. Let us just say that he put me into a position where I couldn't refuse."

"He blackmailed you?" asked Catherine, astounded.

"I'm not prepared to say how he did it, I'm afraid. Not unless I'm under oath." She cleared her throat. "But I didn't kill him."

Catherine couldn't have been more surprised. In fact, she was shocked. The dean was in a very sensitive position. Her invitation for a man with Severn's views to speak to the students would appear to have her endorsement. The parents of the Somervillians, not to mention the Bursar, would be horribly upset. Dean Godfrey could lose her job quite easily over such a move.

She said as much to the dean. The woman bit her lips. "I am and was aware of that, Miss Tregowyn."

"Do you know how he found out about your secret?" Catherine asked, her voice quiet.

"He . . . he must have had me investigated," said the dean.

"So that is how he works," Catherine said. "You know, I very much wonder if his investigator was Dawkins."

"It would make sense," said the dean. "I didn't kill him either. Do you know how it was done?"

"Apparently, he was stabbed just like Severn. It was in the newspaper this morning." Catherine stood. "I am so sorry for your situation. It must be wretched. You can be certain I won't add to your woes by telling the police."

"If they are doing their job, I expect them shortly."

"They think they have their man. It may not come to that."

"Well, I don't wish Mr. de Fontaine ill, but I am not guilty, so I am not going to confess anything."

"Why did you tell me?" Catherine asked.

"I have been so afraid. It was a relief to talk to someone I could trust. I can trust you, can't I?"

"You can, of course," said Catherine, glad she didn't have to share information with Harry anymore.

"Let's just say, I'm not sorry he's dead, and we don't have to worry about him anymore. Tell me, how are your students this term?" the dean asked.

Still stunned, Catherine changed directions with difficulty. "They are a brilliant group. I am enjoying them immensely." She shifted in her chair. "I have just one more question. What do you think of Oliver Anderson?"

The Dean laughed, genuinely this time. "He's the oddest pacifist I've ever met, and I've met a few."

"Yes, I thought that myself," said Catherine. "Did he strike you as the sort that would fall for blackmail?"

"Heavens, no. He's led a blameless life, I'm sure," she said with a deep sigh. "But then, I'm certain most people would say the same about me."

The dean was clearly uncomfortable, so Catherine decided she wouldn't learn anything else from her.

"Thank you for seeing me, Dean. I appreciate your being so open with me."

* * *

When Catherine left the dean's office, she decided to go directly to the jail to speak with Red before any more time had passed.

"The blackmail idea was correct," she told him. "Severn was blackmailing at least one person, not for money but for influence. I can't give you any other details. I gave my word."

"Bad luck for me, I guess," Red replied.

"The person only told me because they were worried about you, but they think the police will be on to them soon."

"Well, good job, my dear."

"I thought that would buck you up a bit. There are doubtless more victims out there. What I need is access to Severn's appointment book."

"That's not going to happen. I'm sure the police have it. But I'll mention it to my solicitor next time I see him."

"Well, the only other thing is to try to follow up on that train ticket stub again. But I can't do anything there until Thursday afternoon after my tutorial."

"How is Lord Rutherford getting along with his sleuthing?"

"I should check in with him, I guess," said Catherine. "I'm sorry, I don't have anything that will get you out of here."

* * *

Catherine used the telephone box outside the jail to ring Lord Rutherford at the Randolph. He agreed to meet her at the Cheshire Cat for dinner. He was very fond of their meat pies. She took the bus to the pub at the west end of Oxford. It felt very odd investigating without Harry. There was an actual pain in her heart, especially when she went to places they had been together often, like the Cheshire Cat.

Sitting at a high table, she nursed her shandy, trying to fight off her self-consciousness. It wasn't the done thing for women to sit in restaurants or pubs alone. After twenty long minutes, she finally spotted the tall thin man making his way to her table.

"What kind of pie would you like?" he asked her.

"Pork, if you please."

"Right-oh," he said.

When he returned with the pies and climbed up on the stool next to her, she felt a little more comfortable.

"How is your investigation coming?" she asked Lord Rutherford.

"Anne is after me to go to Wales and follow up on the train ticket you and Bascombe found."

"She has spoken to me about it, as well."

"I think she has a bee in her bonnet," he said. "The man was in disguise. It won't tell us anything." He sipped his pint and ate his pie with disgraceful speed.

"What has Harry had to say about the cipher translation?"

"I say! You talk to him a good deal more than I do," the peer said.

"Not lately. I have ended my engagement."

"What?"

"I think you heard me, my lord," Catherine said, trying to sound businesslike.

"But why? I have known him all his life. He's a good chap." He tried to look into her eyes, but she put her head down, staring at her dinner.

"Excuse me, but I don't think it is any of your business," said Catherine. "Have you heard anything about Lord Severn blackmailing people in exchange for their influence?"

"What's that?" Picking up his lager, he took a long drink.

Catherine knew he had heard her perfectly well. "You have heard something, haven't you?" she asked.

"I might have done," he said. "But I'm not at liberty to say. The person involved is not a murderer."

"How can you be certain? What would Holmes say about the matter?" she asked.

"I have applied his methods. The person is not guilty of murder." He looked over at her. "I say, are you finished with your pie? I hate to leave you here, but I have another engagement."

Catherine knew without a doubt that he was lying. Was he trying to protect Anne?

"Yes. I am finished," she said. "Thank you."

"I think this whole thing is a Bolshie plot," he said. "For what it's worth. All the pieces have come together for me. I think they have the right man in jail."

"What pieces are you talking about?"

"The code, the appointment set up for five o'clock. I am sure the man who came was the man called 'Red,' in disguise. He got that train ticket ahead of time and dropped it to throw us off."

"And I think you are covering for your daughter," Catherine said. "I think you are very afraid that she did it."

He pressed his lips together. "You dislike Anne because she has bewitched your Harry."

Without any further communication, he left her sitting at the table staring after him.

Catherine pushed her pie plate away and finished her shandy, seething. What Lord Rutherford said was undoubtedly true. She did dislike Anne. But her former fiancé was responsible for his actions; she couldn't blame Anne.

When Catherine left the pub, it was dark and cold. Even though the distance was only a short way to her flat, she felt uneasy and had the bartender call for a cab.

Cherry was waiting for her at the door when she walked in. "Oh! I was that worried about you, miss. Dr. Bascombe has been ringing all afternoon."

"I'm fine. I should have let you know I wouldn't be in to dinner. It was a last-minute invitation." Taking off her hat and gloves, she handed them to the maid and then shed her coat.

Cherry had lit a fire in the sitting room. Catherine went there to warm herself while going through the post. There was nothing of any interest. Unable to shake her feeling of unease, she realized suddenly that, angry as she was, she was missing Harry.

Wills was in Africa, and her parents were very self-sufficient and were only rarely in touch with her. Besides Cherry, Harry had been the only one who cared for her on a daily basis. He had noted her comings and goings, praised her work, listened to her woes. And she had done the same for him. She missed caring for Harry as much as she missed being cared for.

But she was forgetting Dot. Placing a trunk call to her friend, Catherine found she wasn't at home. She felt bereft.

With the nights drawing in, October could be a melancholy month. She wondered if she should get a dog. She had grown up with dogs in Cornwall. They had made splendid companions. A dog never let you down, was unfailingly loyal. But was it really fair to have a dog in a city flat? She thought not.

Thinking of marrying Harry, she had, of course, thought there would be children and had looked forward to raising them. She knew that was terribly unfashionable, but those were her feelings. She and Harry had even discussed it. They had wanted to have three. Dr. and Mr. Bascombe would have been lovely grandparents.

CHAPTER SIXTEEN

Harry showed up unannounced.

"Catherine . . ." Harry said as Cherry left him in the sitting room. "I've been trying to reach you all day."

She was sitting in an armchair. He took the one across from her on the other side of the fire. "I've been out," she said. "Working on this wretched case. Red's in jail now, you know."

"Yes. It was on the news. I wanted to tell you that I've read this ridiculous cipher translation. There is no way a German wrote the text that was supposedly decoded from it. The grammar is all wrong. Wrong genders, wrong verbs. The construction was English, not German. As we guessed, it was a plant."

Catherine looked at him and was surprised to see the pre-engagement-party Harry. The angst was gone from his features—his face was relaxed. Was it just because Anne had been released?

"I'm certain you are relieved that the charges against Anne were dropped," she said.

"Yes. And I owe you an explanation, Catherine. I hope in time you will be able to forgive me, but I certainly understand if you find it difficult." Leaning forward with his elbows resting on his thighs, his hands clasped, he said, "I am not in love with Anne. In fact, I now realize that it is an excellent thing she married my brother."

"Why the *volte-face?*" she asked, holding her breath.

"I remember what misery she brings. As you have seen, she has no empathy and consults only her own wishes. When I was young, I would have stood on my head for her. Seeing her so suddenly, I had no time to prepare. I didn't realize there was unfinished emotional business there."

Catherine found herself in tune with his words. He had been very patient while she worked out her feelings for Rafe. She owed him some understanding. "I think I know what you mean. It was the same when I saw Rafe. I hadn't ever closed the door with any sort of finality. But the fact is, Harry, our history together is very short compared to your history with Anne. There is no getting around that."

"Yes. But I am remembering now why I went off traveling, leaving her for a year. I would never have admitted it, but I needed to get away from her. Anne and I were too enmeshed. I no longer had my own plans, my own opinions. I was chafing at my bonds. I needed a complete separation to regain my perspective. Does that make sense?"

"I'm afraid it does," said Catherine, thinking of the entanglement she had experienced from the time Rafe came to stay when she was ten years old. It had only ended last year. "It's rather a puzzle how we ever survive our first loves, isn't it?"

"You do understand. I was angry with James when I returned and found them married and gone off to Germany, but now I will be eternally grateful. It's different for him. He is so absorbed in his work that Anne cannot exercise the sort of suffocating hold on him that she had on me. He's like quicksilver. He loves her in his own way, but he is not mastered by her if you see what I mean."

"Are you certain you have really untangled yourself?"

He stood and pulled her to her feet. "Yes. You are the one for me. With you, I can be myself—a better self than I am without you. I want to be with you because I have made a conscious choice with my head and my heart. Not because I am driven or compelled by my baser emotions. Do you think you can ever forgive me for treating you so badly?"

"Are you certain you love me enough to marry me? You make it sound as though you are a bit cold-blooded where our relationship is concerned. I'm not sure what we have is sufficient to stand against all your Heathcliff passion for Anne."

In answer, he brought his lips to hers and gave her a kiss that curled her toes. "Does that feel cold-blooded?"

"No," she said, relieved. She kissed him again. "But it is going to take me awhile to believe in it. I think that the enduring kind of love is bone-deep. I'm not sure we have that yet."

"Will you ever believe in what I feel for you?" Harry looked almost desperate.

"I hope I will. But it may take some time. I'm not ready to resume our engagement yet."

"You still want to call off the wedding?" he asked, his forehead pinched.

"Let's just postpone it for now. This has really shaken me, Harry. It's going to take a while to have confidence in your feelings for me again."

He smoothed her hair. "I will try to be more forthcoming. I think I was just afraid to put my whole self on the line. I am beginning to see that now. Have patience with me."

"If you have patience with me," she promised, kissing him lingeringly.

"The immature boy-Harry is gone and will not be returning. There's nothing there for me anymore. I will wait as long as it takes for you to be convinced of my love. I am willing to try to prove myself to you."

"You had best leave now," Catherine said, "while my resolve holds"

Chapter Seventeen

Catherine met Harry at the pub after her Thursday morning tutorial, as arranged. She had rung her mother the night before with the news that the wedding was postponed. Fortunately, no invitations had gone out. Her mother grumbled, but Catherine thought she was secretly relieved.

The memory of how fast things between her and Harry had gotten bad would haunt her for the next while. She wasn't ready to wear her ring again.

"It turns out that Dean Godfrey had a motive for Severn's murder," she said as she ate her second pub pie in as many days. "I won't discuss the details, but she didn't even discuss them. She's waiting for the police to discover that she had scheduled the earl to speak to Somerville students this coming Sunday. That was his demand."

"Ah hah! Blackmail, eh? Surely she wouldn't have invited him under any other circumstances."

"That's why she's waiting for the police to show up. But they might never make the connection because they think they have their man in Red."

"What other suspects do we have?" Harry asked.

"Well, we have Oliver Anderson," Catherine said. "You know, I think we were so carried away with tales of Anne and Winston

Churchill that we might have missed something he said. At the time, something seemed off, but then I lost hold of it because of the Churchill news."

Harry brought out a notebook from an inside pocket. "I wrote down some notes afterward. Let me see," He read over them swiftly. "Here's something: I got the impression that he knew Severn in the war. I don't know what he said that gave me that idea, but I have a big question mark."

"But he told us he'd never met him," said Catherine and sipped her cider. "I remember that part well."

"I think that's why I have this question. I guess we're going to have to dig him up and question him again."

"Maybe he can join us here for a drink before dinner. He's at Merton, right?" Catherine asked.

"Right. I'll just go outside and give him a call from the telephone booth on the curb. Then, I'm afraid I must run. I have a meeting with a student this afternoon."

"I must say, it is wonderful to be working with you again," said Catherine. He steered her with his arm at her back as they left the pub together.

"Likewise, darling," he said, smiling and looking into her eyes. "I look forward to working with you for a very long time."

* * *

Professor Anderson met Catherine and Harry at the Eagle and Child late that afternoon. It had turned brisk, and he was wound up in a bright red scarf that matched the color of his nose. "My, it has turned cold!" he said, rubbing his hands together after he removed his knit gloves.

"Yes," agreed Catherine, who had worn her sable coat and matching hat. The cold weather reminded her of Christmas.

Sitting at their favorite booth, Catherine ordered another hot cider. Harry went to get the drinks.

"The weather reminds me of the Christmas holidays. Do you have children, Professor?" she asked.

"Yes. I shall go over to France to spend Christmas with them. They are at the Sorbonne."

"How did you meet your wife? You said she was French?"

He suddenly became hearty. "It was a love story for the ages. She was my nurse in the war."

Catherine had not been aware that French nurses had worked with British soldiers, but she said nothing. She had suddenly remembered what he had said that had slipped her mind last time they had spoken.

Harry joined them, and he asked, "Did you know de Fontaine is now in custody for Severn's murder?"

"Yes. I heard it on the BBC. Your sister-in-law is no longer in jail, I take it?"

"That's right, but de Fontaine is a particular friend of Miss Tregowyn's, so we are continuing our investigation. She is certain he is innocent. He said he rarely carries the card case that was discovered at the scene of Dawkins' murder."

"I'm sorry to drag you out on such a cold night," said Catherine. "The thing is, I remembered something you said last time we spoke that I wanted to ask you about."

"Oh, yes?" said Anderson.

Catherine continued, "You said that Severn was beastly to his men in the War. Did you serve under him?"

The man's face suddenly grew red, and he pulled his shirt collar away from his neck. "No. No. No," he said with a smile that was a grimace. "I didn't mean to give that impression. It's just that I knew men who were. I heard complaints."

"That surprises me," said Harry. "I thought complaining about a superior officer was close to grounds for a court-martial in wartime."

He smoothed the back of his hair. "Well, it was just the odd grumble. One of those things that everyone just knows. He had a reputation for being a hard taskmaster. Those things can't really be kept quiet. They come out in the end, you know."

"Hmm," said Harry. "Interesting. Can you tell us anything else that you heard at the time?"

"I really shouldn't have repeated that. I don't know anything else," the professor said. "The War is getting to be a long time ago."

"Twenty years," mused Catherine, trying to soothe him. "That is a long time." She decided a change of subject was called for. "You know, Professor, I don't even know what it is that you teach."

"Astronomy," he said. His high color began to recede, and he took a long pull at his lager.

Harry took up the conversation. "What is next on the program for your anti-fascist league now that Severn is dead?" he asked.

The professor drummed his fingers on the table. "Not certain. I'll have to talk to Anne. I'm sure it's not the first thing on her mind."

It proved that getting him to talk about anything was difficult now. Catherine got the impression that they had shaken him badly with their questions about the War.

Something distinctly rotten there. He's scared to death.

When he made an excuse to leave after only ten minutes, she knew for certain something was wrong.

Harry agreed. "I don't know how to go about finding what he's got in his craw that's so disturbing."

"I don't suppose military records are open to the public," she said.

"No, but we can go down to Hampshire and present the problem to my father. He's very active in his regiment's reunions and that sort of thing. Maybe he's heard something about Severn's reputation. If he hasn't, maybe he could sniff around. We could leave after our tutorials tomorrow."

Catherine sipped the last of her cider. "I would enjoy seeing your parents again, but I feel guilty leaving when I haven't done anything for Red."

"Look at it this way: Finding the murderer will help Red. There's something off about Anderson. And you've already found out Dean Godfrey was the victim of blackmail. Maybe Anderson was, too."

"Good, then. I'll go with you to your parents. It occurs to me that we also ought to visit the ninth earl and see for ourselves whether or not he could possibly be the murderer."

"You're right."

* * *

Harry kissed her on the cheek outside her flat before catching a cab. When she went inside, she found Anne Bascombe waiting for her in her sitting room. Cherry had given her tea, and she was looking through Catherine's copy of the *Times*.

Her guest looked up as Catherine came into the room.

"Hello!" said Anne. "I just wanted to come by and thank you for all you are doing to solve this wretched murder."

"I am very glad you have been released, although that had nothing to do with me," Catherine said.

"Yes. Poor Red. I am convinced he's innocent."

"He's been set up," said Catherine. "He never uses that card case they found at the scene."

"I don't find the Oxford police terribly intelligent," Anne said. "I say! You're not wearing your engagement ring!"

Catherine instinctively covered her left hand with her right. "We've decided to postpone the wedding."

Anne's eyes lit. "Oh!"

Catherine decided no further explanation was necessary.

When she said nothing, Anne smiled and said, "I must say, I hope you can work things out. "

Remembering the handholding in the jail, Catherine couldn't resist saying, "Do you?"

Anne's smile was too bright. "Well, yes, of course. I want more than anything for Harry to be happy."

"Tell me," said Catherine coolly, "What do you know about the ninth Earl of Severn?"

"Is he a suspect?" asked Anne.

"He's formerly of St. Athan, Wales."

"Is he really! The place is so unlikely. It can't be a coincidence. That must have been his train ticket in the shrubbery!"

"Or else our suspect in dungarees had just been visiting him," said Catherine. "Perhaps he was a hired killer."

"Oh! That is rather shattering. Where do we go from here?"

Catherine disliked that "we." She said, "Harry and I are going down to Hampshire tomorrow to chase another lead. Tell me, did you know that Dean Godfrey had asked the Earl of Severn to speak at Somerville on Sunday evening?"

"I don't believe it," Anne said firmly. "It must have been someone else's doing."

"You might want to bring it up with her," Catherine said.

"But I know her very well. She would never have let the man within a mile of her students."

"So I would have thought," said Catherine. "And how well do you know Professor Anderson?"

"I know him very well also. Don't tell me he has done something to place himself under suspicion. I won't believe it!" Anne was sitting erect in her outrage.

"Do you know how long he has been in this country?" asked Catherine.

"Quite a while. Since his wife died back in France."

"And how long ago was that?" Catherine rose to put more coal on the fire. While she did this, Anne was silent.

"Have you any idea?" Catherine asked again.

"I always assumed it had been years. But now you mention it, I could be wrong. Oh, my. Shall I look into that?"

"It would be a help," Catherine said.

Anne bounded up from her chair. "I will do that. Anything else?"

"Nothing, right now," said Catherine, amazed at the turn-about on Anne's part. Had Harry taken her to task for treating Catherine like an underling?

* * *

Harry admitted that the trip to Hampshire was as much about explaining the postponed wedding as it was about the wartime record of the eighth earl of Severn. "I know I'll have to stand up and take my scold, and it's far better that we get everything out in the open in person. They like you awfully, Catherine. In a way they have never liked Anne."

"That is nice to hear," said Catherine, grinning. "Although I really wouldn't mind a bit if they take you to task. I imagine you got away with a good bit when you were growing up."

Harry grimaced. "Not as much as you might think. Eldest son and all that. And the village doctor hears everything, so I had to mind my p's and q's, believe me."

On the drive down, they also discussed ninth earl and how they might best approach him. They decided the best plan was to assume alternate identities, perhaps looking to buy his home now that he would dwell in Woodstock.

"I wonder if a simple idea of the present earl's height and the height of the dungaree man would resolve it?" said Harry. "The birder said he was quite a tall man."

Catherine said, "I wonder if the police are doing anything to try to identify the dungaree man. They took all those fingerprints on the door. Oh! I forgot. He was wearing gardening gloves."

"Since they arrested Red, I would say they think they got their man," said Harry, his voice grim.

"But he has only been formally arrested in the murder of Dawkins," said Catherine.

"But they let Anne go. That says something about their

thinking," Harry said. "Let's o make another go at St. Athan. You're far more diplomatic than Anne. Let's see what we can find out about the new earl."

"I think you were raised on detective stories," said Catherine.

"You're right. Have you ever read *The Riddle of the Sands?*" Harry asked. "It was topping."

"Poor Red is languishing in jail," she reminded him.

"We may get him off for the murder of Severn. Don't you think the same person killed both men? We're working on the premise that blackmail was involved in both cases, aren't we?"

"You're right. But I still think you are trying to redeem yourself from the mess you made of your last trip to Wales."

"You know me too well," he said.

* * *

Dr. Bascombe was at her clinic when they arrived, but they were welcomed warmly by Harry's father in the sitting room. Catherine was pleased to see Lord Rutherford standing at their entrance, as well.

"My dear young lady," said Mr. Bascombe while shaking her hand. "How lovely to see you again. Harry dragged you off before I could say goodbye last time you were here." He looked at his son with a raised brow.

"Sorry. We were a bit thrown by Anne's arrest," said Harry. "All I could think of was getting back to Oxford. I shouldn't have behaved so precipitously."

"How is Anne doing?" his father asked. "Ford tells me she's been released."

"Yes, " Harry said. "They now have another of our friends in jail. He was framed, so we're still on the job." He turned to Anne's father. "Good to see you, my lord."

"He's no Bolshie," said Harry. "He's homegrown. But yes. He is a Communist. A good friend of Anne's, as a matter of fact. They were working together to expose the earl of Severn as a dangerous lunatic."

"Politics makes strange bedfellows, they say," said Mr. Bascombe, then asked, "To what do we owe this visit of yours, eh? Not that I'm not happy to see you."

"We wanted to tap your memory, Father," said Harry. "And as long as Lord Rutherford is here, we can tap his, as well. It's about the War."

"Why don't we all sit down?" suggested Mr. Bascombe. "What do you need after your journey? Tea or something?"

Harry and Catherine sat together on the sofa. He deferred to her. "Catherine?"

"No, thank you," she said.

"Me neither, said Harry. Turning to her, he said, "Why don't you tell them what you've heard from Oliver Anderson?"

Catherine appreciated Harry's efforts to bring her into the con-versation. "First of all, to put you in the picture, Oliver Anderson is another member of Anne's anti-fascist league. We are investi-gating him because he knew Anne was going to see the earl that afternoon," she paused.

"You think he or she saw an opportunity to kill Severn and have Anne take the blame?" asked Lord Rutherford. "Why?"

It sounded regrettably far-fetched when the peer put it that way.

Catherine plunged on. "Blackmail has come up as a possible motive for the murder. We were trying to find out if Mr. Anderson had any personal dealings with the earl."

"Right," said Harry's father. "Go on."

Catherine continued, "He let drop during our conversation that the Earl of Severn treated his men abominably during the War. It was one of the reasons he disliked the man so much. When we asked if he was in the earl's regiment, he became very uneasy and flustered and turned the subject."

Harry said, "We thought we'd see if there were ever any rumors about the earl in this regard. We thought you would probably know, Father."

Mr. Bascombe looked at his son for a moment, then raising his eyebrows, he consulted his friend, "Did you ever hear anything, Rutherford?"

"Scattering rumors like that in wartime could get you court-martialed," said Lord Rutherford.

"This isn't wartime," said Catherine, convinced the veterans were reluctant to speak.

There was an uneasy silence. Finally, Harry's father said, "Yes. Despite everything, there *were* rumors that he was ill-tempered. Not only that, but he ordered his troops to go 'over the top' when it was clearly a suicidal move. Desertions among his men were high. And when the men were inevitably caught, of course, they were executed."

Catherine was paralyzed with horror.

Looking at her, Harry said, "How utterly beastly."

Lord Rutherford shrugged. "It was a beastly war."

Harry's father looked down at the carpet. "A lot of men died."

If Oliver Anderson was a deserter and Severn knew it, it would certainly be grounds for blackmail. But do we really want to expose him?

"Is there any sort of amnesty for deserters now?" asked Catherine.

Harry's father looked up and met her eyes, "No. They would be sent to a convict prison. It's considered unforgivable cowardice even now."

"Where could we find a list of deserters?" Harry asked

"There are military records, of course," said Mr. Bascombe. "But you wouldn't be allowed access."

"I would," said Lord Rutherford. "One of the committees I am on in the Lords is still tracing deserters."

Catherine thought of Anderson as she had last seen him. Pale. Afraid. With the way she felt about the War, could she really turn him in? But what if he had committed murder to cover it up?

I don't know if I can do it.

Lord Rutherford obviously had no such qualms. "I will find out if this Oliver Anderson is on the list. That would certainly be motive for murder."

Catherine thought she was going to be sick. "What if he was just badly shell-shocked? They didn't understand things like that then. It would have been murder to shoot someone for that reason."

"This is why women aren't sent to war," said the peer.

"I agree with her," said Harry. "Father?"

"What about the millions of men that stayed and fought and died?" asked Mr. Bascombe. "I tend to think that if deserters weren't punished, we wouldn't have had a single man left on the Front."

"That is as big a condemnation of the War as I have ever heard," said Catherine quietly.

An uncomfortable silence filled the room. Into it swept Sarah, pulling a scarf off her white chignon.

"Harry! Catherine! What a nice surprise!" she cried.

Harry rose and went to his mother. He kissed her cheek. "We had some business with Father and thought we would come down. Don't worry. If it's not convenient, we can turn around and go back after tea."

"Absolutely not!" she said. Turning to their other guest, who had also risen, she said, "Ford, it's good to see you. Why is everyone so solemn? Has someone died? Is Anne all right?"

Her husband smiled. "No. Nothing like that. Anne is fine. Ford says she's been released."

"Well, thank the Lord for that!" said Harry's mother. "I think we all need a nice cup of tea." She rang for the butler. When he appeared, she said, "We're ready for tea, Fredericks."

Catherine was exceedingly uncomfortable. Not only had

nothing been decided about Mr. Anderson, it was now time to divulge the other reason for their visit. But she was not about to do so with the unsympathetic Lord Rutherford in the room.

As soon as the tea cart was wheeled in and Sarah began to pour, she said, "So how are the wedding plans coming?"

Catherine looked at Harry, who had raised his brows in question. She wet her lips and said, "There's been a bit of a hitch, I'm afraid. We've decided to postpone it. It seems Harry and I have a few things to work out."

Harry's father looked back and forth between his son and his fiancée. "You're not wearing your ring. Have you called the whole thing off?"

"No," said Harry in robust tones. "Nothing like that. I've just been a bit of a fool, but Catherine has forgiven me. All will be well."

His mother's brow was puckered as she studied her son. He was looking steadily at Lord Rutherford. The man must have realized he was *de trop,* so he stood.

"Must be on my way. Thank you, Sarah, but I haven't time for tea. I've stayed too long." He kissed his hostess's cheek and was gone in a matter of seconds.

"Well! What did I interrupt?" Sarah asked.

"Nothing you need to bother about," said her husband. "I see we have lemon sponge. The gods are smiling on me."

Her hostess handed Catherine a cup of tea fixed just as she liked it and said, "So I take it Harry has been misbehaving?"

"No, really!" said Catherine, feeling as though she were trying to extricate herself from a bog. "We just realized we got engaged in a bit of a rush. There are still things we don't know about one another."

"Well, in his defense, I must say that Harry often puts the cart before the horse when he gets excited about something, but he always makes good decisions in the end," said the doctor.

Catherine sensed Harry squirming. He then took out his pipe and filled it. "That's lovely to hear," said Catherine. Making another effort, she said, "There are things in both our pasts which we need to settle. We want to make absolutely sure we know what we're doing."

"That sounds reasonable," said Mr. Bascombe. "Marriage isn't to be taken lightly. And if Harry has been the fool he says, all the more reason to take some time and make certain he doesn't make a habit of it."

"Exactly," Catherine said and exhaled in relief. She decided she liked Harry's father very much. As for the doctor, Catherine saw the dawning of understanding on her face and knew she needn't go into excruciating detail.

After tea, Sarah Bascombe left to talk to the maid about readying bedrooms for Catherine and Harry, who decided to go for a walk.

"Phew!" said Harry as soon as they were away from the house and headed for the barn. "Thanks to you, that went off better than I expected."

"Don't count your chickens," said Catherine. "I wager anything your mother wants a private talk with each of us."

"Well, let's enjoy ourselves in the meantime. I think when we're married, we ought to get a dog. Our spaniel just had puppies a few weeks ago."

CHAPTER EIGHTEEN

As they fondled the newborn spaniels, Catherine said, "Anne's father was a bit brisk. I don't think he likes me very much."

"It's his manner. He claims to be a misogynist like Holmes. He makes an exception for my mother. She's his 'Mrs. Hudson' I think."

"I understand that he's a Life Peer. Why did the king grant him a peerage? What exactly is it?"

"He's a viscount. My father told me why once. Let's see if I can get it straight: 'He performed an act of extraordinary valor which helped change the course of the War.' He got the Victoria Cross and the viscountcy, so it must have been something really exceptional." Harry was dividing the puppies up into male and female camps, but the dogs weren't cooperating.

"So, he would probably hold Severn in great disdain," said Catherine, absently petting the pup in the lap of her best suit.

"Yes, he does. And, as you could tell, he doesn't think much of deserters, either. He's active in the Lords. All the Sherlock Holmes business is just a hobby. Don't be taken in by it. He is brilliant and brave. However, he wasn't much of a father."

"Oh?" Catherine looked up, keen to hear about Anne's childhood.

"Anne could never do enough to please him. He vastly preferred his son, but Eric died when he was eighteen. Some kind of heart condition that had never been detected. Rutherford has enshrined his memory."

"Hmm, sad. I wonder if he knows about the work Anne did for Churchill in Germany. Surely that would make him proud." She held the puppy up to her face. It was such a silly little thing with its tiny pink tongue. Catherine brought it close and held it against her shoulder as though it were an infant.

"She didn't marry as he wished. He wanted her to marry into the peerage. He had the fellow all picked out, but Anne couldn't see it."

"Oh! I'm surprised a man like that is such close friends with your family if he disapproves of his daughter's marriage to James."

Harry stood up, clearly finished with the pups for the moment. "Oh, that's water under the bridge by now, I think. Plus, like I said, despite his misogyny, he's always had a bit of a soft spot for my mother."

"Ah! You don't say. That's interesting. What happened to his wife?" Catherine let the puppy she was holding join its littermates, and Harry helped her to stand.,

"Spanish flu. Years ago," he said. "He never remarried."

Sounds like Anne didn't have it easy growing up. Maybe that is what makes her so driven.

They walked over to the horses. Still a country girl, Catherine admired Harry's mount—a chestnut with a nice broad chest and a white star on his forehead.

"Would you like to go riding?" Harry asked.

"I'm not dressed for it!"

"I meant tomorrow morning before we go to Wales." He was grinning at her.

"I'd love a ride, but I brought nothing but skirts. I don't know that we decided to go to Wales."

"I thought we might find out a little about this heir and determine whether he could be our Dungaree Man."

"Yes. You're right. He's got the best motive. Especially if he wasn't terribly well off. Do you think you can move around that little town without putting anyone's back up this time?"

"How about if I leave the questions to you?"

"Sounds like an admirable plan."

* * *

While Catherine was freshening up for dinner, there was a knock on the door.

"It's Sarah Bascombe, the doctor said. "May I come in?"

Wearing her dressing gown, Catherine answered the door. "Yes. Do come in. I'm just trying to do something with my hair. There are times when I wish it were long like yours. It is so much more elegant."

The doctor settled herself on the edge of the bed while Catherine resumed her seat at the dressing table.

"I just wanted to talk to you a little bit about Anne. Am I right in presuming her relations with Harry are the reason for the problems between the two of you?"

Surprised, Catherine said, "Well, it wasn't exactly Anne, but more the effect she had on Harry. I had never seen him like that. Certainly, he never demonstrated the passion for me that he evidently feels for her. Our relationship has always been more superficial."

Catherine looked at the woman's reflection in the mirror. Harry's mother leaned forward as she said, "I know what you think you saw, but in observing Harry's dealings with the two of you, I think your relationship is the more healthy one. To be perfectly frank, I never wanted Harry to marry Anne."

"But you hardly know me . . ."

"I am trained to observe people. When Harry is with you, he's himself. When Harry is with Anne, he is always disturbed. She demands utter devotion and always manages to create drama. She played my two boys against each other all their lives."

Catherine put down her brush and turned on her stool to look at Harry's mother directly. The older woman had settled into a wing-backed chair by the fire. "Yes, but James won, and it has damaged Harry's relationship with him. There is still drama."

Sarah's forehead was creased in earnestness. "Well, I suppose you will have to see how it plays out, but I think Harry knows what he wants now. He wants you." She looked down at her hands. "As for Anne, there may be another reason why she's tried to get Harry back. She is unhappy with James. I don't know how long it has been going on, but I think something happened in Germany. James has toughened up his hide. She no longer has any power over him. I'm amazed they are going to have a child."

Surprised over Sarah's confidences, Catherine said, "How very sad. That must be why he never spends any time at home."

"Yes. So Anne has taken up politics."

"And she tried to take up Harry. I think I really believed she would succeed," said Catherine. To her surprise, Harry's mother put an arm around her and hugged her shoulders. "I am glad he has realized how foolishly he behaved."

"I know something about relationships like Harry and Anne's. I had one myself. I must admit Harry was very patient with me. But I never knew about Anne until the engagement party. That night, the change in him was so marked that I almost couldn't believe what I was seeing. I never thought Harry would show such passionate feelings—it was almost like he wasn't in control of himself."

"Yes. I noticed. He regresses to schoolboy tendencies in Anne's presence. You know what I mean—the desire to slay dragons for one's beloved. I don't think he even realizes it. What has he said?"

"He explained that she wasn't the right person for him. He doesn't seem to like how she makes him feel, but I think he still loves her."

"I can see why you are postponing the wedding."

"It's something only time can decide," Catherine said. "I will see how it all plays out. But I'm not the desperate type. I love Harry, but I don't want to be a consolation prize."

"I understand. I agree with you completely. I just wanted you to know that I'm on your side in this. It is my strong opinion that no one would regard you as a consolation prize."

"Thank you. That means a lot to me."

"How are your parents handling this? I'm aware that they might not consider Harry's social standing good enough for a baron's daughter."

She described a time when Harry had helped rescue her in a public and dramatic way. "My father likes him."

Sarah Bascombe laughed. "That sounds like pure Harry. I'm glad."

* * *

Her conversation with Harry's mother was very much on Catherine's mind as they sat down to dinner. She listened as Harry recounted the steps they had taken in their investigation. He seemed entirely the old Harry.

"I don't understand why the police aren't doing any of these things," said Harry's father.

"They think they have their man in Red de Fontaine. As you noted in Anne's case, they tend to make arrests very quickly on circumstantial evidence. I think they were afraid Red would bolt."

"And what makes you so sure that this man, Red, a known Communist, is not guilty?" Harold Bascombe asked.

Catherine answered. "There's nothing to tie Red to the Severn murder. They have no evidence whatsoever. The only hitch is that he doesn't have an alibi. At least not one he was willing to share with me." Pausing, she took a sip from her glass. "As far as the Dawkins' murder goes, Red's card case was found at the scene. It's not something he ever uses. He only has it because it is of sentimental value. His mother gave it to him when he graduated. I know him quite well. He isn't a violent man, despite his politics. The police have taken a wild leap, not only linking the two murders but citing politics as the motive in both cases."

"Absurd," Harry's father interjected, throwing his napkin down on the table.

"It does seem weak," said Catherine. "We are using blackmail as a motive in our investigation. We know of at least one case where Severn blackmailed someone into getting them to use their influence on his behalf. But Red's sins are in the open. He's never denied being a Communist. He's immune to blackmail, as far as I can see." Folding her napkin neatly, Catherine placed it on the table.

"Well, it would seem that the earl hit a nerve somewhere," said Harry's mother.

"Except in the case of his cousin and heir. That could just be a case of straight-out greed," said Harry.

"Now there's a motive I can get my teeth into," said Mr. Bascombe.

* * *

Friday morning, Catherine and Harry got an early start for their journey into Southern Wales. The cook had packed them lunch for the five-hour drive. As Catherine took her leave of Sarah, Harry's mother whispered in her ear, "I hope you find the confirmation of Harry's feelings you're looking for."

When they were on the road north to catch the highway to Bristol, Harry said, "Have secrets with my mother, do you?"

Catherine forced a little laugh. "She came into my room last night while I was getting dressed for dinner. She'd guessed that your feelings for Anne were at the bottom of our postponement. She was just telling me she hoped I got the answers I was looking for."

She saw a muscle flex in Harry's jaw. "It sounds like you were pretty candid with her."

"Most of the time, I'm pretty candid," Catherine said in surprise. "You know that."

"So you told her I made a fool of myself over Anne?"

"No, not at all. She'd guessed that your feelings for Anne were behind it. I just told her that you were a different person than I'd ever known when Anne was concerned. I said I was holding a watching brief, more or less, and that I needed time. She thought that was reasonable."

Catherine saw Harry's hands tighten on the steering wheel. "I see. I guess I'd hoped that you were feeling a little more positive than that. You make me feel like you're looking at me under a microscope."

She winced. "Sorry. I don't want you to feel that way. It's just that I've had my trust breached. I've seen this other person in you. One that is capable of a whole array of feelings you've never shown me. I didn't like seeing those feelings. I need to make sure which person is the real Harry."

"And you explained this to my mother?"

"Not really. I didn't need to. She didn't like Anne's effect on you. She guessed how I felt. She tried to reassure me. I told her I just needed time."

Catherine felt tension coming off Harry in waves. "I'm not a performing seal," he said bitterly.

"I don't want you to perform, Harry. You've got to understand. I just want you to be yourself. If what you told me about your feelings for Anne is true, then you don't need to worry, do you?"

"Maybe I'm too self-confident, but I don't have those feelings of doubt about you and Rafe."

"Good, because you don't need to. That was adolescent Catherine. No one else brings out that side of me."

"That's it! Why can't you understand that it's the same for Anne and me?"

"I just need to be sure," Catherine said. Was the reason for her request for time feeble? She didn't know how it looked to an outsider, but it was very understandable to her.

"Let me know when I've got the green light, all right?"

His tone was so bitter; she didn't want to be trapped in the car with him all the way to St. Athan. She decided she must change the subject. She grabbed one at random, "I wonder what Lord Rutherford did to get a viscountcy."

For a moment, there was silence. Then Harry broke into laughter. "I know when I'm being carefully handled. All right. I'm done being cross."

"I do love you, Harry," said Catherine. "I just want to make sure it's me you want to be married to for the rest of your life."

They were on a well-traveled road, but Harry turned off onto a secondary road and then a small lane.

"What are you doing?" she asked.

"This!" he said, pulling her to him.

He kissed her like a man starving.

"Was that passionate enough for you?"

"That will do for starters," she said. "But let's save the main course for a time when we're not in a motor car."

He laughed.

* * *

St. Athan was not Catherine's idea of a holiday town. The day was overcast, but even so, she could tell the town wouldn't be terribly inviting on a sunny day. The buildings all seemed as gray as the sky. It had an abandoned feel to it. There was a small tea shop on the short high street.

"Let's start there," said Catherine. "Perhaps we'll meet some friendly people. We can hardly claim to be tourists. What should our story be?"

"We are looking for a place for our honeymoon?" suggested Harry, pulling up the parking brake.

Catherine laughed. "You've got honeymoons on the brain! Be realistic. This is hardly a romantic spot."

"It all depends on the company, I guess," Harry said, deadpan.

"Really! How about this: we're looking for a place to open a bed and breakfast inn. Does anyone know of a place that's suitable that we might be able to purchase?"

"Jolly good. Let's hope the Ninth Earl of Severn is looking to sell the family home now that he's come into his inheritance," Harry said, kissing her cheek.

On the inside, the tea shop was cheerier—yellow walls with red tables and chairs and lots of electric light. The yeasty sugary smell endemic to bakeries assailed her as she noted a group of ladies knitting together at one of the tables. An obvious mother-daughter pair took up another table with the daughter's little girl sitting up in a pram teething on a piece of toast.

A cheerful woman called from behind the display case. "Have a seat, luvs, and I'll be right with you."

Catherine eyed the pastries on the shelves behind the glass. Her mouth began to water. Someone was a gifted baker.

She and Harry sat just one small table away from the knitting group. Harry smiled his best Douglas Fairbanks, Jr. smile. "What's good, ladies?"

"The scones are light as a feather."

"The sticky buns are the very best."

"You came to the right place for lemon pound cake."

"Hmm. How will I ever decide?" said Harry. "Perhaps one of each and a slice of pound cake?"

Catherine asked, "How is the jam roll?"

"You'll love it," said the young mother.

Their hostess came out with her order pad. "I can fix you up a tray with all my best dainties," she suggested. "And a pot of tea. Earl Grey?"

"Yes, please," said Catherine. "And perhaps you could answer a question for us?"

"I can try," the hostess said with a laugh. "I make no promises."

"We are scouting around, looking for a property that we might convert into a Bed and Breakfast in St. Athan. Do you know of anything that might become available that might not yet be listed?"

"Well, no, but these ladies know everything that goes on around here." She pointed her pad to the knitting group.

"Well, it depends on how much you are willing to part with," said an elderly woman with improbable red hair. "I know of a home that should be on the market soon. Belongs to a genuine earl. Not that it's fancy or anything. He never planned on coming into the title."

"Oh," said Harry. "Sounds a little too grand for what we have in mind, eh, Doris?"

"But, Bert, it would be jolly good fun to have a look, don't you think?" asked Catherine.

Harry laughed. "Is it open to view, by chance?"

"Well, the new earl is still in residence. His ascension to the title took him by surprise. He has a little stamp business, and he's trying to wind things up before taking possession of his new home. You wouldn't think he'd take such a long time over such a thing, would you? I mean, he'll be moving into a grand estate, from all I hear. Why can't he just take his business with him?"

"One would think so, yes," said Harry, eyeing the triple-tiered stand of baked goods their hostess had set on their table. "Do you think he'd be willing to let us have a look?"

"Oh, my yes. When you've finished your tea, I can just take you around and introduce you," the redhead said.

"Jolly good," said Catherine with her most devastating smile. "Imagine our luck!"

Yes! Imagine our luck. First inquiry out of the gate! But then it's probably the biggest news around here in years.

* * *

One look at the new peer was enough to see why he thought he'd never come into the earldom. The man was eighty if he was a day—small, stooped, and bald. Not at all similar to the figure of Dungaree Man. He even had a squint.

His home was cluttered, stuffy, and smelled as though a window hadn't been opened in years. But if they had really been looking for a Bed and Breakfast property, it would have been ideal. It was a sturdy stone structure that looked like the Victorian vintage, with many rooms on its three floors.

The new earl greeted them cordially, leading them into a shabby sitting room. "May I interest you in a cup of tea?" he asked.

Madge, their new red-headed friend, said in a loud voice that indicated the new earl was somewhat deaf. "We've only just come from Pearl's."

Catherine might be wrong, but she thought she detected a coyness in her manner. And why not? The man had just come into a fortune, and as far as it appeared, he was without a wife.

"Well, I'm sorry about it, but I'm not really going to sell up. My nephew and his wife will be taking up residence here when I leave. It's just a matter of me getting packed up. As you can probably tell by the clutter, I've lived here most of my life."

"Madge told us you have just seceded to an earldom!" gushed Catherine. "It's like a fairy tale."

"You could have knocked me over with a feather. My cousin was twenty years younger than me," said the ninth earl. "But then you've probably read about him in the newspapers. It seems he was murdered, poor chap. The eighth Earl of Severn."

"Crickey!" said Catherine, channeling Dot. "I did read about that! Imagine! Will you feel altogether safe living there?"

"Do they know who did it?" Harry asked.

"There's some talk about a Communist plot. They've arrested someone. Madge, do you know anything about it?" their host asked the redhead.

"Some agitator. It was political anyway. The eighth earl was a bit of a fascist. But it was no call to go killing him! 'Course we're happy for his new lordship."

"Of course," said Catherine. "We wish you well, Lord Severn." Unfortunately, she could think of no way to extend their conversation in her persona as "Doris." Harry's "Bert" was likewise handicapped, and so they took their leave.

"Well!" said Harry, once they were back in his Morris. "That couldn't have gone better for us. I think we can cross the ninth earl off our list of suspects. I don't think he's the sort to go about hiring killers, and he certainly hasn't got the physique to be Dungaree Man!"

"I think you're right," said Catherine. "The question is, who did that train ticket belong to?"

"It was a false clue to lead us to the heir. That's the only explanation I can think of."

Catherine said, "But whoever it was who laid that little trap had never met the heir, obviously. As you said, there's no way he could have been mistaken for Dungaree Man. Seems quite careless of him."

"Perhaps he was afraid of arousing suspicion by engineering a meeting with the heir. We were fortunate to have the chips fall so nicely in our favor," Harry said.

"It may prove to have been his critical error," said Catherine with a sigh. "Must we drive all the way back to Oxford today? We won't arrive until the middle of the night!"

"I daresay we could find an acceptable place to stay in Cardiff," said Harry with a lascivious grin.

"Separate rooms, Bert," said Catherine pertly. "I don't go sharing rooms with just anyone, you know."

CHAPTER NINETEEN

By the time they had returned to Oxford on Sunday, Catherine was very tired of traveling by motorcar. "If another trip to Wales should appear in our future, I should be very happy to take the train," she said.

"Meanwhile," Harry reminded her, "we had decided we must go visit Red and see if he has any thoughts on our recent discovery."

"Poor man is probably miserable," said Catherine.

However, when they arrived at the jail, it was to find Red was far from miserable. He had begged some foolscap off a sergeant and had been busy reconstructing the case from his point of view.

After greeting Catherine warmly, and Harry a bit less so, he asked what they had found out.

"Well," said Catherine. "It has been interesting. Lord Rutherford, who is Anne's father, was there at Harry's home, so we had his opinion as well as Harry's father's on what kind of leader Severn was during the war. We certainly had no idea Rutherford was such a great war hero."

"Hmm. I didn't either," said Red. "So what did they have to say about our friend, Severn?"

"They only had rumors to go on, but I guess the rumors were bad enough that they could both remember them after all this time. Severn was reckoned to show very little regard for his men," Catherine told him.

Harry summed up the specifics they had heard, "He didn't spare them. He sent them into 'no man's land' on the slightest provocation. Many were killed. Both Rutherford and my father explained about what happened to deserters—they were mostly executed if they were caught."

"Of course, that led us to wonder if Anderson was a deserter," Catherine said. "He married a Frenchwoman and lived in France after the War up until she died. Maybe Severn knew and was blackmailing him. Lord Rutherford has access to military files, being on some special committee in the Lords. He's going to check up on Anderson for us."

"But Anderson hasn't any money!" said Red.

"But he does have sway with a huge number of pacifists who belong to his organization," said Catherine. "There are things I know about the way Severn worked. I won't give you specifics, but he was after people of influence."

Harry said, "I've always understood that the pacifists see the Communists as a tremendous threat to the peace of this country. You haven't made any secret about your plans for a Revolution."

"That's true enough. But it won't be like the Bolsheviks or the French revolution," protested Red.

"You can't expect your average pacifist to understand the difference. Revolutions mean blood," said Harry.

"And there are probably far more organized pacifists in this country right now than fascists. Have you had any unexplained mischief?" asked Catherine.

"There are always anti-Red demonstrations. Occasional acts of violence that are blamed on us, but which we've had no hand in."

"That's the sort of thing we're looking for, I think," said Catherine. "At whom is the violence aimed?"

"The government. And it's been getting worse lately. I was always inclined to lay it at Severn's door, even if he did express horror at the acts, disclaiming them altogether."

"Interesting," said Harry. "Kind of like when Hitler blew up the Reichstag but blamed it on the Communists."

"We do go in for the odd bit of scare tactics at our demonstrations, but we stop just short of violence," Red acknowledged. "It's ironic that I'm now supposed to have killed Severn. No doubt wherever he is, he's relishing it."

"Well, we won't let him relish it a bit longer than we can help," said Catherine. "Though we're still a long way away from identifying Dungaree Man."

"How do you know it's not the heir?"

"We met him," said Harry. "He's at least twenty years older than Severn, a small and infirm specimen. And he's genuinely amazed that he ever came in for the title. I think the whole idea cows him. He lives very simply. I can't see him masterminding this circus for the life of me. He is a philatelist, for heaven's sake."

"Hmm," said Red. "Pity."

"Back to Oliver Anderson," said Catherine. "He's the right size."

"And you don't think his being a pacifist would prevent him from committing murder?" asked Red.

Harry and Catherine exchanged looks. *Should we tell him?*

"He's not the genuine article," Catherine heard herself say. "He reports to Mr. Churchill. He's actually a Churchillian spy, reporting on the pacifist camp. They all hate Churchill, you know."

Harry looked annoyed at her breach of confidence. Red said, "How do you know he's telling the truth? That's a convenient sort of lie—taking him out of the extremist column."

"Anne knows," said Catherine. "Just take her word for it, if you can."

"Well, I must say, that rather surprises me," said Red. "You think he still could be Dungaree Man?"

"If it turns out to be true he's a deserter, and if Severn was blackmailing him over it," she said.

"Are they still shooting deserters?" Red asked.

"No. But they sentence them to a lifetime of convict labor," said Harry.

"Hmm," said Red. "Well, what's next on the agenda?"

"I'm not so sure we should tell you. You have to be able to claim ignorance," said Harry.

* * *

When Harry took her back to the flat, he brought her suitcase in, greeted Cherry, and followed Catherine into the sitting room. "Well, Doris-Luv, what's next?"

"I'm afraid I must cogitate on everything while we wait to hear from Lord Rutherford about Oliver Anderson. Unfortunately, Bert, I do my best thinkin' when I'm takin' a hot bath. Sorry, Luv, but there it is."

Harry gave her a rousing kiss. "Sure I can't change your mind?"

"Certain-sure, I'm afraid."

He took leave with a heavy show of reluctance, and Catherine went into Cherry in the kitchen.

"Anything new in our lives?" she asked the maid.

"Dean Godfrey telephoned. When I told her you'd be gone for the weekend, she said she'd call back tomorrow."

"No one else?"

"No. Will you be in to dinner then?" the maid asked.

"Rather. I'm starved. Have you a chop and some potatoes?"

When the maid tried to interest her in an Italian risotto she had discovered, Catherine restrained a shiver and said, "Oh, I don't want to put you to any trouble. Just a chop, veg, and potatoes will be ripping." Cherry's adventures with the culinary arts were not to be taken on an empty stomach. "And right now, I am ready for a bath. I'll draw it. I'm dying to try Dot's new Damask Rose Soak."

Thinking of Dot reminded her that her friend knew nothing of her reconciliation with Harry. Catherine resolved to place a trunk call after dinner.

While lounging in her heavenly scented bath, she thought about the case, but she was so tired from her journey that she almost fell asleep. Perhaps she could afford to take just a small break. Cherry rapped briskly at the door, announcing dinner, startling her awake.

The lamb chop was cooked perfectly—a miracle—and one thing Cherry never failed at was fried potatoes. The veg—green beans—was overcooked but tolerable. Catherine congratulated Cherry on the meal over her final course of cheddar and biscuits. Afterward, she settled in the sitting room and placed the call to Dot.

"Darling!" she trilled. "I'm sorry I've been out of touch!"

"You're back with Harry, aren't you?" her friend said with a laugh.

"Yes. Provisionally. The wedding is still postponed, but the engagement is back on."

"Why the postponement?"

Catherine went through her thought processes and doubts with her friend. When she was finished, Dot said, "I have two words for you: Remember Rafe."

"Oh, I know. Harry was so patient with me. Do you think I'm asking too much of him?"

"Well, I don't think any man really likes being put on probation. It takes him back to boarding school and all that."

"I just think I need more time. I haven't even seen him with Anne enough to know if he still has that schoolboy passion for her. I'm afraid he won't be able to help himself."

"How would you feel right now if you were to see Rafe?"

"I'd be civil to him but very wary. He has such a way of drawing one in."

"So," said her friend, "Be prepared for Harry to act the same way with Anne. That's a normal reaction. Have you spent much time with him since your reconciliation?"

Catherine related the high points of their weekend together.

"He informed me he felt like a performing seal."

"Darling," said Dot. "You're rather pushing it, I'd say."

Catherine stood up from the couch and ran her free hand through her hair. "I'm just skittish, that's all. I don't want to make a mistake."

"Are you sure you're not trying to punish him a little? I know that would be a temptation if I were in your shoes."

"Maybe I am, a little. He hurt me so badly, Dot."

"But it wasn't intentional, Cat. You've got to help him get past it. I know it takes a big heart and a lot of faith to do that. But you've got both those things."

"I know. That's part of the problem. Think of all those times I forgave Rafe! I can't even count them."

"In what way is Harry like Rafe?"

Catherine bit her lip hard. "He was inconstant."

"You have me there," Dot said. But tell me this: what was Harry's intention? Do you really think he wanted Anne to get divorced and marry him?"

"How do I know that?"

"Or was he just acting on instinct to get her out of a mess with no real plans for the future?"

Catherine thought of the scene in the jail when she had come upon Harry with his hand over Anne's. But hard on that vision came the confusion on his face when Anne started giving her orders.

"I think you may be right. I don't think he likes her very much right now. He realizes she was using him. He caught on when she started using me."

"There you have it, Cat. Don't hold that over his head forever. I'm sure he's not proud of it."

"You're right."

"Now! How is the case going?"

"Well, we eliminated the heir . . ." she told Dot all of the new twists and turns their investigation had taken since she had last talked to her. "I'm not sure where we're headed next," she concluded. "How's Max?"

"He's lovely. He's taken an interest in my business. He found a representative for me in the L.A. area."

"That's topping! Any discussion of your future?"

"No. We kind of avoid that. I'm thinking maybe, once my business is off the ground, we could live part of the time here and part of the time there if he got a teaching position."

"That sounds reasonable. He seems so even-tempered."

"Well, so did Harry! So, who knows?" said Dot with an uneasy laugh. "I guess I'm not the best one to be giving you advice!"

"Well, we'll struggle through together. When are you going to be at Oxford next?"

"At the weekend. It's my turn to travel," said Dot.

"Well, you've got a bed here whenever you need it!"

"This call is costing you a fortune. I'll talk to you when I see you. Write if you have time!"

"Will do. Cheerio!" said Catherine. When she hung up, she felt very much restored to herself.

Chapter Twenty

Catherine was having her roll and tea in the morning when the telephone rang. Cherry answered and was big-eyed as she handed the receiver to her mistress. "Po-lice!" she mouthed.

"This is Detective Sergeant Paul. Do I have Miss Tregowyn?"

"Yes, Detective Sergeant. This is Miss Tregowyn speaking."

"Detective Chief Inspector Kerry would like to meet with you this morning at nine o'clock. Could you be here by then?"

"Yes. If I hurry," said Catherine, annoyed. She hadn't met the new DCI, and he'd started off by being presumptuous. That didn't speak well for their future relations. "I'll ring off now so that I can finish my breakfast." Handing the receiver to Cherry, she buttered her last bit of bun, topped it with marmalade, and chewed it in a leisurely manner. She wondered if Harry was to appear also.

When she had finished her tea, Cherry outfitted her in her black and white tweed suit with her ivory silk blouse that had the tie at the neck. She covered her head with her sable hat and donned her fur. Cherry rang for a cab as Catherine pulled on her gloves and stepped into her walking pumps.

The police station was at the other end of Oxford from Somerville, so the cab was necessary since the DCI had given her no time to walk or take the bus. She walked in through the City

Hall, miffed but precisely on time. As soon as she announced herself to the desk sergeant, Harry came through the doors.

He raised both eyebrows in her direction, then winked. Taking a deep breath, Catherine realized she needed to calm down.

Soon the man who proved to be Detective Sergeant Paul came to take her and only her back to see the DCI.

The policeman stood at her entrance. She had not really taken note of his appearance on the night he had arrested Anne. Now she noted that he would have passed as an ascetic type—tall, thin, early gray hair, wire-rim glasses—were it not for his sun-tanned face. Holiday in the South of France? He gave her a brief smile that showed grooves on either side of his mouth that had once been dimples.

He nodded at her, "Miss Tregowyn. Thank you for coming. Please be seated."

She sat on a stiff office armchair.

"I asked you to come in to talk about a man you have visited here in the jail whom we have arrested for murder—Alexander de Fontaine."

Catherine was familiar enough with the law to know that he couldn't compel her to answer any questions at all. She would have to weigh each question and determine whether it would harm her friend.

The DCI began. "Mr. de Fontaine is a Communist. He does not try to hide that fact. Are you a Communist as well?"

"My politics are my own business," she said reflexively. Then, realizing that wasn't helping Red at all, she said, "I am a Liberal."

"Our investigations have revealed that you are a friend of Mr. de Fontaine."

"I am. He has a jazz band. I sang with his band for a while when he was short a singer. It was a year ago."

"At that time, he was a murder suspect as well," the DCI said, his manner severe.

"He was innocent," she said. "He is innocent now."

"I understand that it was you who exposed the guilty party at that time. Then, last winter, you came to the aid of a young student Garrison Nichols and proved him innocent of theft in a very dramatic manner."

She merely nodded.

"Do you see yourself as a detective, Miss Tregowyn?"

"I am a tutor at Somerville College. I occasionally embark on inquiries—scholastic and otherwise."

"I would call them rather adventures. In each of those 'inquiries,' you were very nearly murdered yourself. Why haven't you learned to keep to your own business, which is not crime but *poetry?* You have had some luck so far, I don't doubt it, but you are not a trained investigator. Sooner or later, your luck is bound to run out."

Now he had her temper up. "You sneer at my profession. I happen to know an excellent solicitor, Mr. Spence, of Lincoln Fields, London. We had an eye-opening discussion not long ago when he was so good as to praise my analytical mind. He told me that the word-by-word analysis of poetry had prepared me well for that type of thinking. He went so far as to declare that more solicitors should be as analytical as I have the good fortune to be."

DCI Kerry smiled derisively. "I have the misfortune to be related on my mother's side to the Irish poet, James Joyce. I have never encountered such disarray in anyone's mind as in Mr. Joyce's. And yet, he is a poet of great renown."

"I don't suppose you asked me here to speak about Mr. Joyce, but just for the record, I am not overly fond of him either."

The DCI smiled again, but it was a perfunctory effort. "So if you don't think Mr. de Fontaine to be the guilty party, who do you suspect?"

"We are trying to discover the identity of the man who let himself in by the study door at the time of the murder. I assume you have seen the sketch which your sketch artist made?"

"Ah, yes. You did show great presence of mind to question the Birders, I must admit. I did look at the sketch. Have you had any luck identifying him?"

"Not yet," Catherine admitted. "We discovered a train ticket to Oxford in the hedge near where he was seen. I think it is likely that the murderer accidentally pulled it out of his pocket when he pulled out his gloves to open the study door. It was dated the day before the murder. St. Athan in Wales was the starting point." She told him about Harry and Anne's aborted investigation in St. Athan. Then she said, "We went down there again this last weekend because we determined that Severn's heir was from St. Athan."

The DCI's eyes were a cold blue. "We have met with the heir. He knew nothing of or about the murder."

She continued, "We wanted to compare him to the sketch to see if there was any resemblance. We, too, were able to disqualify him. The man in dungarees was large, both in height and girth."

By the time she had finished, the DCI was frowning. "Have you considered the possibility that the heir hired the man in dungarees to kill the eighth earl?"

"Yes, we did. But the new earl seemed completely innocent and genuine."

"Hmm," said the DCI. "We agree with you there."

The DCI waved his hand. "As for that train ticket, it seems a bit too lucky. I'm not sure someone didn't drop it precisely to implicate the heir."

"We have considered that as well, of course," said Catherine. "However, we can't afford to discount it. I believe it also eliminates Mr. De Fontaine. He is too short to have been the man in dungarees. Would you consider completing the task that Dr. Bascombe started? Seeing if anyone in St. Athan can identify the sketch?"

The policeman bridged his fingers in front of his face. "I agree that it would be a good idea if only to eliminate the possibility."

"It is a very small place. If Dungaree Man is known there, I think you will find out," said Catherine.

Resettling himself in his capacious leather chair, the DCI said, "These observations of yours are overly elaborate, I feel.

Mr. de Fontaine has no alibi for the first murder, and he has only a trumped-up alibi for the second. What sort of motive do you think would drive a person to commit this murder?"

Catherine swallowed. She hadn't counted on disclosing this, but now she could see that it couldn't be avoided. Sitting up straighter, she unconsciously gave a slight toss of her head. "We believe that Severn was a blackmailer and that Dawkins was murdered because he was taking up where his employer left off."

The DCI shook his head. "No. The man was rolling in it. That is out of the question. Really, Miss Tregowyn, you disappoint me."

Annoyed, Catherine kept her mouth shut. She didn't want to tell him about the dean's experience with Severn or the possibility that he had been blackmailing Oliver Anderson as well.

The policeman said, "I'd like to remind you that you have no official standing in this investigation. I won't tolerate your getting in the way of our finding a killer. As you should know from your past experience, it could be hazardous to you as well. Now, I would like to see Dr. Bascombe."

Catherine stood, and trying to draw her dignity around her, she left to walk home while Harry had his interview. She passed him in the lobby and thought she must have looked particularly quenched, for he gave her another wink.

She was glad of the walk as an opportunity to spend her temper. Scarcely noticing her surroundings, Catherine went over her unsatisfactory interview word by word. Of course, the man had seen her as nothing but an amateurish interloper, but she wasn't at all impressed by anything the police had done. Would they even bother showing the sketch around St. Athan?

When she arrived back at the flat, Cherry told her Hobbes, the porter at Somerville, had rung and wished for her to ring him back.

"Is everything all right with you, miss?" he asked when she had him on the line.

"I'm very well, thank you, Hobbes," she replied, puzzled by his concern.

"It's just that the police called, wanting your telephone number at that flat of yours when they found out you didn't live at college. Are you involved in one of your inquiries, then? Or are they interfering where they don't belong? I felt that bad about giving your number, but I didn't want them to ring through to the dean!"

"You did exactly the right thing, Hobbes. Don't worry. Dr. Bascombe and I are involved in another inquiry. The police have one of our friends in jail. I don't know how they manage to do that with such frequency!"

"Well, just as long as it's not you in jail. How could you solve things then?" he asked with a booming laugh. "Good luck to you, then!"

Catherine thanked him, grateful that he had given out her number, so they hadn't rung through to Dean Godfrey. Sitting down at her desk, she attempted to rein in her thoughts about the case and concentrate on her tutorial for the next day. She had essays to mark, and they would move on to Wilfred Owen, another of the war poets, so she needed to brush up on his poetry.

> *What passing-bells for these who die as cattle?*
> *—Only the monstrous anger of the guns.*
> *Only the stuttering rifles' rapid rattle*
> *Can patter out their hasty orisons.*
> *No mockeries now for them; no prayers nor bells;*
> *Nor any voice of mourning save the choirs,—*
> *The shrill, demented choirs of wailing shells;*
> *And bugles calling for them from sad shires.*
> *What candles may be held to speed them all?*
> *Not in the hands of boys, but in their eyes*
> *Shall shine the holy glimmers of goodbyes.*
> *The pallor of girls' brows shall be their pall;*
> *Their flowers the tenderness of patient minds,*
> *And each slow dusk a drawing-down of blinds.*

Catherine traced the poem on its page with a tender finger. Owen's poetry always put her right in the trenches. How could anyone, after reading his heart-wrenching words, ever want to sacrifice another generation to this same fate?

So immersed was she in her work, she wasn't even aware of the knock at the door. It was a surprise when Cherry interrupted her to announce a visitor: James Bascombe.

Startled, she stood up and greeted Harry's brother.

"Hello, James. Take a chair, won't you? I've lost track of time, I'm afraid. Have you had luncheon?"

"Yes, thank you," the tall, scholarly-looking man said. "I don't mean to disturb your work. I just wanted to thank you for getting Anne out of that beastly jail."

She smiled at him. How different he was from Harry! His whole expression was diffident, and she had the feeling that he didn't communicate with ordinary people very much.

"It wasn't I!" she said. "It was the murderer who got to poor Gerald Dawkins while she was safely locked up. Won't you have a seat?" she prompted him again.

"Have you had any success finding the man who did it?" he asked.

"At this point, we are still discovering suspects . . ."

He broke in, "Harry has treated you damned badly, I'm afraid. He and Anne have been living in each other's pockets ever since they were young. That's all it is. I knew things would be like this when we came back to England. I don't know why she chose me, to tell you the truth. We haven't got much of a marriage. Next to Harry, I am a stick in the mud, but my work is important. And it will be even more important should we have another war."

Catherine didn't know how to reply to his first statement, so she concentrated on the second one. "It's some kind of drug, isn't it?"

"Yes. Sulfa. It will end up saving limbs and saving lives. It would have made a tremendous difference if they'd had it in the trenches. It would have saved tens of thousands of lives. It's a marvelous discovery. Man by the name of Domagk. German fellow. I hated to leave Bayer Labs, but it was time. Anne had gotten herself into a mess, and if I hadn't gotten her out of the country, it would have been prison camp for her. Cursed Nazis. We are working on how to deliver the sulfa in a form that will be the most helpful."

"Marvelous," she said. "Tell me, do you think there will be war with Germany?"

"If it were up to the scientists like me, here and in Germany, we'd have a chance at avoiding it. But the Nazis are like virulent influenza. They are invading every part of life in Germany. And soon Germany will be too small for them. They want *Lebensraum*. They will start by retaking the Rhineland. Then, if no one stops them, they will go on to take Austria. The German people have given Hitler a clear mandate. He will go on and on until he is stopped."

Goosebumps rose all over Catherine, and she grew sick to her stomach. Harry's brother didn't spare her. He went on to discuss how life in Germany had changed since the Nazis had come to power.

Finally, she said, "Have mercy, James. You are talking about my worst nightmare!"

All at once, he looked like a boy who had been given a scold. "Oh! Sorry. I'm afraid I do go on about the subject."

There was an awkward silence. Finally, he said, "I just mainly wanted to reassure you about Anne and Harry. She takes his devotion as her right. But it's not. I've talked to her about it. To be honest, she's not the most faithful of wives, but I think things will be better in future. One might not think it, but she listens to me. And now that we're going to have a family, there are other things for her to think about."

Catherine couldn't think of one thing to say except, "Thank you, James. I'll bear what you say in mind."

He stood and offered his hand. "Harry and I don't always see eye to eye, but I certainly agree with him about you. Insist upon his treating you well. I hope you'll be very happy."

She shook his hand and thanked him again. Finally, he took his hat from the hat tree, put it on his head, and exited.

Catherine sat weakly back in her chair. What a disconcerting fellow James was! He was almost too rational, but he meant well. Imagine his letting it drop that Anne wasn't "the most faithful of wives"! The net effect of his visit was to unsettle Catherine. Anne was even more unscrupulous than she had thought.

She went back to her War Poetry. Fortunately, she had last year's analysis of the Owen poem to rely on.

* * *

Harry called at 3:00 and gave her an account of his interview with Kerry.

"He sent a couple of sergeants down to Wales with the police sketch of Dungaree Man, at least. I'll be interested to see if anything comes of it."

Cherry thoughtfully brought warm cups of cocoa to them and tended the fire. There was a north wind that always seemed to whistle straight into the flat. Catherine and Harry sat next to each other on the sofa and sipped their beverage.

"Your brother was here today," she said.

"James? Here? The deuce! Why?"

"He wanted to put me wise about you and Anne. I got the feeling they'd had words on the subject. I know that you will find this hard to believe, but he inferred that Anne was unfaithful."

"The deuce!" Harry's brow became thunderous. "I know James is a straightforward chap, but imagine saying something like that about your spouse!"

"James doesn't strike me as a suspicious sort," Catherine said. "I don't think he would have brought it up if it weren't true. He was rather 'by-the-way' about it, not emphatic or anything."

"Huh!" said Harry. "Well, I can say with a surety, she's not adding me to her conquests."

Catherine was happy that he didn't feel it necessary for him to stand up for Anne. Leaning over, she kissed his cheek.

He also talked to me about Germany. He scared me, Harry. And just on the day when I was channeling Wilfred Owen. I don't know what to think. I really don't."

"I know what you mean. But it's not as though the responsibility for what to do about Hitler is on your shoulders."

"That's part of the problem, for I'd like to be able to do something. I don't see peace on the horizon," she said woefully. "I may have to change my stance on rearmament."

He put down his mug and took her into his arms. "Who knows what will happen? All we can do is live one day at a time. We can't take counsel from our fears. If war comes, we will worry about it then."

Catherine took a deep breath. "You're right. Now. What direction should we take on this investigation?"

As though on cue, Cherry entered with an envelope. "This was just delivered by a messenger." She handed it to Catherine.

"What did he look like?" she asked.

"He was just a lad," Cherry said. "He didn't even have a coat. If I'd had a child's coat, I would have given it to him."

"Thank you, Cherry." Catherine opened the envelope. The letter was written in block capitals.

I UNDERSTAND YOU ARE LOOKING INTO THE MURDER OF THE EARL OF SEVERN. HE KNEW DEAN ELIZABETH GODFREY WELL. SHE IS NOT WHO SHE SEEMS.

A WELL-WISHER

Catherine put a hand to her lips. "Oh no." She handed the letter to Harry.

"Well, this is a turn-up for the books," he said after reading it.

"This is where we could use one of those P.I.'s they have in

America. I don't even know where to start." Catherine ran a hand through her hair.

"She didn't tell you why she was being blackmailed, did she?" asked Harry.

"No. Not a clue there," said Catherine. "It was something so private, she had no intention of sharing it."

"What do you know about her? She replaced the old dean last year, didn't she? Isn't she rather young for the post?" asked Harry.

"Yes. And as far as I know, she has never been married," Catherine said, her forehead creased in thought.

"Is she an Old Girl?"

"I've always just assumed she is. All of the administration is made up of Somervillians. I guess the thing to do is to get hold of the Oxford *Mail* from when she was hired. They would have gone into detail about her past. The school would have published something, as well, but I don't want to be seen going into their archives at this point. It would rouse suspicions."

"It's off to the *Mail,* then," said Harry. "We need to think like P.I.s. What else?"

"It all depends on what we see in the *Mail.*"

* * *

The archives of the Oxford newspaper made Catherine sneeze. "All right," she said once she had managed her sneezes. "The new dean came during Michaelmas Term last year. The same time I started."

They located the newspaper with the dean's biography easily enough.

The new dean of students at Somerville College is Elizabeth Godfrey, lately the dean of students at Thane College for Women in York. Born in New Zealand, she came to this country to attend Bishop's School for Young Ladies in Hampshire.

Upon her graduation from this elite academy, Dr. Godfrey attended Somerville, where she graduated with a first in Classics.

Scholars recognized her work in that field, and she co-authored a book of Classics for Young People. She received her Doctorate in Education at Somerville and took her first employment at the Thane Academy.

"Does anything strike you as odd about this?" asked Catherine.

"Offhand, I'd say it is a creditable biography."

"Yes. But there is no mention of family. She didn't just sprout from the head of Zeus, I don't imagine."

"Good point. I know the Bishop's School for Young Ladies. My mother gives guest lectures there from time to time. I think she also tends to their health. It's her alma mater."

"That's topping!" said Catherine. "Can we go down to Hampshire after our tutorials tomorrow? We can come back here on Wednesday in time for our lectures."

"I'll just telephone the mater," Harry said. "Just one snag. Anne is down in Hampshire, staying with my parents."

Catherine was annoyed. "Why doesn't she stay with her own father?"

"She likes mine better. Anne and Father are good friends. As soon as she was released from jail, she went down there. James isn't much company for her right now."

CHAPTER TWENTY-ONE

Catherine's tutorial on Wilfred Owen went exceedingly well. Her students were sobered by his poetry and anxious to study the other poets of the period. Catherine planned to have a reading of the War Poets Wednesday week. Harry would recite the poetry, taking samples from all the tragic poets. Last year, it was very well received.

She and Harry started for Hampshire soon after luncheon.

"I wonder if we're ever going to find out the results of the police canvassing St. Athan," Catherine said as they left Oxford behind them.

"I'm also anxious to hear from Lord Rutherford about whether or not Oliver Anderson was a deserter," said Harry.

"I don't have much hope there," said Catherine. "He wouldn't come back here without changing his name, I don't think. The risks are too great."

"That's probably true," said Harry. "He probably changed it long ago, when he was living in France."

"This case is growing to be an octopus," said Catherine, leaning back against the seat in Harry's Morris. "I wonder how Severn found out Dean Godfrey's secret."

"Maybe when we know what it is, we can figure that out."

Catherine put her hand on her hat as Harry increased his speed.

They were driving with the top down today as it was gloriously sunny and temperate—one of those fall days that gifted them with a blue, blue sky and air so clear you could see for miles.

She was beginning to enjoy the drive south to Harry's home. She loved the undulating fields dotted with sheep, which represented Harry's father's livelihood. At this season, leaves were changing on the trees that lined the highway and divided the fields into a crazy quilt.

She hoped Anne wasn't going to make any trouble.

They drove straight to The Bishop's School for Young Ladies, lodged in a Tudor building at the end of an avenue of plane trees. Catherine presented her card to the porter at the door. Using his telephone, he informed the head-mistress, Miss Johnson, of their arrival. The porter, in maroon liv-ery, led them to a neat office overlooking the remains of a flower garden. The headmistress was short and compact with a head of graying hair.

"Good afternoon, ma'am," Catherine said. "I'm Catherine Tregowyn from Somerville College, and this is Dr. Harry Bascombe from Christ Church. We are doing a series of articles on the administrators of Somerville College. We wonder if you might help us with some background on Dean Elizabeth Godfrey, a student here a number of years ago. She was in the Somerville Class of 1924.

The woman's face creased in a wide smile. "I'm Mrs. St. James. And oh, yes. I remember dear Elizabeth very well. Such a sad beginning to her life here and such a triumphant exit. She was a magnificent scholar, and her life was a sermon."

"Sad beginning?" Catherine prompted.
"Oh, my yes. It's no secret that Elizabeth lost both of her parents right before she started here. It happened back in New Zealand. I'm not privy to the details." The woman flashed a quick smile and interlocked her fingers before her. "The Brook family sponsored her. Mrs. Brook had taken her under her wing. You see, Elizabeth had been sent here by her parents. With only

a chaperone—she traveled here all the way from New Zealand. I believe she was terribly brave." The headmistress sighed. "Shortly after she arrived, her parents were killed. They had had some sort of arrangement with the Brooks for Elizabeth's care, and Sadie Brook had become her dearest friend. Both girls were twelve at the time. The family just swept Elizabeth up and watched out for her ever after."

"What a brutal thing to have happened!" exclaimed Catherine. "I had no idea."

She wondered if this was the core of the story. "And where do the Brooks live?" she asked.

"Oh, fortunately for Elizabeth, they are a local family. Mrs. Brooks has passed, sadly. Sadie and her husband live in the family home now and look after her father."

"Perhaps my parents know them," said Harry. "My mother is the GP around here. Dr. Sarah Bascombe."

"Ah, yes. I thought I recognized the name. Dr. Bascombe treats our girls when they're ill. We are very fond of her."

Miss Johnson ordered tea, and they sat down to a comfortable coz about Elizabeth Godfrey's career at the Bishop's School. Catherine learned that Elizabeth had worked as one possessed as a girl, determining that she wanted to go to Oxford at a young age. She won all the prizes in Classics her final year. She was not strong, however, and didn't do well at games. Miss Johnson confided that she was a nervous child. Elizabeth was very highly strung, jumping when one touched her unexpectedly, startling when one entered a room where she was alone. If she were reprimanded for any reason, she would break into tears."

"It is amazing to me that she has overcome that kind of loss to become the dean of one of the most elite women's colleges in the Kingdom," said Catherine.

"I marvel at it. Truly I do," said Miss Johnson.

Their visit was soon ended, with false promises made by Catherine to send a copy of the article on Dean Godfrey to the Bishop's School.

"If even part of that history is true," said Catherine, "I can see how Dean Godfrey might treat any threat to her position."

"Yes," said Harry. "She is the only one we know of, so far, that gave in to the blackmail. However, she may have killed to keep Severn from soiling the young Somervillian's minds with his propaganda."

"You're right. Do we keep pushing to try to find the secret?" asked Catherine, reluctant to go further.

"I think so. One can never have too many facts," said Harry. "I wonder if my mother remembers her."

* * *

Harry's mother greeted them with delight. "What is this? How lovely to see you both! But what is the occasion?"

"I don't suppose you could give us dinner and a couple of beds?" asked Harry. "We were down here making some inquiries at the Bishop's School."

"How extraordinary," the doctor said. "But of course, you must stay. On the condition that you tell us what all this is about!"

"We shall," Harry promised. "We're actually hoping you can help us a bit."

"Oh! Well, I shall if I can. Come into the sitting room. I have Anne here. We're knitting baby things."

Catherine steeled herself.

"Oh!" Anne greeted them, springing up from the sofa. "Harry! Catherine! What are you doing here?"

Catherine held her breath as she watched Anne start to go to Harry and then stop herself.

"Inquiries. Believe it or not," he said.

"Would either of you care for tea?" asked Sarah Bascombe.

"We've just had it at the school," said Catherine. "But thank you."

"Well, sit down and tell us what this is all about!"

Catherine and Harry sat together on another sofa, and she gave him a nod to begin the story.

"Well, we've been investigating Dean Elizabeth Godfrey because Severn was blackmailing her, but she wouldn't tell us why. We wanted to know if she had a motive for murdering him." He informed them of their research efforts which had brought them down to the school.

"Lord Severn was a blackmailer?" Harry's mother exclaimed.

"Yes. We've suspected it, but Dr. Godfrey is the first victim we have confirmed. The headmistress of the Bishop School was a lot of help. It seems Elizabeth came here from New Zealand to attend The Bishop School for Young Ladies when she was about twelve. But right before she started there, she got word that her parents had died. She was staying with the Brook family, who apparently lives near here. Elizabeth had become close to their daughter, Sadie, who would also start at Bishop's school."

"I've been the GP for the Bishop's school for a long time," said Sarah. "I'm also the doctor for the Brook's family. What was the girl's name again?"

"Elizabeth Godfrey," said Catherine. "Do you remember her?"

Harry's mother pursed her lips. "I do, as a matter of fact. She was a puzzle. I don't know how much I should say."

"This is a murder investigation, Mother," Harry reminded her.

"Do you really think she could be a murderer, though?"

"She was very distressed over Severn's blackmailing her, as anyone would be," said Catherine. "She wouldn't tell me what he had on her, but it must have been quite a big secret for her to agree to have him speak to the Somerville girls. Then he was killed before he could give his speech."

"And," added Harry, "She was one of three people who knew Anne had an appointment with Severn that afternoon. She could have set Anne up to take the fall for the murder."

"Don't be ridiculous," Anne scoffed. "Elizabeth would never do such a thing."

"Yes," said Sarah. "I do see."

Getting up, she wandered to the French doors to look at the remains of her husband's flower garden. The first frost had come the night before, and all the flowers were dead, their stalks black and depressing looking.

"Well, I didn't really ever find out the answers to my questions," the doctor said. "I have watched her achievements as the years have passed. She's an extraordinary woman, and if I'm right, she overcame a great deal."

"You have me curious," said Anne. "Elizabeth is my friend, and I must confess I've wondered why she never got married. Until recently, she lived a very solitary life as the dean. However, lately, there has been a man in her life. Mr. Oveson."

Sarah Bascombe said, "The first time I met her, she was only twelve. Something—I don't know what—had frightened her very badly. Amanda Brooks called me out to her home. She said that Elizabeth had just arrived from New Zealand, and she was really in a bad way."

"How?" asked Harry.

"She was in the corner of her room, curled into the fetal position. She wouldn't speak. The family very much wanted to help her, but they didn't know how." Dr. Bascombe shook her head. "It was very sad. I felt she belonged in a mental institution. I didn't have the first idea how to take care of her."

"It sounds like something horrible must have happened to her on the ship from New Zealand," said Anne. "How awful."

Harry's mother continued, "The Brooks were devoted to her. I told them that wrapping her tightly in warm blankets might help. That's what you do for a traumatized infant. She was petite for her age. I suggested that Amanda Brooks try to hold her in her arms, on her lap in a rocker if possible."

"How long did it take her to get better?" asked Catherine, moved almost to tears at the thought of the strong, seemingly confident Elizabeth Godfrey in this condition. Could such a person have grown up to be a murderer?

"I consulted with my professors in Edinburgh about what I

could do to take care of her, but no one gave me any sound suggestions. It was months before she spoke. Eventually, after about six months, she started attending school as a day student. The thing that really puzzled me was that she spoke without a trace of a New Zealand accent. Her speech was pure Oxbridge. I don't even know at what stage of her illness she was told that her parents were dead. I never learned anything about them or how they died. The Brooks fostered her, of course."

"That is heartbreaking," murmured Catherine. "The Brooks family—were they relatives or something?"

"I never learned. But how else would Elizabeth have ended up with them? There had to be some connection."

"What year was this?" asked Harry.

"Let's see," said his mother, thinking. She brightened. "It was about twenty years ago. Right in the middle of the War."

"1915. So, she was born in '03. It might be worth checking the birth certificates in Britain for that year since you have doubts about her citizenship," said Harry. "We can do that at Somerset House."

"It's a longshot," said Catherine. "When did Amanda Brooks die?

"She had a stroke last year," said Dr. Bascombe. "In the summer. August, I think."

"Perhaps we can find a connection to Elizabeth if we look up the death certificate. It will have Amanda Brooks' mother and father's names on it,'" said Catherine.

"Death certificates are available in the county," said the doctor. "It should be on file in Winchester."

"Too bad we have to go back to Oxford in the morning," said Harry. "That's an excellent idea, darling."

"Actually, the *Hampshire Chronicle* probably has her obituary. We have those at the library. It's open until eight," said Harry's mother.

Harry stood. "Come, Watson! The game is afoot!"

Catherine scowled. "Just watch who you call Watson!"

Chapter Twenty-Two

The town library was an unpretentious red brick building on the square. Catherine felt a bubble of excitement in her middle as they entered and asked for the back issues of the *Hampshire Chronicle*.

A small gentleman with wire-rimmed spectacles fetched the bound copies for August 1934, for Catherine. Harry decided to look through July, just in case his mother's memory was playing her false.

It was a dirty job. Newsprint covered Catherine's fingers as she paged through the issues. She soon realized all obituaries for the week were printed on Sundays, making her task more manageable. Finally, she found it in mid-August.

Amanda Leslie Brook, born Amanda DeFurrier, died on Wednesday following a short illness . . . Catherine scanned through the tribute until she came to more family information. Mrs. Brook was pre-deceased by her brother, Alvin, and her sister Mrs. Irene Stanton (Frederick).

"Harry! I've got it!"

"Spiffing!" He read it over her shoulder as she copied down the family information.

They made it back to Harry's family home just in time for dinner.

"Did you find it?" Anne asked. Catherine nodded, imagining

that Anne did not like feeling left out of the investigation, but she was hiding it well.

Or at least Catherine thought she was. Anne's first question over dinner made her wonder.

"Have you rescheduled your wedding yet?" Anne asked.

Before Catherine could reply, Harry said, "Not yet. Catherine's father's been ill. It's his heart. We're hoping he'll rally in time for a spring wedding."

His lie took Catherine's breath away. She wasn't sure how she felt about it, but she was very glad she didn't have to stammer through an answer that Anne didn't even deserve.

"Ah!" Anne replied. "So it's still on?"

Harry's mother looked daggers at her daughter-in-law. "Of course!" she said. "What made you think otherwise?"

Anne's skin flushed. "Well, Pardon me, I'm sure," she said, employing the accents of a Cockney shopgirl.

"We did find the obituary!" Catherine announced during the awkward silence.

Dr. Bascombe asked, "Did it give Amanda's family name?"

"Yes. Rather posh. DeFurrier."

"DeFurrier, DeFurrier . . ." repeated Harry's father. "I know that name. Something unsavory."

"1915 . . ." said Sarah. She paused, her forehead drawn. Suddenly her eyes opened wide. "Oh heavens! That poor child!"

"What?" asked Catherine and Harry in chorus.

"Yes. That's it, Sarah," agreed Harold Bascombe. "It was a huge story at the time. It ran in one form or another for months. A very prominent Cambridge professor shot his wife and himself in front of his children. One daughter disappeared before the police came on the scene. She was never found."

"Elizabeth must have run away and eventually rung her aunt," said Sarah Bascombe. "How dreadful. What a dreadful thing for a child!"

Catherine's mind reeled with shock. "It's no wonder she changed her name."

Harry said, "Nowadays, they think the kind of mental illness her father must have had is hereditary. She would certainly never be given charge over all those students if the truth were known."

"And that's the thing," said Catherine. "How did Severn come to know such a closely held secret?"

"We may never know," said Harry. "But it gives Elizabeth Godfrey a huge motive for murder."

"Are we going to tell the police?" Catherine asked, assailed by a wild urge to start biting her fingernails.

"Let's wait and see if we can establish how Severn might have known her secret and thus become a threat to her," said Harry. "We have no right to ruin her life if she's innocent."

Catherine tended to agree with him. For the first time since she had begun doing these types of investigations, she had more sympathy for a possible murderer than she did for the victim. "She is too small to be our Dungaree Man anyway."

"If she's guilty," said Harry, "she hired him to do it, I suppose."

"I think we had better read those accounts for ourselves," said Catherine. "The Bodleian Library has back issues of the *Times* into the Middle Ages, I think."

"Is there anything I can do?" asked Anne. "I'd love to help."

Catherine exchanged a look with Harry. He appeared to be annoyed. "Nothing at the moment," he said. "Anne, I think this goes without saying, but it's very critical that you say nothing of this to anyone, including James."

"Why, how could you think I would be so indiscreet?" Anne asked.

"I just want to make certain you understand the nature of the situation." Then he turned to his parents. "Sorry, everyone. We're being the most terrific bores."

"Not at all, dear," said his mother. "I am glad we could help, but I am most awfully glad you're not going to give up the poor woman just yet."

"Let's play bridge or something," said Harry.

* * *

Catherine didn't sleep well that night, thinking of their discovery and how it could upend the career Dean Godfrey had fought for so hard. Surely, she wasn't a murderer! Catherine taxed her mind until well after 2 a.m. trying to come up with another suspect. Was Red really innocent? And what about Oliver Anderson? Or could Dawkins have killed his employer, after all, only to suffer death at the hand of someone he tried to blackmail as his boss had done?

At least Harry seemed to be keeping Anne at arm's length. But from the wounded look in her eye when he refused to allow her to help, she wondered if Anne would leave it at that.

Morning came far too early, but they needed to get back to Oxford for their 11 o'clock lectures. When they arrived, Catherine had only enough time for a quick change of clothing.

She felt groggy at the podium, and her lecture was not as compelling as she would have liked or as good as the War Poets deserved. Foregoing luncheon, she went back to her flat and slept.

When she woke, she had essays to mark for the next day's tutorial. They were well-written for the most part. Her students thought Rupert Brooke's poetry to be from an earlier age, as the poet himself appeared to be. Most of them picked up the fact that this illustrated clearly how the war had provided a complete schism with the past.

Catherine wondered what another war would do. Would it plunge them into change so complete that the life she was living now would one day prove to be a lost age? She hoped she would never find out.

Just before tea Lord Rutherford rang.

"I just wanted to let you know that I've gone through all the records available on known deserters. Oliver Anderson's name hasn't come up. That doesn't really prove anything, however. He most probably changed his name. But you think he was in Severn's regiment?"

"Yes," she said.

"If I could get a look at him, I might recognize him. That was my regiment, as well."

"I could invite him along with some other people in for drinks. Would you be available tomorrow night?"

"I would be. What time?"

"How about six o'clock?" she asked.

"I'll be there."

"I expect he looks quite different now. He's bald, and he wears a beard."

"I can still give it a try," the viscount said.

After they rang off, she rang Harry and told him the plan.

"Sounds just the ticket," he said. "Do you want me to ring Anne and get Anderson's telephone number? Should I invite her, as well?"

Catherine deliberated only a few seconds. "Yes. But you might want to warn her that her father will be here. I don't know how she feels about that."

"She doesn't get on with him, but they are civil to one another. Who else should we invite?"

"James?" she asked.

"I'll give him a ring. Anne would probably like to invite the dean. How would you feel about that?"

"Is Anne going to be able to keep quiet about the dean's past?" Catherine asked.

"I'll remind her that those facts are absolutely not to come out. I can't think of anything that would be more distressing to the dean."

"Right, then. Speaking of the dean, she may like to bring a guest. Of the male persuasion."

"You can mention it when you ring her," said Harry.

"I shall. Let's begin at six o'clock. I'll see you then. I'm going to spend tomorrow at the Bodleian with the *Times*. I shall probably need spectacles by the time I'm finished."

"You would look charming in a pair of specs. Meanwhile, I'll pay our friend, Red, a visit and see how he's getting on."

* * *

The following morning, Catherine was at the Bodleian at opening time. A helpful librarian in the periodical section assisted her in ordering the correct month and year of *Times* editions in the archives. A telephone call to Harry's father that morning had pinpointed the month of the murder-suicide as September, right before the Cambridge Michaelmas term. After paging carefully through the old newspapers (wearing the obligatory gloves), she found in the *Times's* most boldly permitted headlines:

CAMBRIDGE PROFESSOR MURDERS WIFE AND KILLS SELF.

The initial article read:

Dr. Alvin DeFurrier, 36, professor of Medieval History at King's College, shot his wife, Josephine née Winthrop, and himself in the presence of at least two of his children. His third child, a twelve-year-old daughter, was missing at press time.

Friends of the professor indicated that his mood had been unstable, and he had been drinking heavily since the end of Easter Term. Dr. Defurrier was a favorite among his students who expressed shock and disbelief at the manner of his death.

An intense search continues for the missing daughter, Olivia, who is small for her age, with blue eyes and long blonde hair worn plaited. Anyone with information concerning her whereabouts is asked to call the police.

The following days' articles included quotes from Charles S. Myers, the Director of the Psychology Laboratory at Cambridge, stating that "the commission of such a vicious act as Dr. DeFurrier's was a direct result of a frenzied consciousness likely aggravated by the consumption of alcohol or drugs." The two children known to be present during the murder/suicide have been put into the custody of relatives. Dr. Myers has given his opinion that they will undoubtedly need psychoanalytic treatment. At present, no news was to be had regarding the missing daughter, Elizabeth.

Many inches of print quoted politicians, fellow Cambridge scholars, and the police decrying this "evidence of the war on public morals among leftist academics."

Catherine read enough to know that Elizabeth's location was never uncovered and that she was presumed dead. Sure that the police would have interrogated her aunt regarding the location of her niece, Catherine decided that Mrs. Brook had likely lied to protect Elizabeth from the police, the press, and other relatives.

By lunchtime, Catherine had concluded she wouldn't find anything new and thanking the archivist for her help, she went off to her flat for luncheon. Cherry was involved in a frenzy of cleaning to get ready for the cocktail party, so after eating a boiled egg and an apple, Catherine went off to the market to buy cheese and biscuits. Harry was bringing liquor and wine.

What news would tonight bring? Catherine had a queer presentiment. She felt that the investigation was about to break wide open.

Chapter Twenty-Three

James and Anne were the first to arrive.

"My dear, what a cunning little flat!" the woman said. "And how lovely that you have a gramophone. I do so love jazz." For some reason, Anne was speaking in the manner of an empty-headed debutante.

Harry came in with the liquid refreshments just as Lord Rutherford arrived.

Everyone placed orders with Harry, acting in a convivial way as Cherry passed around biscuits with cheese. Elizabeth Godfrey arrived with Mr. Oveson. Catherine was glad that the dean had brought him.

"So lovely to see you again," he said. He had the sharp eyes of an observer who took in everything at a glance.

Dr. Oliver Anderson was the last to arrive. Catherine paid attention to the viscount's manner as he saw Dr. Anderson for the first time. There was no change except for a slight narrowing of his eyes.

Surprisingly, the Merton professor showed a definite reaction. *His* eyes grew rounder as Anne introduced him to her father. Dr. Anderson became a bit skittish, scratching the back of his neck and swallowing convulsively.

Did Rutherford recognize him, and did Dr. Anderson know

that he was being pegged as a deserter? It certainly seemed so. Elizabeth Godfrey appeared to notice his discomfort and tried to put him at ease by introducing Mr. Oveson and conversing with the professor about his students. Anderson took her cue and began sharing anecdotes about one of his students who brought his Siamese cat to his tutorials.

James was speaking to his father-in-law about sulfa while Anne cornered Harry. Catherine could not decide which discussion to join. At length, she went to listen to the latest developments in James's world.

Rutherford spoke to Dr. Anderson away from the others, while James talked about sulfa being developed in cream form. Catherine smiled at him. "Ingenious!" she said. She shouldn't have put the volume up so high on the gramophone. It made listening in on other conversations impossible.

At length, Rutherford concluded his conversation with Anderson and came over to Catherine. "I was in touch with the Chief Constable today. I think they may have decided to give up on the man your birder saw, Miss Tregowyn. They canvassed every address in St. Athan, and no one saw the man in the sketch."

"Hmm," said Catherine. "That is interesting. Thank you for telling me."

The peer wandered off to get another drink from Cherry, who was minding the liquor.

James said in a low voice, "I need to speak with you in private."

Surprised, Catherine noted that his features suddenly had a grim cast. She couldn't imagine what he needed to say to her, but she replied, "Come with me into the kitchen, then. It seems more cheese and biscuits are wanted."

Once they were away from the others, James said, "Anne informed me tonight that she's leaving me. She seems to think she and Harry can make a go of it. I thought I should warn you. Anne is used to getting what she wants."

Catherine's mouth went dry. Of everything he might have said, this was the last thing she expected. "Does Harry know anything about this?"

"I imagine she's telling him right now. When Anne makes up her mind, she doesn't hesitate to barge ahead."

Hands shaking, Catherine forgot all about the biscuits. "I must say, she's got a nerve."

"You can't tell me you didn't see this coming," James said. "You've postponed your wedding."

She gripped the counter. "But how do you feel about this?"

"I'm a dull dog compared to my brother." James looked apologetic. Catherine wanted to shake him. "We had our troubles in Germany. As a matter of fact, I doubt the child is mine. You know, it's ironic. As much as she hates them, she's probably going to have a child that's half Nazi. I should have divorced her long ago."

Catherine was so shocked, it was a moment before she found her voice. "Well, Anne may find that Harry isn't hers for the tak-ing," she said. Vaguely remembering her task, she focused on placing biscuits on a serving tray. They insisted on eluding her shaking hands and ended up on the floor.

"Bother!" she said, going in search of the broom. At that moment, Cherry entered the kitchen.

"What are you doing, miss?" she said. "Let me take care of this mess. You can go back out to your guests. I don't know what you were thinking. I can manage this."

Duly reprimanded, Catherine and James left the kitchen. She realized Dr. Anderson was looking for her.

"I'm just going to take my leave," he said. "Papers to mark, you know." He thrust his glass at her and went after his coat and hat. It wasn't hard to see he was rattled and anxious to be gone.

Catherine's interest was divided between the Merton professor heading for the door on one side of the room and Harry and Anne in earnest conversation in the other. She felt at a loss.

The dean and Mr. Oveson walked over to her. "My dear, you look as though you've seen a ghost. Is everything all right?" Dean Godfrey asked.

"Oh, I'm all right," Catherine said. "Just feeling a bit light-headed for some reason. It happens sometimes." Into her crowded consciousness came an image of a little blonde schoolgirl watching her father slay her mother. She wanted to reach out and clasp the dean's hand in comfort.

Instead, the dean reached out to her, placing a hand on her arm. "You should see a doctor, dear. We can't have you getting ill!"

It was impossible to believe this woman could have inherited some kind of murderous inclination. She sincerely hoped not. Mr. Oveson was looking at the dean with frank admiration.

"I just had a thought," said Catherine. "If you are interested, my fiancé will be performing the works of the War Poets next Wednesday morning here at Somerville. He has a gift for the oral interpretation of literature."

"I'm a drudge, by comparison, I'm afraid."

"A reading by Professor Bascombe is not to be missed," Catherine said. "He had them standing in the aisles in Hollywood."

"Hollywood?"

Catherine told him of their summer semester at UCLA, and for a while, they discussed their impressions of America. Overson had been there often in a professional capacity.

Then he said, "Elizabeth tells me you and Harry are amateur sleuths. You are trying to find Severn's murderer?"

"We are. Presently, we're concentrating on the earl's murder with the hope that his murderer killed Mr. Dawkins as well."

"Your friend, Red, is in custody. You don't believe he did it?"

Since he really seemed interested, she said, "Not according to the evidence we've gathered so far."

"Hmm. That's interesting. Apparently, the police don't agree with you."

The man raised an eyebrow, and she could tell that he thought her audacious. The thought crept into her mind that if he was Dungaree Man, he was a bit nervy himself. She drew herself up and said, "We've proved them wrong before."

"Is that so?" He grinned.

"Yes, as a matter of fact. My job leaves me with a lot of extra time on my hands," she said sweetly. "I like to stay busy."

At that moment, Lord Rutherford came over to say his farewells but ended up conversing with Mr. Oveson. Catherine watched the viscount as he spoke. There was a new tension in him—a rigidity in the way he held his shoulders, eyebrows pulled into a frown. Did he think poorly of Dr. Godfrey's friend? Had he recognized Anderson? Would he tell her?

After a few minutes, the dean came up to her and said, "We must be on our way. How lovely of you to invite us. I am enchanted by your flat. I do so love Art Deco. But I'm worried about you. Get some rest, dear."

She and Oveson left. Rutherford said only, "I'll ring you tomorrow," before he left himself. Only Harry, James, and Anne remained. The latter looked around, surprised to see the rest of the company had gone. She said, "Come, James. It seems it's time to leave. Jolly short party. But thank you, Catherine."

Catherine smiled with difficulty, saying, "It was nice to see you. Thank you for coming."

Once they were out the door, she said the first thing that came to mind, "So, Harry. Are you going to take Anne up on her offer?"

He looked uncomfortable. "So, James has talked to you? Jolly bad form—asking a bloke to marry you at your fiancée's cocktail party. Not to mention her husband standing a few feet away."

"I agree," Catherine said, her voice brisk. "But then, James says she's been unfaithful to him, so apparently she has few scruples. He doesn't even think the baby is his. You won't believe this, but he said the child is probably 'half Nazi.'"

Harry was nonplussed. "Oh, I say! He must be completely shattered. Poor bloke!" It was a moment before he could continue. "So she was carrying on with a Nazi? Are you sure it wasn't just James slandering her for being unfaithful?"

She put a gentle hand on his arm. "I don't think so. It's probably just as well you didn't marry her when you had the chance."

"Well, I'm afraid I gave her a shock tonight," Harry said, shaking his head. "I told her that she had best stick to James. I hope she doesn't continue to accost me in social situations. I missed everything. Did Rutherford appear to recognize our Dr. Anderson?"

"Not so I could tell," said Catherine. "But Dr. Anderson left almost as soon as he met the man. He looked terrified."

"Rutherford is going to ring me tomorrow. I had a short conversation with Mr. Oveson. You know, he's an engineer in Severn's works. Funny how everything comes back to the earl," Harry said, narrowing his eyes. "I wonder if Oveson is fond enough of our dean to have shot Severn for her?"

"A thought. Harry, is this case curdling our brains?"

Harry said, "No. I think Anderson is the likeliest for our culprit. But not for long. I imagine Dr. Anderson will make a hasty exit from Merton in the middle of the term. He's probably running for his life."

"Rutherford did say he'd spoken to the Chief Constable, and they had no luck in St. Athan with the police sketch of Dungaree Man," said Catherine as she helped Cherry retrieve glasses from tables.

"I require sustenance," Harry said. "A meat pie from the Cheshire Cat sounds just the ticket. We can put our heads together."

* * *

The low-beamed ceiling of the pub and the wood-burning fire gave the hostelry a welcoming feeling. Catherine sat upon a stool at one of the high tables.

"Steak and kidney pie for me, please," she told her fiancé.

"Right," said Harry. "Coming right up."

As they ate their comfort food in the womblike atmosphere, Catherine eventually had an idea. "If our Dungaree Man wasn't wearing his disguise in St. Athan, I imagine he assumed it in Cardiff where he would have had to change trains for Oxford."

"He could have done that in the Gentlemen's Cloak Room," said Harry. "He would have hired his bike in Cardiff, too, presumably."

"Yes. But what would he have done with his other clothes?" said Catherine. "He must have brought his dungarees, etc., in a suitcase, one imagines. Then he would have put his gentleman's clothes in the suitcase once he'd dressed. Don't you think it logical that he would have put that suitcase in Left Luggage? He couldn't have carried it with the bicycle."

"Brilliant!" said Harry. "And the ticket was one way. There was no reason for him to go back to fetch it. It must still be there!"

"But why wouldn't he use the rubbish bin?"

Harry said, "Train stations are busy places. Someone might have remarked a man putting a perfectly good case in the rubbish."

"Well, I've heard tell that after a certain interval, the powers that be in Left Luggage give the whole lot to the church jumble sale or some such thing after a couple of weeks. Hopefully, if there is such a thing, it's still there."

"Shall we put the police onto it?" asked Harry.

"I think they've had just about enough of us. Shall we go to Cardiff in the morning?"

"Let's!" said Harry gaily.

"It's rather a long shot," She reminded him. "Let's take the train this time. It's far less tiring than motoring." Catherine was finished with her excellent pie. She sipped her still-warm cider and smiled at Harry.

"I say," Harry said. "You don't suppose we ought to tip off the police about Anderson, or whatever his name is, possibly making a run for France?"

"We haven't got anything but a hunch. They don't take kindly to hunches," said Catherine.

* * *

193

Though it was early, Catherine decided to ring Rutherford before they left for Wales. To her great disappointment, he wasn't in, and the Randolph hadn't a clue where he had gone. He did remain a guest, however.

"Anne rang this morning," said Harry when he and Catherine were aboard the train and settled in a first-class compartment. "She wanted to see me. When I told her I'd be out for the day, she began to cry and said James had left her. He's staying with a friend while he looks for another flat. He's actually taken leave from his job."

Though Catherine was selfishly pleased at this news, she didn't think it would be kind to let Harry know that. But before she could think of a reply, he said, "You know, despite our differences, James is a good fellow. He deserves a wife who loves him."

Suddenly, she remembered. "But what about the child? What is she going to do about the child?"

"Blimey. Forgot about the child. I guess we must hope they can work things out between them. Maybe James's actions will force Anne to think about someone other than herself for once."

Catherine said, "She has to know that there can be nothing, ever, between the two of you. I think it would be a good idea if we go ahead with the wedding the way we had planned."

Harry took her hands and looked into her eyes. "Are you certain, Catherine?"

"I think you're going to have to be a bit more forceful with Anne."

"I shall be. I'm terrifically appalled by my schoolboy behavior. I shall endeavor to remember my age." Harry kissed her lingeringly. "I can't believe I nearly lost you."

"That was a very satisfactory kiss, but I think you're out of practice," she said.

Harry proceeded to show her more fervently the way he felt. It was all very lovely.

By the time they pulled into the Cardiff station, their wedding date was confirmed, and their honeymoon to the Costa del Sol was thoroughly planned.

Upon disembarking, Harry insisted that they make their way through crowds of weekenders to the telegraph station, where they sent telegrams to both their families. Harry wanted everyone to know their wedding date was fixed. Only then was he ready to proceed with their business at the Left Luggage Office. They waited in a queue to speak to the worker who was manning the Office.

"Are you the usual person in charge here?" Harry asked.

"Seven days a week, guv," the worker said.

"Oh, excellent," said Harry. "I can't believe my luck. We're trying to solve a murder. A particularly nasty one. This is the man we suspect." Harry pulled out the photograph of Dungaree Man. "Obviously, he was wearing a disguise. You can see that for yourself. The beard, the hair, even the eyebrows. Matter of about two weeks ago. Do you keep the luggage that long?"

"Blimey! You don't think there's a body in one of them suitcases do you, mate?" Catherine was surprised to hear London in the man's voice.

"No. Nothing like that. But there may be a clue. When do you give up the luggage?"

"There'sa warning, there is. After two weeks, we pitch it."

"Do you remember this fellow?"

"I might." There was an avaricious gleam in the eye of the worker. Harry extracted a guinea from his pocket and placed it on the counter. The fellow's eyes gleamed, and he took up the coin. "I remember. Awful nice case for such a dodgy-looking character. Calf's leather. I was getting ready to toss the contents and keep it for myself. Would have if you hadn't come today."

"May we see the case?"

The worker went to the back of the office and picked up an expensive-looking case sitting alone next to the rear door. Catherine's heart speeded up, and she clasped her gloved hands together and brought them up to rest against her lips.

Once the case was on the counter, Harry paid the man who signaled them to move aside so he could wait on his next customer. Harry took up the article, and they moved over to one of the benches. He held the case on his lap. It was locked.

"Hold on," said Harry, bringing out his penknife. "This shouldn't be too much trouble."

Catherine bit her lip as he dealt with the locks. When they snapped open, he passed the case over to her. She opened it.

Inside was a large, crushed Fedora hat, obviously never meant to be worn again, a pair of gentleman's tweed trousers and matching jacket. The tailor's name had been carefully cut out of the suit and the hatter's label out of the hat.

"Well, that lets Red out," said Catherine. "He doesn't patronize a tailor." There was a yellow linen shirt and a brown tie. Everything was wadded up without regard for wrinkles. It was evident they had been disposed of, never to be worn again.

"The man who wore these was tall," said Harry. "I reckon they would have fit Dr. Anderson perfectly."

"We had better call DCI Kerry. We don't want Anderson to leave the country! We might already be too late," said Catherine.

"Don't let's get ahead of ourselves. We don't even know if the man was a deserter. I suggest we put a trunk call through to Rutherford," said Harry. "You do it. He likes you. No reason to tell him about our treasure here."

Catherine spied a row of red telephone boxes near the exit from the train station. "I'll be back in a moment."

"I'm just going to tell our friend at the counter that we'll be rescuing this lot from the church jumble sale. I'll give him my card in case anyone comes looking for it."

CHAPTER TWENTY-FOUR

To their vast disappointment, Rutherford was still not in.

"Anderson could be halfway to France by now!" moaned Catherine.

"You're supposing he's guilty. We don't know that," said Harry. "Even if he is a deserter, we still don't know that he killed Severn and Dawkins."

"It's clear as can be that Severn would have blackmailed him into using his influence with the pacifists. Anderson was probably supposed to back Severn by saying that he was for a strong, independent Britain that could be achieved without a war."

"Darling, your mind is ever-inventive, but you must remember patience is a virtue," Harry reminded her. "Maybe he said something to Anne, though."

"I'll try her," said Catherine.

When the woman answered the telephone, it sounded as though she had been crying. Catherine said, "Anne, we are down in Wales. Did your father happen to tell you anything about Dr. Anderson this morning?"

"I don't know what you're talking about. He went to the horse races today."

When she had rung off, Catherine asked Harry, "Do you think she was telling the truth?"

"As far as she knows it," Harry replied. "It really doesn't strike me that he would confide in Anne. Remember, he's Sherlock Holmes. Inscrutable."

Midway through the afternoon, as they were eating ham and eggs in the dining car, Catherine said, "You know, Harry, both Anderson, and the dean had huge secrets Severn could blackmail them over. But Anne? He didn't blackmail her so much as threaten her. I hate to slander her this way, but suppose he knew that Anne didn't care about anyone but herself. She wouldn't cease her campaign against Severn for her husband or her father. I think he blackmailed her over her personal problem. If her lover was a Nazi, he might have known him. Severn did business with the Nazis."

Harry toyed with his food. "That's a bit of a stretch," he said.

"But can you imagine if it came out that she was having an affair with a Nazi? It would violate all of her principles!"

"It fairly makes me ill," said Harry, pushing away his plate.

"Do you suppose she's mentally ill? Something is amiss with all of this," said Catherine. She pushed her plate away, as well. "There must be more to the story. Remember, Dr. Anderson said she was a spy for Churchill. Maybe her affair, or whatever it was, had something to do with her spying."

"That's generous of you to assume she had a expiating motive," Harry said, his whole face pulled down with disgust.

"I think it goes a long way toward explaining the inexplicable," she said, reaching across the table and putting her hand on his forearm. "I don't think she's a wholesale hypocrite. I think she's very sincere in her political beliefs. We should look on a map and find how far Bayer Labs is from Krupp and the other armaments manufacturers that Severn would have traded with. She may have been spying on them. I think it's reasonable, Harry. I really do." Catherine sliced her ham into smaller and smaller pieces as she thought. There must be a way to find out about Anne's German affair.

It was late afternoon by the time the train pulled into Oxford station. Catherine and Harry had debated all the way home for the rest of the journey what their next course of action should be.

They started by calling Lord Rutherford once more from the train station. This time he was at home and agreed to meet them at the Eagle and Child.

* * *

He kept them waiting, however. Catherine was on her second cup of cider by the time they saw his lean figure stride into the pub. He ordered a pint and then joined them in their inglenook.

"To my knowledge, I never saw the man before in my life," he pronounced as he sat down. "I guess it was too much to hope things could be that easy."

Catherine could not believe it.

"The devil!" Harry said.

"I'm beginning to believe Dawkins was the guilty party," said Rutherford. "Then he took over the blackmail game and got himself killed."

Catherine asked, "What about Dungaree Man?"

"He may have been just what he looked like. A gardener. He wanted to ask Severn a question about the gardens."

"And the train ticket? And the clothes we found at the Cardiff station today in left luggage?"

"Hmm," said Rutherford. "Rather too much evidence to explain away, isn't there? I must be off my game."

They hadn't told Rutherford about Dean Godfrey, and Catherine hoped Harry wouldn't do it now. There was no point in ruining the poor woman's life if she was innocent. This whole thing was just a game to the viscount. He wouldn't bother about such a small matter as a woman's reputation.

"Well," said Rutherford, "Perhaps, in this case, the police have got it right. De Fontaine could have done it easily."

"That still doesn't explain Dungaree Man," insisted Catherine.

"Perhaps the bloke was a fellow Bolshie. Maybe he and De Fontaine cooked it up between them," said Rutherford.

"But what would be the motive?" Catherine asked, annoyed.

Rutherford dismissed her question with a wave of the hand. "Maybe something as simple as class warfare. 'This is a warning to you industrialists if you don't allow the unions to organize in your companies.'"

Harry intervened, "I'm afraid you're reaching now, my lord. They haven't claimed responsibility, which they'd do if your motive held up."

"Tell me about these clothes you found," said Lord Rutherford. "What made you think of looking for them in Cardiff Left Luggage?"

"It was the next logical step," said Catherine with a bit of shrug. She explained their reasoning. Then, she said, "The clothes are rather ordinary—a suit of tweeds, all labels cut out. Tall man. They would have been a perfect fit for Anderson."

"Maybe we shouldn't be so quick to discount him then," said the peer. "Maybe he wasn't a deserter, but maybe he had another reason for stabbing the fellow."

"I guess we need to dig a little more," said Catherine.

"I'll do so from my end, as well," said Rutherford.

It was late when they left the pub, but Catherine had had an idea dawn halfway through the discussion with the viscount. She had thought it would never end. She didn't want to discuss it with him.

As they drove back to her flat, she said to Harry, "We haven't properly considered Stanley Oveson. If he were being cast for a part in a Hollywood movie, his character would be the strong, devoted type. What if he became outraged by Severn's manipulation of Elizabeth? She might not even know about it. In fact, she probably wouldn't."

"I won't say that hadn't occurred to me," said Harry. "But I can't really see the man getting his hands physically bloody."

"He wore gloves!" Catherine said impatiently. "You won't be

too happy about this next bit, I'm afraid," said Catherine. "He's a Christ Church man. Old school tie."

"The devil!" Harry said. "Well, I guess that makes it easier. We have all the class books in the library. I can find him there. From there, we'll do a little background check. Stanley Oveson, here we come."

"First, we need to take these clothes to the police. Whether they like it or not, they should get Red off the hook. Dungaree man wasn't a gardener. He was real, and he dressed like a Toff in his other identity. Red would swim in these clothes."

* * *

The police were not pleased that Harry and Catherine had removed the clothing from the scene where they were found, even when they explained that the left luggage custodian had taken a fancy to them and was ready to add them to his wardrobe.

They insisted that Catherine and Harry give signed statements about where they had recovered this evidence. Performing this chore made it very late when they finally left the station.

They made plans to research Stanley Oveson the next day after services at the Christ Church Cathedral. Hearing the choir always set her up for the week ahead.

As she lay in bed after her fiancé left that night, she tried to make sense of everything they knew, but she fell asleep instead.

* * *

The choir was particularly marvelous Sunday morning. Afterward, Harry invited her to a Sunday dinner of roast beef and Yorkshire pud at Christ Church. He had put in time that morning looking for Stanley Oveson in the college year books.

"The write-up said he'd graduated with a first in Engineering in 1921," said Harry. "He's from a little village in Hampshire quite close to the Baker school where the dean attended. It's possible they knew each other during their teenage years. He may know everything about her background."

"That's interesting," said Catherine. "I think he must. Could he be her avenging angel? We have never determined how Severn found out about her past. I wonder if Elizabeth knows."

"Well, I don't think she'd welcome questions from us on the subject," Harry said. "But you're right about the avenging angel part. Considering the way he was looking at her Friday night, he's devoted. I can picture him taking Severn apart, limb by limb."

A server approached Harry. "I'm sorry to interrupt, sir, but there is an urgent telephone call for you. You can take it in the Junior Commons Room."

Alarmed, Catherine looked at Harry's face. "I guess I'll have to wait here for you. I hope it's not bad news."

"I'll come and find you after I see what this is about. You don't want to miss the trifle."

When Harry returned, his face was pale and rigid. "That was the hospital down in Hampshire. My parents were hit by another motorcar, and they are in critical condition. I've got to leave right now to go to them."

The big dinner she had eaten turned leaden in her stomach. She said, "I'm so sorry, darling. I'm coming with you. Let's go this minute."

Harry had parked his Morris in the college car park, which was a stiff walk from the Christ Church. Catherine tried to keep up with Harry as he took long strides.

Once they reached his motor, she didn't wait for him to open her door but scooted in beside him. Sunday traffic was light, and they were soon on the road going south. Harry drove fast. Terrified, Catherine held on to the seat with both hands.

Five miles out of town into the Oxfordshire countryside, he rounded a curve going fifty miles an hour . There in the road in front of him appeared a massive lorry going about a third his speed.

"Harry!" Catherine cried.

He stood on the brake. The motor kept going forward. Before Catherine could realize what was happening, they were upon the back of the lorry. She flew forward, her head crashing through the windscreen. The last thing she saw was the back of the lorry coming toward her head.

Chapter Twenty-Five

The pain in her head was so terrific, Catherine couldn't open her eyes. She tried turning away from the light that was bright even through her eyelids, but she couldn't move. Where was she? Something was squeezing her head like a vice.

Wait. Was that her mother's voice? Why couldn't she lift her eyelids?

"Catherine. Darling. You've got to wake up. You're getting married in two months." There was a pause. "Unless you change your mind again, you wretched child."

She heard her father cursing Harry. "What did he think he was doing driving so fast on a country road?"

She couldn't answer. She just wanted to go back to sleep. So, she did.

The next time she woke up, Catherine was alone. She was able to open her eyes. Blinds were closed, and she didn't recognize anything. A small light burned over the doorway. Her head hurt so badly she closed her eyes even against that small bit of illumination. She was terribly nauseous. Someone walked into the room and began fiddling with something on her arm. She heard a pumping sound and felt pressure around her bicep. Catherine opened her eyes.

"There you are," said a cheery voice. "And your blood pressure is still low, but it's coming back with the transfusion. How is the head?"

"Horrible," she croaked.

"Now that you've awakened and we know you're not sliding into a coma, we can give you some morphine for that. I've got it already to go here. It's going to go into your arm by way of this IV. You're lucky to be alive, young lady. Very, very lucky. They had to cut you out of the motorcar with a saw."

"Motorcar?" she asked. A horrible fear clutched at her heart. She almost couldn't breathe. "Harry?"

"Ah! Well, memory loss is common when you have a blow to the head. You have a concussion, I'm afraid. But your parents are here—all the way from Cornwall. You've been unconscious for over two days. You're in the Radcliffe Infirmary getting some of the best care in Britain."

Two days? She didn't even know what day it was. "Harry?" Catherine asked the nurse.

"It's in the wee hours of Wednesday morning. Can you feel the medicine helping your head?"

"Not yet," she said.

"It'll take the edge off your pain. You'll see."

Her head felt funny. She reached up and touched it but felt only stiff and itchy fabric, even on her face. Gauze. She was almost completely covered.

"Your head is bandaged," said the nurse. "You went through the windscreen on the car. But you are going to be all right, Miss Tregowyn."

Her left arm was immobilized and strangely heavy. *What happened to me? What is wrong?*

"You have a concussion, a fractured arm and some contusions on your head and face," the nurse told her. "You were very lucky, ducks."

She tried to move out of the bed, but the nurse restrained her. "You're not going anywhere. You've had a miraculous escape, but it's going to be days, weeks before you'll be back to your normal life."

"Parents?" she asked.

"Yes. And glad they will be to see you've awakened. Let me get them for you. It bears repeating. You are a very lucky woman!"

Her headache was receding a bit. But she wanted answers.

When her mother walked up to her bed, Catherine almost didn't know her. She wore no makeup, a sort of turban on her head, and there were heavy bags under her eyes.

"Thank the Lord you're awake!" she said. "They didn't know if you'd ever wake up again, darling." For one of a handful of times, she could remember, her mother was crying and kissed her on the forehead. Of course, it was covered in bandages so that Catherine couldn't feel it.

Her father went around to the other side of the bed and caressed her shoulder and unbroken arm.

"Harry? Where's Harry?"

Her mother laid a hand on her shoulder. "Harry is going to be all right, we think. He's on the men's ward. You were in a horrific motor accident. You hit the back of a lorry. It's a miracle you're still alive, darling."

"Harry?" she asked again.

"He was driving. He's still unconscious. We don't know where you were going or why, but the driver of the lorry you hit said you were in a tremendous hurry to get there."

"Harry's unconscious?" The heartbeat she could feel pounding in her head speeded up.

"He went through the windscreen, too."

"His parents?" The pain in her head was almost blinding.

"Yes," said her mother smoothing her cheek where the bandage did not cover it. "They're here. Decent people. His mother has been very helpful in letting us know what to expect. She's the one who called us about the accident. I still think it's odd that she's a doctor. Imagine! A female doctor!"

"What's wrong with Harry?" She tried to raise her hand, but it was all too hard.

"Most of your injuries are to your head, but your shoulder was dislocated, and as you can see, your arm was broken. Harry's injuries are a little more extensive, but the doctors have said both of you should have been killed," said her mother. "Is Harry normally a reckless driver?"

"No," said Catherine. Her head felt dull and foggy. "Don't remember." Everything felt futile. "Harry?" she asked again.

"Darling," her mother had turned to her father. "Go check on him, will you? Just talk to the nurse on the men's ward."

"All right," said her father. "But he's a reckless bounder."

"You have something called whiplash," her mother told her. "You were thrown back when the motor hit the lorry, and then your head whipped forward. The nurse told us it's very painful, but I expect you know that. That is why you have that neck brace on."

"Father's heart?"

"It's all right. Thank the Lord. By the time they called us, they had stabilized you with transfusions. Apparently, head wounds bleed tremendously. A coma was still a possibility, though."

She was almost asleep again by the time her father returned. "He's still unconscious, according to his mother. She would like to see you if you're up to it."

"Yes," she said.

Harry's mother came into the ward a few minutes later. "Oh, my dear! I'm so glad you are awake! You had us worried."

"Harry? Will he . . . live?"

"If he doesn't lapse into a coma. Those are caused by bleeding on the brain. He didn't hit his head as hard as you did because of the steering wheel, but he has cracked ribs and a broken collarbone. And he managed to break a leg. The damage could have been so much worse. I just can't imagine what he was thinking of to be driving that fast! The police said there aren't even any skid marks, so it looks like he didn't even try to stop before he hit the lorry."

Catherine had a glimmer of memory, and she shut her eyes against it. "Harry. Brakes. No brakes."

"No brakes? What do you mean?" her father asked.

The sides of the bed seemed to be crowding in on her. "So tired. Sleep."

* * *

The next time she woke, her parents had gone. Catherine felt something urgent pressuring her into speech. "No brakes," she said to the nurse. "No brakes."

The nurse bustled off and returned with her mother.

"Police," Catherine repeated. "No brakes."

"Your father's ringing them," Catherine's mother said.

Catherine relaxed. "No brakes," she said.

* * *

It was several days before Catherine was able to do anything but sleep on and off. The thoughts persisted, going round and round in her head until even with all the drugs in her, she hadn't been able to sleep well.

But when Saturday morning dawned, she finally felt less fuzzy and had been given the news that Dot was on her way.

Before Dot arrived, Catherine had a visit from DCI Kerry.

"The nurses said you were cogent," he said. "I have some information. This was no accident," he said. "This must be connected with the poking around you and your fiancé have been doing. We're dealing with an uncommonly clever and vicious individual. I'm putting a constable outside your wards.

"I've examined the clothing you retrieved. Very impressive. My men have gone down to interview the Left Luggage bloke and take his statement. Has there been anything new you've stirred up since last we talked?"

She told him about the drinks party.

"What happened there? It sounds like something from Agatha Christie."

"We didn't learn anything startling. I suppose if we ever find the murderer and he fit the clothes, that would be another strike against him. But at this point, I don't know why someone would try to kill us."

Since the ruse to trap Dr. Anderson had failed, she didn't mention it. Nor did she confess what she had found out about Dean Godfrey.

Fortunately, DCI Kerry couldn't see much of her face, so it was easy to keep these two things from him. She only hoped Harry would do the same when he regained consciousness. *If* he regained consciousness.

Her torturous worry over Harry superseded all Catherine's pain and discomfort. Her love for him had laid her open to fears she had never felt before. So much of her life intertwined with her fiancé's, she thought that a great piece of Catherine Tregowyn would languish and die if Harry were to die.

Dot was a welcome sight. "Darling, I've been in Yorkshire for my job. I didn't know. I rang your flat this morning, and Cherry told me about the smash-up."

The first thing she asked Dot was if she could check on Harry to see if he had awakened. While she was gone, her mother arrived. "Darling, I'm so glad to see you're awake. How is the pain?"

"My head hurts," she said.

"I brought you some croissants this morning. The rolls here are like stones."

"Thanks. How's Father?"

"Your father has gone to the police station this morning to check on their progress. They found out somebody cut your brake lines. He's checking to see how they're coming on the investigation. He's out for blood."

Dot returned. "Harry's still unconscious," she said. "I met his mother. She's a lovely woman."

"Hello, Dot," said Catherine's mother. Catherine read disapproval in her mother's eyes. Was there something they weren't telling her?

"What's wrong with Harry?" she asked.

"His injuries were a little more extensive than yours, darling. But there isn't anything to indicate he's not going to wake up," her mother said. "Do you want me to go get Dr. Bascombe to come and see you?"

"Yes, please."

When her mother left, she said to Dot, "Tell me the worst. No one will tell me."

Dot wet her lips and whispered, "He leg is rather badly smashed up. He also has head injuries and broken ribs from the steering wheel. Dr. Bascombe feels he's still unconscious because of the pain."

"Someone cut the brake lines. We hit a lorry."

"So someone *caused* your accident? They were trying to kill you!"

"Yes, I guess so. Have you got your compact, Dot? I need to see my face in the mirror."

"There's nothing to see," Dot told her. "You're wrapped up like a mummy."

At that moment, Sarah Bascombe appeared with her mother. "Dear one, I know you're worried about Harry. Don't be. All the indications are positive."

"But he's still unconscious!"

"It's probably because of the pain. I'm convinced men don't deal with pain as well as women do."

At that moment, the nurse interrupted and sent her visitors out to the lounge.

"You're to have a bed bath this morning, and I need to change your bandages."

* * *

Dot stayed during the day, allowing her mother to get a bit of sleep in Catherine's flat. Her father returned to say that the police had come up with naught. Catherine's memory of the case began to return and with it the realization that someone was trying to kill them and had nearly succeeded.

She longed to see Harry, though he was unconscious. His mother soothed her. His father sat in the visitor's lounge along with her father, apparently taking turns cursing the ineptitude of the police.

While she was eating her luncheon—a repulsive Salisbury steak—Dean Godfrey appeared, her eyes cloudy with worry.

"My dear, I am so sorry for this. What a wretched thing! Is Dr. Bascombe conscious yet?"

"I don't know," replied Catherine, trying for a bit of stoicism. "His mother seems to think he will recover any time. She's a doctor. Who could have done this?"

"Don't you have any idea?"

"It's fairly obvious that it's connected to our investigation of the earl's death," Catherine said.

"I suppose so. They're sure it wasn't an accident?" The dean looked like she hadn't slept. Her eyes were red-rimmed and looked almost bruised underneath.

"At least you are alive!" said the Dean.

"I am, but what about Harry?" Catherine's eyes filled with tears.

"Oh, I'm sure he'll come about! He has to!" the woman's voice was high, and she brought a handkerchief to her eyes. It occurred to Catherine that Dean Elizabeth Godfrey was terrified.

"What's happening with my tutorials?" Catherine asked.

"I thought maybe you could give me the reading assignments, at least. So they can keep up. We've organized some of the other tutors to cover your tutorials."

"I appreciate that. They have a syllabus with all the assignments through the end of the term. I hate to miss them," Catherine said.

"I know you'll return as soon as you can. You're a fighter."

Catherine's heart felt heavy as she thought about Harry. Would he come about?

Chapter Twenty-Six

Dot returned to her bedside as soon as the dean had left. "Poor woman," her friend said. "She is really broken up."

"The reason isn't far to seek. She's afraid Stan did it."

"Stan?"

"Her beloved Mr. Oveson. She must think we were on the point of having him arrested for the earl's murder."

"Were you?" Dot asked, sitting up straight.

Catherine sighed. Everything seemed to hurt in her, including her heart. "He's a suspect. The dean has secrets he's trying to protect. Or maybe he thinks the dean did the murder, and we're about to arrest her."

"The dean!" Dot's eyes were round with shock.

"I know it seems far-fetched, but the earl was blackmailing her." Catherine felt horribly weary.

From her purse, Dot whisked out a little crochet envelope. From it, she pulled a crochet-edged handkerchief. "Lavender," she said, handing the cloth to her friend. "I'm developing a line of sachets. Lavender is supposed to calm you."

Catherine put it to her nose and breathed the pungent scent.

At that moment, Sarah Bascombe showed up pushing a wheelchair. "Harry's come round!" she announced. "He wishes to see you! Let me take you quickly before the nurses catch me! They're having their tea."

Catherine was very weak, but Dot helped her into the chair and covered her with blankets. She began wheeling her friend while Sarah led the way.

Harry was bandaged in the same way Catherine was, but she could never mistake those eyes. "Darling!" she whispered hoarsely. "You had me worried. Thank the Lord you're awake! Now we can start figuring out who did this!"

"Is that really you, Cath?" he said, his voice scratchy and thin.

"It is. We both look like we've escaped from an Egyptian museum!"

With her right hand, she grasped hold of his right hand and brought it to her lips. "James will be so pleased you are well. He was quite worried about you."

"So mother says. He's been to see me every day."

Catherine realized the weight had freed itself from her chest and disappeared. "I only have a minute before the nurse sees me. Standing with Dot's help, she stretched over the bed rail and kissed Harry on the lips. "Welcome back, Harold Morris Bascombe, Jr.!"

"Uh oh," said Sarah. "Here come the nurses. We'd best be on our way!"

On a whim, Catherine pressed her lavender-scented handkerchief into Harry's hand. "I love you!" she whispered, just before Dot whisked her off down the lane between beds in the men's ward.

She received a half-hearted scold from the nurse in passing, but Catherine just grinned.

To her great surprise, just before dinnertime, her nurse told Catherine she had a male visitor in the visitor's lounge and asked her if she could manage another trip in the wheelchair.

"Do you know who it is?"

"Viscount Rutherford. He says it's urgent."

Her pulse quickened. He must have news about the investigation. "All right. Have you prepared him for how I look?"

"Yes. He's most agitated."

When Catherine was wheeled into the patient's lounge, she saw Harry's neighbor dressed in a bottle green jacket and looking very fine. He registered shock at her appearance.

"My dear girl!" he pronounced.

"Yes. I know it's bad," she said. "But you are looking fit!"

"How's Harry?"

"He just regained consciousness. He had me scared. He's jolly well banged up, but nothing that can't be mended. We were very lucky, they tell us. Our brake lines were cut."

"My dear girl!" he repeated. "Have the police been told?"

"Yes. But I haven't much faith in them, unfortunately."

"Well, I've come to tell you that I'm concerned about Anne. Apparently, according to her maid, she's disappeared. "Gladys hasn't seen or heard from her since the day of the accident."

Catherine felt bowled over with astonishment. "Anne? Why would she disappear?"

"I only hope she wasn't in any way concerned in your accident. I stopped in at James's work. They're separated, you know."

"Did he know anything?" Catherine asked.

"No. She hasn't been in touch with him."

"Do you have any idea where she would go?" Catherine could hardly take in the information.

"She has her own money. I set up a trust for her when she was married. I suppose she could be anywhere. Even outside the country."

"I hope she's all right," said Catherine. Her head pounded as she tried to comprehend what he was saying. He was obviously agitated, holding his hat by the brim and circling it around with his fingers.

Through her anxiety for Anne, a thought teased her but wouldn't come through her brain fog. "Oliver Anderson," she said finally. "Has she possibly gone away with him?"

"Anderson? Why on earth would you say that?" The viscount's brow contorted. "Though it is odd now that you mention it. He has disappeared as well."

The drinks party at her flat two nights before they were injured came back into focus. She had expected Dr. Anderson to take flight, but not Anne.

"Has she ever told you that she was spying for Churchill while she was in Germany?"

"What a preposterous idea! Why do you say that?" Rutherford asked.

"Anderson told me. He met her down at Chartwell one day. They were both being debriefed."

"How absurd. The chap must have been telling tales to make himself appear important. Who could he possibly be spying on?"

"I don't know," she prevaricated.

"Well, it all sounds a bit suspicious to me. Anne, a spy? Who would she spy on? She's a little nobody. Especially in Germany. She didn't even speak the language."

His contempt for his daughter was obvious. Though Catherine was certainly not fond of Anne, she found herself feeling sorry for her.

"Well, I'm sorry, Lord Rutherford, I have no idea what has become of Anne. Maybe she's afraid of the murderer for some reason. Or she just might be trying to teach Harry or James a lesson."

"Or she might be the murderer after all," said the man darkly. "Though I hope that's not the case. She's my daughter, after all."

As the details of the case came slowly back to her, she was bound to agree that things weren't looking very bright for Anne or Oliver Anderson. But she couldn't stand this cold-blooded man another second.

"I'm afraid I'm feeling quite dreadful, Lord Rutherford. Please ring the bell for the nurse. I may faint."

Her nurse arrived, all a-flutter. "I suppose you've had too much," she said. "Heaven knows I don't wish you ill, but you mustn't try to do too much too soon."

* * *

Dot left while she ate dinner and returned afterward with more gifts. She brought some of her lavender lotion and talcum powder. "This'll make you feel fresher. I don't know about you, but I can't stand the smell of hospitals."

Catherine told Dot about Anne's disappearance.

"She probably knows nothing about the accident and thinks she's making herself more interesting to Harry or James," Dot said.

"We've definitely been friends for too long. That's exactly what I told her father."

"Or, maybe she's the murderer, after all. Have you thought of that, love?"

"Her father certainly has. I thought at first that he was like my father, but you know what? He's worse."

"Oh, you're father's coming on. He's here, isn't he?"

"Speaking of parents, they're sleeping in my flat. That leaves you out in the cold."

Dot preened herself. "I'm already booked into the Randolph for the night. Thought I'd treat myself to make you wildly jealous."

"I'd settle for an old-fashioned coaching inn with a privy compared to this place," Catherine said. "Thank you so much for coming. You've done me a world of good. Especially now that Harry's come round."

* * *

Sunday was Catherine's best day yet. She could feel her strength returning and managed to visit Harry during visiting hours that afternoon after Dot had left for London. She told him about Anne's disappearance and her father's disdain of her.

"I, on the other hand, can believe Anne was a top-notch spy," he said. "She's more devious than a barrel full of snakes. But you'd best let James know."

"I shall if you think that's the right thing to do."

"Have the police made any headway on our phony accident?"

"They haven't taken me into their confidence, but I doubt it."

By that evening, she was ready to look in a mirror. All she saw were white bandages covering her head and two black eyes. Looking a bit closer, she saw a thin line of stitching down the side of her head near the ear down to the jaw.

* * *

Early that evening, her nurse notified her future brother-in-law would like to visit her in the patient's lounge. *James*? Oh, yes.

She told her nurse she would see him. Sitting in her wheelchair, she was covered with blankets when she was wheeled into the patient's lounge. James stood up when she entered. She thought he looked better than he had since she'd met him, even with the worry stamped on his features.

"It's good to see you, James," she said.

"Oh, I say, Catherine, are you in pain?"

"Just a headache. Everything else is much better now. Harry got the worst of it."

"I'm sorry to tell you that none of our friends have seen Anne. I haven't the faintest notion where she has gone."

"You didn't need to come to the hospital to tell me that," she said.

He finally sat down. "I wanted to finish telling you what I started to tell you at your flat. At the drinks party. It might give you more of an idea of what Anne is like these days. Harry doesn't really know what she is like anymore. He still sees her as he did when they were undergraduates. He has a somewhat idealized perception of her."

"I think he has gotten somewhat wiser in that department lately. We have patched things up between us," said Catherine.

"I'm glad. The fact is, Anne changed a lot while we lived in Germany. I'm probably at fault there. My work consumed me. But it's like the chicken and the egg. Which came first: her not being home at night or me working late? At any rate, not one to be idle, she began to mix with the wives of the Germans I worked with. She learned the language very well during the years we were there."

He paused, stood, and walked around the room. "The fact is, she was soon mixing in circles I knew nothing about. We weren't that far from some of the factories that manufactured weaponry. It horrified Anne the number of weapons they were selling to the Nazi party and then the government when they were in power. She got the idea to 'infiltrate' the circle of Nazis within the Krupp factory."

"How dangerous!"

"It was, and I knew nothing about it. Unfortunately, they were an immoral bunch. She began to dispense sexual favors to the Nazis who were closest to Hitler. She was appalled by what she found out.

"She quite openly shared what she found out with Churchill by sending letters to Chartwell."

"And they found her out?" Catherine couldn't imagine doing anything so brave and so heedless of her own danger.

"It was inevitable. Anne took no precautions. And her friends were wives of these men. One of the wives was jealous of her husband's attentions to Anne, as you can well imagine. She began to follow her. Eventually, she stole Anne's correspondence out of her handbag. When Anne noticed, she was frightened for her life.

"She came to me and laid it all out. I took emergency leave from Bayer and got her out of the country that very night. We left everything behind and came here to Oxford.

"What you cannot imagine is how betrayed I felt. Finding out that she had fallen pregnant only made it worse. But I worked and worked and tried to forget. She had become addicted to danger. I have the feeling that Earl Severn found out from his friends at Krupp, who were quite good customers of his, what she had done. I think he held it over her head and threatened that she publicly withdraw from her anti-fascist tirade or he was going to publish in the *Times* what a slut she was. So, she killed him."

Catherine felt as though her insides had turned to a seething mass of anger. This was the woman she and Harry had been protecting with their murder investigation? Had it been Anne who tried to kill them, and when she failed, had she run off to who knows where?

"You think Anne tried to kill Harry and me?"

"I do."

Catherine raised her chin. "I am very glad you left her, James. She isn't a good person."

"She isn't."

"You must go to the police, James."

"I can't do it. I am a coward. All I can think of is what it would do to my career, my future, everything I have worked for. Sulfa will change the course of medicine. It will save millions of lives when the war comes. And it will come. That much I learned from Anne. She learned Hitler's whole blueprint. But then, anyone can read it in his book: *Mein Kampf.*"

Catherine was ill. Her scalp prickled, an angry flush of heat spread from her chest down to her belly.

"James, I'm going to be sick." She managed to get to her feet and stagger into the visitor's cloakroom, where she vomited into the sink. Sinking to the floor, she shook all over and broke out in a cold sweat. James threw open the door.

"I'm so sorry. How horribly selfish of me." He had wheeled her chair to the door, and he helped her back into it, piling the blanket on top of her trembling body. Then he wheeled her back to the ward.

"Tell Harry," she said. "Tell Harry right now."

The nurse took one look at Catherine and rushed to her aid. "I just need to get to bed. So silly of me. I was sick in the cloakroom. Did too much today."

Chapter Twenty-Seven

Catherine couldn't sleep. She could only go over James's story, again and again, to experience over and over the horrible truths he had told her. Anne had betrayed her husband, her father, and had tried to kill her and Harry. But what about Dungaree Man? No wonder Anne had wanted them to pursue those false clues. She still couldn't figure out where the train ticket came from, who the clothes in the Left Luggage suitcase belonged to.

Had Anne killed Dawkins as well? No, wait! Anne was in jail when Dawkins was murdered. Who had killed Dawkins?

Then there was the whole issue of Nazi rearmament and determination to go to war. How could Catherine live in such a world? How could Hitler and his Nazis do that to Europe again?

She needed to talk to Harry worse than she'd ever needed anything.

When morning came, she hadn't slept at all. Her bandages were removed to reveal that she had places on her head where clumps of hair had been shaven to stitch up the scars on her scalp. There were scars on her face, too. She barely glanced at them, and couldn't bring herself to care.

"You are tremendously fortunate," the nurse told her. "There is a superbly gifted surgeon here at the Radcliffe. He does facial reconstruction after accidents or birth defects. You will eventually only have thin white lines which you can cover with makeup."

She was so listless and non-communicative, the nurse told her mother, "I'm afraid she's fallen into a dark melancholy. It sometimes happens a week after something this catastrophic. The night nurse said she was vomiting, had chills, and was shaking all night. I'm going to give her a sedative. Maybe she'll be better after some good sleep."

She just stared at the wall as the nurse tended to her. Afterward, she did feel herself falling into a void of senseless sleep. She didn't wake up until Tuesday morning.

Harry sent her a written message via a young orderly.

> *Darling Cath,*
>
> *I am desolated that you have fallen ill. James's story was hard to hear, and it is difficult to know what course to take. Unfortunately, the DCI is coming on Tuesday Morning at 10:00, and we are to meet him in the Patient's Lounge. Why don't you leave it to me to answer his questions? I can only pray that I will know what to say. This is so difficult—I don't even know what to say to my parents.*
>
> *All my love,*
> *Harry*

Harry looked much better than he had any right to. Seated in the wheelchair with his leg stretched out and rested on a special footrest, he sat straight up as he was bound tightly around his ribs. His scars were worse than hers but still didn't mar his charismatic air. Just seeing him did her a world of good. She smiled.

"I'm afraid I have some very bad news," the DCI said. "Professor Oliver Anderson has disappeared. No one has seen him since your crash. Is there any way you can tell me that these two things are connected? Is there someone who wanted both of you dead?"

Catherine's heart dropped. She opened her mouth to reply when the DCI put up a hand to stop her and said, "Before you speak, I want you to realize that I know you have been keeping things from me. I want everything you know or even suspect. This minute! Detective Sergeant Paul is taking notes." He indicated the unobtrusive man in uniform.

Harry said, "I think you may find that he's gone back to France. We suspect he may be a deserter from the War. It is probably nothing to do with what happened to Catherine and me."

"What gave you the idea that he's a deserter?" asked the DCI.

"He stayed in France after the war and never came back to England until three years ago when his French wife died." Harry tried to look contrite and failed. "We thought the Earl of Severn might have been blackmailing him. We suspected him of the earl's murder."

"And just how would Severn have known he was a deserter?" The DCI's voice held notes of impatience coupled with menace.

"We figured out he was in Severn's regiment from something he said. But we had no proof. Lord Rutherford thought he might recognize him from his company, but it turned out he couldn't."

"Hmph. And what else have you been up to?"

Harry hesitated. "I don't really think it amounts to much," he said finally.

"Let me be the judge of that."

"It would be terrible if it became common knowledge," he temporized.

"Tell. Me."

"Well, there were three people who knew Anne Bascombe was going to be seeing the Earl of Severn the afternoon he was murdered. They were in a meeting together—Mr. De Fontaine, Dean Godfrey, and Professor Anderson."

"Go on."

"I already told you that we eliminated Mr. De Fontaine because he wasn't the right height for Dungaree Man. Professor Anderson was the right height."

"And Dean Godfrey? I suppose you thought she got herself up to look like a man and turned herself into a murdering harpy for no reason?"

"That's the thing. She had reason. She told me Severn was blackmailing her. Under duress, she set up a speaking engagement for the earl with the Somerville women. Were the earl not murdered, it would have been last Sunday."

"Did you find out why she was being blackmailed?" The menace was back in the policeman's voice.

Catherine moistened her lips. "She didn't tell us, but we found out. That is the part that can't come out."

"Miss Tregowyn, unless it proves relevant to the prosecutor, it won't come out."

Catherine took a deep breath. She supposed that the dean would be guilty in that case, and it would need to come out. "Well, we found out that back in 1915, when Dean Godfrey was only twelve, there was a terrible tragedy. Her father, Dr. DeFurrier of King's College, Cambridge, shot and killed his wife and himself. In front of his children. Dean Godfrey ran off before the police arrived and somehow made her way to her aunt's house. She probably rang her, and her aunt came to get her."

The DCI's face remained a bland mask. Catherine forced herself to go on. "She changed her name and was brought up with her aunt's children. They gave out that she was an orphan from New Zealand. If people knew her father was a vicious killer and completely unbalanced, she would never be able to hold a position of trust such as the one she has earned at Somerville. The current thinking is that these things may be hereditary. You know the saying: The apple doesn't fall far from the tree."

"How on earth did Severn ever find this out?"

"I think only Dean Godfrey knows the answer to that. She doesn't know that I know who she is. She has worked very hard to achieve her position at Oxford. What happened when she was a child was in no way her fault, and I don't think she should be punished for it. I speculate that Severn knew the family, and there is a strong family resemblance."

"And Dungaree Man?" asked the DCI.
"The dean has a man in her life. We met him. He is the right height. It's possible he could have done the deed for her. If he did, she might not even know."

"And we can't forget Dawkins," said the Detective Chief Inspector. "It sounds as though he might have had access to the secrets of his employer."

"Precisely," said Catherine.

"Well, you must be on to something if somebody almost killed you. You must have made the murderer feel very threatened. I'm tempted to keep you in the hospital until we wrap this thing up. What's Dean Godfrey's man friend's name?"

"Stanley Oveson. He's an engineer at the Severn precision tool works."

"Hmm. Interesting. I think I'll have him in for questioning. When are you supposed to be out of the hospital?"

"Apparently, I am now out of danger. It's just a matter of getting my strength back," she said.

"Well, I'll have a word with the doctor. This is the safest place for both of you."

"But I have classes to teach!" she protested.

"You can't teach them if you're dead," the DCI said.

CHAPTER TWENTY-EIGHT

Catherine and Harry stayed in the lounge after the DCI left.

Harry said, "I think it's best if we keep on going until everyone but Anne is eliminated. Only then will we know for sure. It's not Anne I'm thinking of. It's James. He's right to be concerned about his career and the importance of his work."

Catherine gulped. After thirty-six hours of sleep, she was better able to see that Harry's words made sense.

"I wonder if Anderson is our killer. Do you suppose he could have tampered with my brakes and then made a run for it?"

"It makes more sense than anything else," said Catherine. Harry looked so good to her. She put a gentle hand up to his cheek. "How are your ribs, darling? You look positively wonderful. It's not fair because I am a hag."

"You could never be a hag. Your hair will grow, and the scars will fade. I love your spirit, Cath. Right now, it is very troubled, and that bothers me. Tell me what I can do."

"You're doing it. Just being you, so I know there's at least one sane man in the world."

"I am trying to take it easy on the morphine. A fellow can get dependent on that stuff, and it's going to be a while before my ribs are healed."

"You are terrifically brave." She kissed his cheek. "If Anderson did the murders, committing two more in such a roundabout way wouldn't seem worse than playing skittles, I imagine," said Catherine. "Harry, darling, I'm so glad we weren't killed. We should have been. Why would Anderson have wanted to kill us?"

"Perhaps he thought we were onto him. You know, it really surprised me when Rutherford didn't identify him as a deserter. I could have sworn they knew each other. Dr. Anderson looked afraid of Rutherford."

"I agree. And there's one thing that doesn't make sense. If he was going to hop it to France, why would he try to kill us? In France, knowing it as well as he must, he would be beyond our reach. It just doesn't feel right to me. Maybe whoever has done these awful things is someone we haven't even thought of yet. A disgruntled workman or some madman from the House of Commons."

"It does seem pretty futile, doesn't it? But someone like that would have no reason to kill us because all we've done is fail."

Lord Rutherford chose that moment to enter the patient's lounge.

"What ho, mates!" he said. He sat down on a chair he pulled over to sit across from where they were on the sofa. The peer kept his coat and hat in his hands as he rotated his headgear through his fingers again. It must be a nervous habit. Everything about the viscount spoke of money and privilege.

He said, "I'm ready to do a séance and call forth the ghost of Conan Doyle to give us a bit of help here! We've got to stop this fellow."

"We were hoping you would have it all figured out," said Catherine.

"Severn seems to have been blackmailing half of Britain. What do you suppose has happened to Anderson? My money's on him for the murder. I couldn't identify him as a deserter, but suppose Severn did?"

He sat forward in his chair. Something teased the edge of

Catherine's consciousness, but then Harry gave a soft curse as he tried to move without jarring his ribs, and she lost the thought.

"Darling," she interrupted, speaking to her fiancé. "I can tell you're in pain." She turned to the viscount as she pushed the call button next to her. "We must get Harry back to his bed. Thank you for your visit. I'm afraid you shall have to crusade along on your own. Our detecting days are done for the time being."

She squeezed Harry's hand. "Too right," he said. "It'll likely be a month before I'm back on my feet. Still, mustn't complain. They've been good to us here."

The nurse showed up in answer to the bell Catherine had rung.

"We're ready to go back. I'm afraid Dr. Bascombe has over-tired himself."

Rutherford realized he'd been dismissed. Standing up, he offered his hand to Harry. "Sorry about the accident, old boy. I hope you haven't overtired yourself. Trust me to run on." He bowed his head at Catherine. "I hope you will both recover soon."

The viscount walked out of the patient's lounge and down the stairs. Catherine breathed a sigh. She followed the nurse who wheeled Harry to his bed and helped him settle there.

"I'll just stay and visit him for a little while longer," she told the woman.

When the nurse was out of earshot, she said, "I can only take so much of Lord Rutherford. He was so nervy and upbeat."

"Is that why you were so anxious for him to leave?"

"His good spirits rubbed me the wrong way. The other day he was worried about Anne's disappearance. Now he doesn't have a thought to spare about her. He only cares about solving this mystery."

Harry grimaced in pain but said, "Rutherford could be right. Even though he didn't recognize Anderson, Severn might have done. The more I think of it, the more I'm close to believing Anderson did put my brakes out of commission."

"He could have. Either him, Oveson, or Anne," said Catherine. "But you are in pain, darling. Enough of this."

"One of them put me in this damned cast? Who was it?"

She leaned forward and kissed his forehead. "Don't bother with it now. We have a long way to go to prove anything. Get your rest, and we'll talk later."

* * *

A new nurse was on duty that afternoon. She confided in Catherine, "Your accident was in *News of the World*. The article said you were helping the police with their inquiries into the Earl of Severn's murder."

Catherine groaned. "Won't that just please the Detective Chief Inspector!"

"I've read about you and Dr. Bascombe. This is the fifth murder you've worked out. I'll do anything I can to help."

"Is there a telephone here I could use?"

"There is one in matron's office. You could use it when she goes to lunch. But you'd have to be quick about it."

"I shall be, I promise. I wouldn't want to get you in trouble."

Catherine's mother arrived, saying, "I can't see your face, Catherine, but I just have the feeling you're hatching a plot. There's an air about you. How is Harry today?"

"He's not doing as well as I am, poor lamb. Cracked ribs are miserable. Would you mind awfully going to Blackwell's and asking for the latest popular mystery? Something by Marsh, Sayers, or Allingham, I think. Maybe all three. He needs a diversion, and he loves mysteries."

"Of course. Would you like me to pick up something for you while I'm there?"

"*News of the World*. You and Father aren't going to be happy, but apparently we've made the newspapers again."

"I don't care." Her mother was not at all a demonstrative woman, but to Catherine's surprise she reached over and squeezed one of Catherine's hands. "I'm so sorry about your face and your hair, darling. But I'm so very glad you're still alive."

"Is my face bad?" Catherine asked, biting her lip.

"You're just lucky you were near the Radcliffe Infirmary. They have the very best man for injuries like yours. You have over a hundred little, tiny stitches. He promised me you would have little to no scarring after you've had time to heal. And, of course, your hair will grow back. You can imitate Veronica Lake with your hair hanging over that side of your face."

"You must be joking, Mother! A Somerville tutor could never get away with imitating a movie star!"

"Seriously, dear, you must give up this detecting business. I appreciate that it's a diverting challenge, but you're not a cat. You don't have nine lives." Her mother gave a little shrug. "One of these days, I suppose there *will* be an end to relatives who end up in jail."

"One can only hope. I have my doctoral dissertation to write. And Harry and I must find a new home here in Oxford."

At that moment, her nurse came to take her vital signs. She said, "All signs are good. You've made wonderful progress, miss."

"I'm getting anxious to leave here, but I don't feel like I can leave Harry behind," Catherine said after the nurse left.

"Poor fellow," the baroness said. "He seems to be bearing up as well as he can, but it's easy to see he's in terrible pain."

"He's a brick," said Catherine. "I wonder . . . do you suppose we could hire a hospital bed and have it put in my sitting room? We could also arrange for a nurse to come and check on him."

Her mother was apparently giving it some thought when the new nurse came to check Catherine's vitals.

"Do you ever release patients to their homes if their families have the means to take care of them?" Catherine asked.

"Sometimes. But you'd have to talk to Dr. Stevens, miss. He's on the men's ward at the moment. I can ask him to come round and speak to you when he's finished."

* * *

By the end of the following day, all had been arranged so that Harry could be released at the same time as Catherine. A nurse from an independent agency had been hired to come in twice a day, as well as being on call, and a hospital bed arranged for. Dr. Stevens would call on Harry at Catherine's flat once in the morning and once in the evening.

"It will do his spirits good to heal at home," he said. "Whatever its virtues, the hospital is not designed to be cheerful. I know he is discouraged and it's not helping his pain. It's my opinion that he misses you, Miss Tregowyn."

After the doctor had departed, her mother sighed and said, "I can see why you want to do this, and I also think it would be the best thing for Harry's recovery, but I can't allow you to be alone with him in your flat. I shall also have to stay with you for the duration. Though I'm sure you don't relish the idea."

Catherine smiled at her mother. Not long ago at all, she would never have expected such an offer. "On the contrary. It will be a bit crowded with us sharing my bed and Harry's hospital bed taking up the sitting room, but I would be happy to have you."

"All right then. I suppose the next thing to do is to get Harry's mother on our side."

Catherine smiled. "I am sure she will think it the best thing for Harry's spirits."

And so it proved. Dr. Bascombe had taken a holiday from her practice in Hampshire while Harry was in hospital.

She visited Catherine after seeing Harry that afternoon and learning of the arrangements.

"This will do wonders for him; I think we'll find. He is going to have to negotiate the crutches, however, so he can get back and forth to the WC. That won't be pleasant given the pain in his ribs, but it will be good for him to have some independence."

Chapter Twenty-Nine

Sarah Bascombe arranged for them to all have tea in the patient's sitting room that afternoon.

Harry was in tearing spirits. "Apparently, we're both to be released tomorrow! I couldn't be more chuffed!"

"I had to do something to keep you out of trouble," said Catherine with a grin. "I couldn't have you falling into the designing clutches of one of these nurses, you know."

"Huh!" he said.

"I have arranged to stay with James for another week," said his mother. "He has returned to his work and taken a small flat near the Oxford canal."

Harry sobered. "Has he spoken to you about Anne, Mother?"

"No. And I think it's best to let sleeping dogs lie," Harry said

"She'd been staying at our house in Hampshire since she walked out on James. No one knews she was there since my parents are here. I got a telephone call this morning from her. She told me she was ringing from the hospital and she has lost the baby. I couldn't help feeling she was happy about it. But maybe it is for the best."

Catherine was very glad for the child Anne lost. How would it be to come into the world with a murderess for a mother and a Nazi for a father? She didn't think that under the circumstances James had any intention of accepting the child as his.

"She will bounce back. She is quite worried at the moment

about her friend, Dr. Anderson," said Sarah Bascombe, "Apparently, he has gone missing, and she's afraid he may have been murdered." "Hmm," said Catherine. "The thought never occurred to me. I assumed he had disappeared because he was guilty of desertion or murder or both."

* * *

Harry's large hospital bed dwarfed the sitting room, just as Catherine had thought it would.

"You are like one of those Arabian princes, reclining on your couch as you receive your women."

He laughed. "I just need jewels on my fingers," Harry said. "Truly, I'm sorry to invade your place like this."

She kissed his forehead. "It's much better than having you in hospital. Did your ribs make the journey all right?"

Though his face was white with pain, he gave her a thumbs-up sign. "You'll have me better in a trice. And your mother has pur-chased me all these delicious mysteries. Just the thing."

Cherry brought them a light meal of cold chicken, tomatoes, and dinner rolls which she had made for the first time. They proved to be a bit heavy, but Catherine congratulated her. It hadn't occurred to her that they were overburdening Cherry. Her skills in the kitchen were sketchy at best.

After lunch, Catherine settled at her desk to go through her accumulated mail. There was a letter from her publisher with get-well wishes, bills, invitations for events already passed, and a thick letter in an unfamiliar hand. It was postmarked from Paris. There was no return address. Catherine opened it with her paper knife.

October 20, 1935

Dear Miss Tregowyn and Dr. Bascombe,

I am afraid I left England precipitously because I realized my life could be in danger. It is no good trying to find me. I shall slip back into my identity in an obscure village here in France. However, I have gone to the trouble of having the letter notarized, in the hope that it could be used as evidence in court, if necessary.

I realized for the first time at your drinks party that I may hold the key to your investigation into the murder of Lord Severn. I imagine he came upon the same information I have in some other manner. It lies with you to make that connection.

During the time I lived in France following the War, I was in a small village where I did not receive news from England. So it wasn't until my return three years ago that I learned the fate of many of my brothers-in-arms. Most of the ones who lived through the War, attempted to take up their former occupations. But for one man, the War provided a perfect vehicle for him to change his life and his circumstances completely. I looked into his face the other night at your drinks party, and I'm afraid I let my astonishment show. Once he recognized me, I knew he was the killer you are looking for. Unfortunately, I knew other things which put my own life in danger. I'm afraid I haven't had much practice in hiding my feelings, and I gave myself away.

The following day I spent in the Bodleian Library among the Times newspaper archives. I learned how my old commanding officer, Major Stapleton, had come to be the Lord Rutherford I was introduced to at your party.

He was awarded a life peerage and the Victoria Cross by King George V for "glorious valor in the execution of heroic deeds which saved the lives of thousands and altered the course of the war."

That credit was stolen from my deceased comrade, Private Billy Baldwin. I was a witness to Baldwin's heroic actions the night of his death. He crossed No Man's Land that night, creeping from mortar hole to mortar hole, crawling between them flat on his belly.

When he got to the German lines, he found a deep crater right next to the trenches. He hid as long as he dared and listened to the urgent conversation and the movement of tanks and artillery right up to the front lines. My friend, the private, had a German mother and was completely fluent in the language. I was his lieutenant and told him his plan was certain death. He said, "We're all going to die anyway. I might as well do some good."

Baldwin learned of an all-out attack that was to take place the next night from that position. The private heard that the German generals knew the British lines to be poorly fortified at that point . Their goal was to force annihilation or surrender of thousands of men up and down the mile-long line of trenches. This would have given them a stronghold so complete they could have moved the German battlelines forward by many miles before the British could have reassembled on their flanks. It would have been a mortal blow to the British, as well as a moral victory. The battlelines had been fixed for months. The act was meant to vitalize the German army at a time when spirits were low, right before the intervention of America which eventually changed the course of the war.

How was it stopped? Private Baldwin was able to escape back along the way he had come, partially because the Germans were so preoccupied with their plan. He got back in time to tell me what the Germans had in store for us. I took him to our senior officer Major Stapleton. The major sent a dispatch at once to the right men who wasted no time in moving in tanks and artillery to our position, where they immediately engaged the enemy in a heavy preemptive attack which succeeded in wiping out the enemy's position that very night.

It was a fierce and horrible battle. Both Billy and I were severely wounded in the night's battle. We ended up next to each other in a makeshift hospital behind the lines. I pulled through. He didn't.

My nerves were shattered with what we now know to be shellshock. I decided the war was over for me and I couldn't go back. When I was well enough, I escaped the hospital and was taken in by a French family a good way behind the lines who had lost their own son in the war. I never went back. I married their daughter and stayed in France for the next 17 years.

When I came back to England, three years ago, I learned that a Viscount by the name of Rutherford had appropriated my friend's heroism. But I was still sick of war. It brought back all my mental anguish; I didn't pursue it. However when I met the usurper in your sitting room and realized Rutherford was none other than Major Stapleton, our commanding officer I was shocked. I could tell he recognized me. I dearly hope that you will be able to bring this crime home to Stapleton.

Yours truly,
Lieutenant Henry Weller aka Oliver Anderson

Catherine's hands began to shake. "Harry, darling. You must read this. It is shocking."

She passed the letter to him. When he had read it through, he whistled. "I have never liked Rutherford. He's excessively full of himself."

"I must send take this to the police immediately."

"You're not well enough. You had best ring them and have DS Paul come here to pick it up."

"You know there was something that bothered me the last time we saw him," she said, before she picked up the telephone. "I wish I could remember what it was."

When the detective sergeant came on the line, she said, "I just received a letter from Dr. Anderson who is in hiding in France. He has some information you need to see. It could go a long way toward solving our case. Could you please come to get it? We're at my flat. I'm afraid I'm still not in any condition to bring it in."

"I have Lord Rutherford with me, at the moment. I'll come when I can," the Detective Sergeant said.

Catherine knew a moment of alarm. He in particular must not know about the letter.

"Please don't speak of this to anyone. It's very sensitive information."

"I don't need you to tell me my job, Miss Tregowyn."

When she rang off, Catherine was troubled. "I should have gone there in a cab!" she told Harry. "I have a horrible feeling."

"Perhaps you should do something with the letter. I was able to hear your whole conversation on the telephone," said Harry. "Rutherford would probably have been able to hear your side of the conversation, as well."

Catherine took the letter and the envelope and went into the kitchen. Her eyes searched the room. Where should she hide it? Cherry had heard their conversation and was watching her.

"How about the oven, miss?"

"Perfect!" Catherine slid the important evidence into the cold oven, hiding it further by placing it underneath a pan.

"Our story is that we sent it to the police already by messenger," said Catherine.

"We are probably getting all fussed about nothing," Harry said. "But better safe than sorry."

It wasn't very long before there was a knock at the door. Cherry went to answer it, as they had planned.

"I'm sorry," she said. "Miss Tregowyn isn't receiving visitors today."

Rutherford's familiar voice said, "The police sent me to pick up a letter." He strode past Cherry and into the sitting room. Catherine had moved quickly to Harry's side and was apparently checking his head for fever, though she was shaking from head to foot.

It would be Rutherford! I must act normally. He mustn't think there was anything in the letter about him!

"Lord Rutherford, I'm sorry, we just sent it off by messenger!"

The man paled, turned on his heel and left in an obvious hurry.

At the same moment, Catherine's mother entered the sitting room from the bedroom.

"Catherine, I've heard everything. I assume this letter he wants will compromise Lord Rutherford. Ring the police and tell them everything. I'll be your messenger. The man will never suspect me. Where is the letter?"

Catherine said, "Mother, it could be dangerous!"

"Just get me the letter. I know how to handle myself."

Catherine's heart was beating so fast she couldn't think. Harry said, "Do it, Catherine. Your mother will go completely undetected, I'll wager anything."

"It's in the oven," Catherine said. She sat down with a thump on her desk chair, her hands shaking. "Be careful, Mother."

"You just ring the police!"

Catherine bit her lip and took up the telephone.

She was put through to the DS. "Sir, Lord Rutherford was here demanding the letter! It is he who is named in it by Dr. Anderson. He is on his way back to the station. He thinks I sent it off by messenger already, but my mother just left to bring it to you. Hold Lord Rutherford or you'll never see him again, I guarantee it!"

"I can't believe the man had anything to do with the murder," said DS Paul. Catherine's jaw clenched. "Read the letter!"

She rang off.

"There's a reason that man isn't the DCI!" she told Harry.

When her mother returned after performing her potentially dangerous mission, she agreed with Catherine. "I had to go directly to the Detective Chief Inspector! The Detective Sergeant wouldn't see me!"

It wasn't until later in the day that Cherry delivered Lord Rutherford's hat to her. "He forgot he handed it to me when he came in."

The hat reminded her of what she had thought the day the viscount had come to see them in the hospital. The hatmaker's name was in it. And it was twin to the hat the police now had that was taken from the Left Luggage Office.

"Harry, doesn't this hat of Rutherford's look overly large?"

"It does. I wouldn't mind laying a wager that it was especially made for him." He looked at the label. "Winston's is a hatter in Bond Street."

"It's identical to the hat we found in Wales, but the tailor's label was cut out. Do you suppose the hatter could identify it as one he made for Lord Rutherford?"

"Certainly. I think the police could handle a simple little inquiry like that. It's the only thing that really ties Lord Rutherford directly to the murder."

Cherry answered the ringing telephone.

"We caught up with him at the Randolph, Miss," the DCI told her. "Getting his travel documents. Now suppose you tell me what we're charging him with. Granted, he has a huge motive, if Severn knew the truth, but we have no evidence that he did it."

"Yes, you do," Catherine told him. She explained her theory about the hat he was holding as evidence. "He was Dungaree Man. The whole thing reeks of Sherlock Holmes."

"Ah! Right you are! I'll have my too loquacious DS get up to Bond Street as soon as you ring off. But I don't suppose you have any idea how Severn managed to find out about his deception, do you?"

"Have you gone through all his papers, yet? There might be something there."

"Severn was the colonel of the regiment. I suppose he knew Rutherford well when he was a major. Maybe someone else who served under Rutherford knew the truth and went to Severn with it. There may be another letter. Possibly from another private."

"That's a good thought. I guess I can't depend on you to do all our work for us. I'm really sorry for your car smash. Rutherford was behind that, obviously."

"Yes," said Catherine, though that had only occurred to her that moment." When he realized who Dr. Anderson was, he must have known he would tell us the truth. If Dr. Anderson hadn't left for France so smartly, he would have doubtless been another victim."

EPILOGUE

THE NEWS OF THE WORLD

PERPETRATOR AND MOTIVE DISCOVERED FOR EARL OF SEVERN'S MURDER!
TENANT ON SEVERN ESTATE CLAIMS VISCOUNT RUTHERFORD
IS MILITARY IMPOSTER
RUTHERFORD ARRESTED

* * *

Woodstock—Police discovered a document among the murdered Lord Severn's papers written by his tenant and former private in the late war, Joseph Buck as he lay dying December last.

"I didn't know how I was going to face my mate, Billy Baldwin, on the other side if I didn't tell what I knew and try to set the record straight," said Buck. "I sent a letter to my former colonel, Lord Severn, begging him to visit me so I could right a terrible injustice."

"Lord Severn sent me a letter saying I should tell my story to his secretary, Mr. Dawkins. Dawkins would write everything I said and Lord Severn would show it to the proper people. Next day, Mr. Dawkins came to my bedside, even though I thought I was dying and feeling terrible, I told him the whole story right there and he wrote it down."

—

The News of the World has obtained a copy of the document that police discovered among the late Lord Severn's private papers:

"*My name is Joe Buck. It was 1917 in the trenches in France. We weren't winning. Both sides were stuck and couldn't advance. My mate, Private Billie Baldwin, decided to do something about it. All on his own, he set out for the German lines one night with his face all mud-died so the moon wouldn't shine on it. He went from mortar hole to mortar hole, crawling on his belly, not making a sound. When he got close to the German lines, he found a giant crater and climbed in real quiet-like. He could hear a lot of commotion and orders being given. He spoke German from his boyhood—his mother being a German.*

He stayed in the crater a long time, until he had the whole story. Billy found out that the Germans had been sending artillery, tanks, weapons, troops and all sorts of things to this spot for days. The next day they would launch an all-out offensive on our position. It would be a surprise attack so big it would kill us all and break open our line and then they could go for miles into France.

Billy sneaked back the same way he sneaked out. When he had made it, he told me what he heard and said we needed to tell the officers about it right away. We went to our commanding officer, Major Stapleton, and Billy told him the whole story. Our major went to the next officer up the line and so forth.

The next day, we attacked before dawn and surprised the Germans. It was all a big victory for our side, but

Billy and I were both wounded. Both of us were in the same hospital tent. That night, Billy died in that tent right near me.

I was right surprised when they said Major Stapleton was a great battle hero. He claimed my mate's heroism, said he did all the things Billy did. At the end of the war, they made him Lord Rutherford and gave him the Victoria Cross for his daring deed to cross No-Man's-Land and get back to the British lines just in time to launch an all-out offensive. They said it was one of the most important battles of the whole war.

Nobody ever said anything about Billy Baldwin. He died just like he lived—a hero nobody ever heard about.

Nobody even asked how Major Stapleton could have heard the plans when I remember him saying before this happened that he hated all Germans and didn't understand a word of their cursed language."

Mr. Buck told our reporter that after he dictated this story to Dawkins, he heard no more about it. Mr. Buck continued, "A few days after I talked to Mr. Dawkins, I finally began to feel a little better and wasn't going to die after all. They sent me home and I took up farming again. I didn't think no more about what I told Mr. Dawkins. Now they tell me Lord Severn used what I said to Dawkins to blackmail Lord Rutherford and that Severn was killed because of it. Since the war, I try not to think anything about it, but I stand ready to read my statement that Mr. Dawkins wrote down to a judge and swear that it's true whenever they want me to."

"They told me my mate, Billy, will receive the Victoria Cross even though he's long dead, for which I am very grateful. Now, when my time comes, I can die in peace."

This new information was wholly satisfactory to Catherine and Harry. "The article does all but call Lord Rutherford a scurrilous rat!" said Catherine. "Not meaning to imply a pun, but the man is a thoroughly bad hat!"

* * *

By the middle of November, Harry's ribs had healed sufficiently for him to be able to tolerate using crutches. X-rays showed his leg was healing properly, and he was allowed, at the end of November, to return to Christ Church and his teaching duties. Catherine missed him at the flat but knew it wouldn't be too long before they would be living together permanently.

Catherine and her mother had put their time together in Catherine's flat to good use, and the invitations had gone out for their small wedding, to be held on the fourteenth of December in the chapel on the estate. There would be a catered luncheon following the service. They had settled upon all the details. A hot-house in Plymouth was to handle the flowers—calla lilies.

As usual when Catherine needed a special dress, she and Dot visited their dressmaker, Madame Devereaux in London. Catherine's gown had mermaid lines, hugging her slim figure until it flared at the knees. Dot, as maid of honor, had a hunter green gown made.

Of serious concern was Catherine's missing hair. The friends visited Monsieur Louis at Madame Delacroix's suggestion. He designed a closely fitted "Juliet" hat that hugged her head and tied under the chin. What hair she had left was allowed to fall from the back of the hat in curls. Catherine declined a hair piece which would have added length. "I want to be as genuine as possible on my wedding day. False hair would make me feel a bit of a fraud," she said.

The press had gotten hold of the wedding plans for the pair that had fired the publics imagination.

SLEUTHS TO WED

Oxford—The News of the World has learned that the detective pair, The Honorable Catherine Tregowyn and Dr. Harold Bascombe, Jr. will be married in December in a ceremony at the bride's home chapel.

Dr. Bascombe is a professor at Christ Church College, Oxford, and the honorable Miss Tregowyn is a published poet as well as being a tutor at Somerville College, Oxford.

The pair are well-known as amateur detectives who have solved several high-profile crimes both in Britain and Hollywood.

As they will honeymoon in Spain, it is our profound hope that they will not come across any dead bodies.

Even in the midst of her preparations, however, Catherine still thought often of Anne. "Now she will never be able to gain her father's approval," she told Harry.

Harry replied, "She blames all her troubles and misbehavior on him, you know. For once, she doesn't want anything to do with me."

"I wouldn't be surprised if she went to live abroad," said Catherine. "But, if she is right and war is coming that may not be the safest place."

"I don't think any place will be safe if Hitler has his way," said Harry.

Catherine was in hopes that she could enter her marriage without the specter of Anne always standing over them, weeping. James had never been acceptable to his snobbish father-in-law and therefore minded little about Rutherford's downfall. As usual, he found solace in his work, for which Harry and his family were grateful.

James's father-in-law had been shorn of his title and his Victorian Cross. Private Billy Baldwin became the last person to receive the Victoria Cross for exceptional gallantry during the War.

As Christmas and her wedding approached, Catherine found herself feeling very grateful. She and Harry had narrowly escaped death. They had overcome the problems in their relationship. Because of the events of the last month, she felt closer than ever to her mother and had a lovely new relationship with Harry's parents.

Catherine knew that struggles were a part of life, but she also knew that, with Harry beside her, she now had twice the strength to face them.

THE END

Other Books by G.G. Vandagriff

Catherine Tregowyn Mysteries
An Oxford Murder
Murder in the Jazz Band
Murder at Tregowyn Manor
The Hollywood Murders
Death of an Earl
*

Romantic Suspense
Breaking News
Sleeping Secrets
Balkan Echo
*

Historical Fiction
The Last Waltz: A Novel of Love and War
Exile
Defiance
*

Women's Fiction
Pieces of Paris
The Only Way to Paradise
*

Genealogical Mysteries
Cankered Roots
Of Deadly Descent
Tangled Roots
Poisoned Pedigree
Hidden Branch
*

Suspense
Arthurian Omen
Foggy With a Chance of Murder
*

Regency Romance
The Duke's Undoing
The Taming of Lady Kate
Miss Braithwaite's Secret
Rescuing Rosalind
Lord Trowbridge's Angel
The Baron and the Bluestocking
Lord Grenville's Choice
Lord John's Dilemma
Lord Basingstoke's Downfall (novella)
Her Fateful Debut
His Mysterious Lady
Not an Ordinary Baronet
Love Unexpected
Miss Saunders Takes A Journey
The European Collection (anthology)
Spring in Hyde Park (anthology)
Much Ado About Lavender (novella)
*

Non-Fiction
Voices In Your Blood
Deliverance from Depression

ABOUT THE AUTHOR

G.G. VANDAGRIFF is a traditionally published author who has gone Indie. She loves the Regency period, having read Georgette Heyer over and over since she was a teen. Currently, she has thirteen Regency titles in print, but she writes other things, too. In 2010, she received the Whitney Award for Best Historical Novel for her epic, *The Last Waltz: A Novel of Love and War*. She has also written Romantic Suspense, and her mystery fans are always urging her to write another book featuring her wacky genealogical sleuths, Alex and Briggie. Her latest work is a 1930's Golden Age mystery series. She studied writing at Stanford University and received her master's degree at George Washington University. Though she has lived in many places throughout the country, she now lives with her husband, David, a lawyer, and a writer, on the bench of the Wasatch Mountains in Utah. From her office, she can see a beautiful valley, a lake, and another mountain range. She and David have three children and seven adventurous grandchildren. Visit G.G. at her website ggvandagriff.com, where you can read her blog, keep track of all her books and her work in progress, and sign up to receive her newsletter. She has an author page on Facebook (G.G. Vandagriff-Author) and on Goodreads and Amazon. She loves to hear from her fans!

Made in the USA
Coppell, TX
20 May 2022

78013924R00144